ACCLAIM FOR JOHN HERRICK'S NOVEL *BEAUTIFUL MESS*

"A creative and fresh romp through one of pop culture's most notorious tales. John Herrick's characters become your best friends. His world is keen, compelling and excessively alive."

— Jeffrey James Keyes, *New York Times* bestselling author

"*Beautiful Mess* is an engaging work of fiction, a compelling and delicious 'what if' about one of the most celebrated and tragic figures in Hollywood history."

— *Foreword Reviews*

"Entertaining ... If you are in the mood for a quick read, this may be the perfect book for you."

— *Bismarck Tribune*

ACCLAIM FOR JOHN HERRICK'S NOVEL *BETWEEN THESE WALLS*

"Herrick will make waves."

— *Publishers Weekly*

"[John Herrick] performs a service."

— *St. Louis Post-Dispatch*

"With *Between These Walls*, John Herrick has crafted an engaging, inspirational story with a resounding message about faith, matters of the heart and above all, inner peace."

— Edge Media Network

"A compelling read from beginning to end … A sophisticated and deftly crafted novel … Very highly recommended."

— *The Midwest Book Review*

ACCLAIM FOR JOHN HERRICK'S NOVEL *FROM THE DEAD*

"Eloquence with an edge. In a single chapter, John Herrick can break your heart, rouse your soul, and hold you in suspense. Be prepared to stay up late."

— Doug Wead, *New York Times* bestselling author and advisor to two presidents

"A solid debut novel."

— *Akron Beacon Journal*

"A solid read with a powerful spiritual message."

— *The Midwest Book Review*

"A well written and engaging story. It moves, and moves quickly. … I don't think I've read anything in popular novel form as good as this in describing a journey of faith."

— Faith, Fiction, Friends

ALSO BY JOHN HERRICK

Fiction

Beautiful Mess

Hit and Run

Between These Walls

The Landing

From the Dead

Nonfiction

8 Reasons Your Life Matters

MONA LISAS AND LITTLE WHITE LIES

A NOVEL

JOHN HERRICK

Published in the United States by Segue Blue.

Book layout by Ebooklaunch.com

Library of Congress Control Number: 2018961030
ISBN-13: 978-1-7324314-0-9 (trade paperback)
ISBN-13: 978-1-7324314-1-6 (Kindle ebook)

Publisher's Cataloging-in-Publication Data

Names: Herrick, John, 1975- author.
Title: Mona Lisas and little white lies / John Herrick.
Description: St. Louis, MO : Segue Blue, 2019.
Identifiers: LCCN 2018961030 | ISBN 978-1-7324314-0-9 (paperback) | ISBN 978-1-7324314-1-6 (Kindle ebook)
Subjects: LCSH: Commercial artists--Fiction. | Automobile mechanics--Fiction. | Man-woman relationships--Fiction. | Fame--Fiction. | Romance fiction. | BISAC: FICTION / Romance / Contemporary. | GSAFD: Love stories.
Classification: LCC PS3608.E7746 M66 2019 (print) | LCC PS3608.E7746 (ebook) | DDC 813/.6--dc23.

PRINTED IN THE UNITED STATES OF AMERICA

Dedicated to the memory of
Bill Vann

Husband, father, friend.
An artist and an inspiration.
Widely considered the godfather of illustration.
He had a passion for the next generation of artists.
Loved by many, may his memory endure in our hearts.

A close friend of my family,
I last saw Bill on the day I interviewed him at his studio for this novel.

I pray this novel is one that would have made Bill proud.

ACKNOWLEDGMENTS

Love to my family.

Thanks to everyone who are part of this book: Ian Pazgon and Gunya Na Thalang provided information about Thailand and Thai culture. Amy Dake's personal photos and experience helped me create the epilogue. Pam Rempe read my first draft, confirmed where I was on the right track, and asked questions. Lorri Hackett provided feedback on the draft, as well. Kathy Wakeman proofed the final draft before publication.

Maryglenn McCombs is "my MG," a supporter and strategic collaborator. Eliot Parker and I are iron sharpening iron.

My "Forever Grateful to You" club includes Marnie Thompson, Felicity Swann, Kelly Corday, and Christen Santoscoy. Phil Lewis gave me my first chance to write for a mass audience in radio as a college student. Dr. Carla Siegfried is more critical and appreciated than she can imagine.

The art community considered Bill Vann the Godfather of Illustration. He was a legend—a man whose commercial work was so widespread, you've probably seen it and never realized it. He had a passion for helping younger artists learn and succeed. Susan and my mom met at Joyce Meyer's weekly Bible studies when I was a kid, back in 1984 or 1985, and she and Bill became a permanent part of our family's life. Years ago, when I experienced eye issues, Bill was genuinely concerned and asked often about their status—he understood how much we artists need our sight. Yet, despite knowing him for decades, I never visited his studio or picked his brain about visual artists and their work until I entered the research phase for this novel. I interviewed him and watched him work. Little did I know that studio visit would be the last time I'd ever see him this side of heaven. Four months later, he passed away. This book represents the last time I spoke to him. He was operating under a deadline at the time, so my final memory of Bill includes not only his friendship, love and talent, but his generosity, for he shared his limited—and, as it turned out, his borrowed—time.

Thank you to the bloggers, reviewers and everyone who takes time to read, support and/or offer opinions on my work. Thanks also to those individuals I've forgotten to mention here.

Readers, you choose to spend your valuable time with my work. That's the greatest gift you could give to me. I appreciate you more than words could express.

Lord, You make this possible. I love creating stories, but I love You more.

Much love. Never give up!

MONA LISAS
AND LITTLE WHITE LIES

PROLOGUE

ONE

FEBRUARY 2007

EVEN ROOM TEMPERATURE feels chilly in the middle of winter, noticed Ryder Flynn. Jack up the thermometers all you want. Cloak it in bright colors and enhance its lighting, but a 72-degree room feels much warmer in July than in February. You can't hide the essence of winter. It's just damn cold.

Or blustery. That's the way Ryder described northern Ohio in early February.

According to the morning news, ten inches of snow had fallen in the metro area overnight. Ryder had learned it was lake-effect snow, whereby moisture evaporated from Lake Erie, traveled a short distance, then fell like powder several miles away. But in downtown Cleveland, adjacent to the lake, he had observed only an inch of accumulation.

Not that the weather mattered to Ryder. He would spend most of his weekend here, inside the ballroom of a four-star hotel.

Twenty-seven-year-old Ryder fought to keep his hands at his sides. He balled his hands into fists to contain any display of exhilaration. Upon closer inspection, browsers might notice his fingers wiggling because, at the moment, he wanted to shout.

Minutes earlier, someone had shelled out a record amount for one of his paintings. Well, a personal record. His watercolor depiction of orchids he'd seen in a greenhouse had garnered him $165. From a distance, Ryder had sneaked glances at the transaction as Chase Patterson, Ryder's friend and unofficial business manager, had bargained with a middle-aged lady, who increased her offer by ten dollars.

In a few minutes, the starving-artist show would close for the night. Its Saturday night crowd had thinned an hour ago. Yet Ryder continued to wander the aisles, past easels and racks filled with framed pictures in a variety of paint mediums. He absorbed the visual evidence which, as he knew firsthand, represented hours invested by other artists who had participated in this show. He eavesdropped on random conversations about price and technique. From the ballroom next door, bass notes penetrated the common wall, which towered above Ryder. He felt the music reverberate against his eardrums as he continued to browse.

A wedding next door, someone had told him.

Back home, acquaintances had urged him to tinker with a self-portrait. Test the waters, they'd suggested. See if he could sell it. After all, his handsome appearance rivaled that of a celebrity, with wavy, sandy-brown hair and a chiseled jaw line to crown his five-feet-ten frame. But Ryder had considered the self-portrait idea ridiculous. He couldn't imagine himself in a painting unless it occurred in the proper context. Whatever that might be.

Ryder taught art classes at a local community college during the week. To earn extra cash, he sold paintings to anyone willing to buy them. But one day, he suspected, his fate would change for the better.

For Ryder, this latest $165 transaction represented a taste of things to come. And that was why he grinned on his way out of the ballroom. After a successful day today, he would see if he could score some more sales tomorrow.

As he strolled through the lobby, he picked up traces of exhaust from cars and limos as they eased outside the hotel's main entrance. He'd heard Bruce Springsteen, who had come to town for a concert, had stayed here the prior week.

Ryder observed a bellhop, dressed in a red jacket and flat-topped hat, who pushed a brass luggage rack across dark carpet etched with larger-than-life rosebuds. The lobby seemed so quiet to him.

He jolted as two hands clapped against his shoulders and gave them a vigorous shake.

"We raked in more than two thousand bucks today, man!" Chase spoke under his breath. He gave Ryder's shoulders a final jiggle before letting go. Although they had agreed Chase could collect twenty percent for negotiating sales and setting up Ryder's participation in the art show, Ryder knew his longtime friend was more excited about the challenge itself. For a year, he'd urged Ryder to try to expand his audience. "So how does it feel?"

"Words can't describe it," Ryder replied. "But right now, I feel hungry more than anything. Want to find a pub and grab a bite to eat?"

"Sure, man. Let me run upstairs to grab my coat, then I'll meet you at the front door." He held out a fist, against which Ryder bumped his own. Chase pointed at him with each hand. "My gravy train. You're my gravy train, buddy!" Chase jested as he jogged toward the elevator bank.

Ryder wandered to the corner of the front desk, leaned on his elbow at the edge of the counter, and, in search of inspiration for future paintings, eyed individuals who strolled through the lobby. An older couple, dressed in black, walked through the rotating front doors. Ryder watched as snowflakes, speckled across their shoulders, melted before his eyes.

At a sudden outburst of laughter, Ryder peered across the lobby and watched a group of three young women gather near the elevator bank. Adorned in peach-colored bridesmaid dresses and hairstyles that had, no doubt, taken hours to get just right, the women appeared to be in their early twenties. Even from this distance, he could pick up features in their eyes and figures that suggested they might be relatives. They huddled and whispered before breaking into another bout of laughter. An elevator beeped. The doors of one elevator opened, and a blond-haired bridesmaid held the elevator while the other two followed her in.

The blond peered around the door. "Lily, are you coming?"

Lily? Ryder found the name tender, yet intriguing.

"Yeah, we're here." Another bridesmaid rushed around the corner, her auburn hair in gentle wisps and pulled up well above her shoulders. A black-suited, twenty-something guy jogged beside her.

Since the guy lacked a tuxedo, Ryder assumed he was Lily's date rather than her corresponding groomsman. Yet Lily and the young man seemed mismatched. Ryder wouldn't have picked them out of a lineup as business partners, much less a romantic couple. But soon he forgot about the guy in the suit altogether.

Ryder leaned forward. He couldn't help it.

Stunning. Lily glowed with bliss. Most observers might attribute beauty to the other three bridesmaids, but the sight of Lily tickled Ryder's heart and triggered within him a sweet ache.

From his vantage point—a weak one, he had to admit—he detected a natural beauty about her. She looked uncomfortable in her bridesmaid dress, but appeared to enjoy the wedding festivities, even though she didn't seem to fit in. The other bridesmaids appeared to have a rapport with each other, a relationship they had honed over the years. Lily, on the other hand, seemed along for the ride, squeezed into the middle of the backseat of a car. She followed her cohorts into the elevator.

He couldn't put his finger on why, but something about her drew him in. And she didn't even know it.

The elevator doors pinched shut. She vanished.

"You ready? I'm craving fried pickles," Chase said as he approached.

Ryder's stare remained unbroken a long moment before Chase's remark registered in his mind.

"Huh?" Ryder turned toward his friend and tried to rejoin the moment at hand. "Oh. Yeah, let's go."

On their way out the front door, Ryder glanced back at the elevator. Once more. The last place he'd seen her.

TWO

RYDER RUBBED HIS eyes. No wonder they felt so sore—one glance at his watch told him it was almost two in the morning. Although he could still hear well, the loud music seemed to have whittled his sensitivity to about 85 percent, as though he'd wrapped his eardrums in cotton.

After dinner, he'd allowed Chase to drag him to a nightclub, which was where Ryder had last seen his friend before returning to the hotel alone by way of a taxi. They would find each other before the art show opened that morning at ten o'clock. Chase might push his limits, but he was never late.

Now, upon entering the hotel, he found the lobby empty except for a concierge at the front desk. The room's silence rivaled that of a funeral parlor. Ryder made a beeline for the elevator bank and pushed the round button to hail a ride upstairs. With a glance around the corner, he found the doors to the art show shut and locked. He detected no pulsating rhythms, which meant the wedding reception had ended, as well.

Ryder heard the elevator tone—followed by the swish of fabric coming from his left. He halted. Listened.

Another swish, like the chiffon of a bridesmaid's dress.

When the elevator doors opened, Ryder wasn't standing in front of them. With one eyebrow furrowed and his ear cocked upward, he eased toward the far end of the elevator bank, then peered around the corner.

More rustling of fabric, then tiny sobs. Step by step, he followed the sounds. On his right, he noticed someone had left open the door to a dark room. Another sob came from inside that room. A female voice.

"Hello?" Ryder whispered. His eyes adjusted to the dark as he brushed his hand along the wall in search of a light switch. At last, he located the switch and flipped it on.

The room was small. He wandered to a far corner, where a desk topped with random clutter sat, a four-star hotel's answer to a dumping ground. When he peeked behind the desk, he discovered a young woman. Weeping, she sat crumpled on the floor with her back against the desk. A peach-colored rose trampled by life.

Ryder darted around the desk.

"Excuse me, are you okay?"

His heart rifted. When he knelt beside her, the first thing he noticed was the scent of alcohol that permeated her dress.

Lily.

Ryder could tell she was drunk. And so alone.

A few inches away sat an upright wine bottle, which he grabbed by the neck and jiggled. Empty. A glass sat beside her, tipped over, its contents also empty, save one last drop, which had begun to dry along the glass's glistening edge. Remnants of cabernet sauvignon had left a burgundy stain on the side of Lily's dress and, judging from her current condition, upon her heart.

Ryder's heart cringed each time she inhaled for another sob. He could tell she'd tried to keep her sniffles quiet and wondered if he'd invaded her privacy. Then again, she hadn't asked him to leave.

Where was the guy with whom he'd seen her earlier?

"Lily, are you okay? Do you need help?" Ryder asked, leaning in to see if he could read her eyes since she didn't want to speak. When she peered into his eyes, Ryder couldn't help but notice a stark departure from the clear, bubbly visage he'd observed near the elevator bank. Now, as he tried to decipher her needs, her eyes welled up with tears. They trickled past her mascara and down her cheeks, leaving behind dark trails. She must have sat here for quite a while before he'd found her, because her corneas had turned a shade of pink—a contrast with the intense, cobalt blue of her irises. In fact, her eyes reminded him of a sapphire necklace on display at a jewelry store. He considered how their tone matched her mood.

On second thought, he was wrong. Such a rich shade of blue spoke of royalty. It befitted a young woman who deserved happiness in life.

And where was her date? Was he the reason she sat here broken and alone?

Ryder sat beside her on the floor and took in the full sight of her face. One glance into Ryder's eyes triggered in Lily a fresh onslaught of tears, and from his soul, Ryder responded before logic could convince him otherwise. He slid his arm behind Lily's back and, to his surprise, she leaned into his partial embrace. And wept.

Ryder drew her closer to his chest, nestled his chin upon her head. The locks of her hair, perfectly styled a few hours earlier, had loosened and fallen to her shoulders. He could tell her hair wasn't naturally curly. He picked up the scent of hairspray. Taking a closer look at her hands, he noticed a slight discoloration of her fingertips, a rust color. A light stain, it appeared more prominent in contrast with skin as fair as hers.

Lily drew her feet underneath her wrinkled dress and wrapped one arm around Ryder's belly. She tried to form a word but grew dispirited and gave up.

"Shhhh," Ryder whispered in her ear as they rocked back and forth. When she trembled in his embrace, he tightened his arm around her, which he hoped would make her feel secure.

This is a convergence of strangers, he had to remind himself. Nothing more. Given her drunken state, he doubted she would remember his presence by morning.

Yet she'd captured his heart.

And someone had broken hers. How?

He felt his adrenaline surge, anger toward whoever had treated her with cruelty and left her in this drunken mess.

Lily. A broken flower.

"Lily, can you stand up?" He waited for a response, but she closed her eyes. "Do you know where you are?"

A soft giggle, momentary and laced with pain, escaped through her rosebud lips before it disintegrated into another series of sobs. An emotional rollercoaster of an evening, Ryder figured.

Lily shivered. The flesh of her shoulder felt a tad cool when Ryder touched it with his knuckle. With one glance above, he found a heating vent blowing hot air, which seemed to cool by the time it reached the ground.

Ryder rose to a crouch.

"Tell you what: Stay here, and I'll try to find someone from your group. You're in the wedding, right?"

Lily nodded, then leaned back and appeared to drift to sleep.

Though hesitant to leave her alone, Ryder didn't know what else to do. He couldn't carry her throughout the hotel, drag her from door to door, until he located her room. Rising to his feet, he took one final glimpse to make sure she was safe, then slipped away. He turned out the light so no one else would disturb her before he returned.

THREE

BY THREE O'CLOCK in the morning, Ryder had left Lily with her relatives and parted ways with her. The thought of never seeing her again chafed his heart as he walked down the hotel's ninth-floor hallway and stuck his key card into the electronic lock of his own room. As he walked inside, his eyes moved toward one side, where a table lamp kept everything aglow.

He wouldn't sleep at all tonight. He couldn't. The thought of Lily lingered in his mind and swayed within his soul. Even at her low point that evening, as dismal as she'd appeared, Ryder had seen an angel when he'd gazed into her eyes.

In his room, he plunged into a sea of plush cushions on the sofa and grabbed a tiny, five-dollar bottle of mineral water from the mini bar. As the carbonated liquid tickled his throat and settled into his belly, its bubbles danced and brought a grin to his face. An unexpected end to the evening. Ryder hadn't stepped foot in his room since morning and noticed he'd left the curtains open. From his vantage point on the sofa, he gazed out the window at the Cleveland skyline, where he noticed lights glowing from a nearby office tower.

Something stirred in his soul, but he couldn't identify its source. Invigoration, perhaps? No, on second thought, he felt...*alive.* Alive, fueled by the memory of *her.*

Something about her had created in him a longing.

The stirring wouldn't cease. An artist's vulnerability. An abstract impression that begged manifestation.

She had disappeared from his life. Dejected at the realization, Ryder sought to keep her memory alive.

With a beckoning in his heart, he moved to the writing desk. From his satchel, which he'd placed beside the desk when he'd arrived that morning, he retrieved a small sketchbook and his favorite pencil. After flipping through the book in a hurry, he found a crisp, white page and focused his attention. With soft, careful strokes, he sketched a figure on the paper.

Lily.

With careful attention to detail, he sketched her countenance based on what he remembered from the first time he'd laid eyes on her, when the bridesmaids had gathered near the elevator.

A glad Lily, content in life. That's who she was.

He wished he had his paint and canvas with him, because this black-and-white sketch could never do justice to those bright, cobalt eyes and the tone of her hair, its auburn shade more red than brown. Creamy porcelain skin and light freckles on her cheeks.

As each detail re-emerged in his mind's eye, Ryder added it to his sketch. He maintained one detail from her latter state: He kept her hair down, so it rested upon her shoulders.

Feature by feature, he emptied his soul upon the paper, where it became one with hers in a manner only an artist could perceive. Ryder savored the friction of his pencil as it scratched the paper's surface.

Absorbed in what unfolded before his eyes, Ryder lost track of time until he sensed a change in the atmosphere around him. He sneaked a peek at the window and discovered the inky night sky had grown a shade lighter.

Sunrise.

Sunday morning. The emergence of a new week.

And a new era for the artist.

PART ONE

MONA LISAS

CHAPTER 1

SIX YEARS LATER

FROM HER PERCH on high, a daytime talk-show host held court inside the confines of a television set. She seemed to look down upon two customers at a suburban location of River City Auto, a local chain of tire-and-auto shops in St. Louis. In the waiting room, the customers, who sat on cheap metal chairs covered with gray fabric, ignored the talk-show host as she spouted advice on how to become the *real* you.

Lily Machara didn't bother to offer the TV host a glimpse as she entered from the garage. Instead, she shook her head and scoffed at the program's nonsense. As if a television personality from Portland had unlocked the secrets of life.

That bimbo can't even convince the tabloids that her kids aren't half-alien, Lily mused about the carefree host. Seconds later, the television audience applauded, and Lily continued her silent commentary. *Thank you. I'll return with more wit and dry humor after a word from our psychic sponsor.*

Her fingers, tinted with dried automotive oil, felt grimy. Lily rubbed her thumb and forefinger together, then clicked to open a customer record on a computer terminal, which sat behind the counter at the forefront of the waiting room. She entered the maintenance tasks she'd completed on a Chevy. Along with an oil change, she had filled its tires with air and topped off the coolant and windshield fluid. A bead of perspiration slithered down her temple as she pecked at the keyboard. Back in the garage, between the machinery and a handful of employees, the temperature had crept at least ten degrees higher. She wiped her brow with the sleeve of her navy-blue coveralls. Twenty feet away, she'd propped open the shop's front door. A March breeze drifted past a row of tire displays and carried their scent through the waiting room. The smell of new rubber kindled in Lily a sense of comfort and continuity.

Unlike men—and cars, for that matter—a new tire had never let her down.

Some women sought ice cream for comfort. Lily, when given the opportunity, preferred to grab a mallet and pound on a vehicle.

Although she worked with her back to the cash register, she heard the scratch of footsteps as somebody approached the counter behind her. "Be right with you," she said without breaking her concentration.

"No rush. I've got a vacation day anyway." A male voice.

With a final click to close the record on the computer, she pivoted and almost blushed at the sight of the customer who had approached her.

Gorgeous.

A couple of inches taller than her own five-feet-eight frame, the man with ash-blond hair gave her a nod as he wrested a key from his key ring. No wedding band.

"Can I help you?" Lily asked.

"My last name's Wilson. I have a two o'clock appointment for an oil change," he replied, then provided his license plate number.

Lily entered the number into the computer, pulled up his customer record, and created a work ticket. A dot-matrix printer screeched to life and spewed the details onto an order form. By the time she ripped the form from the printer and turned around, the Wilson guy had managed to pull apart the spiral of his key ring, but it snapped shut before he could liberate his key. So he tried again.

Another glance at his hand revealed he was a nail biter. No wonder he fumbled with the key ring. She considered offering her help, then opted against it. Many men preferred not to cave in to minor challenges. Some seemed embarrassed leaving their cars in the hands of a woman to begin with.

Bashfulness crept in. Lily felt her body tense beneath her coveralls. She kept her eyes glued to his hands, making her best effort at composure so she wouldn't look nervous around this handsome man. When she was confident he wouldn't notice, she sneaked a glance at his face and admired him for a few seconds as he focused on that stupid key ring. She absorbed his green eyes and imagined them staring into hers. Before she realized it, she touched the back of her auburn hair—a self-conscious habit, her roommate pointed out—which she always wore up while at work. Another bead of perspiration dripped down the back of her neck and cooled in the spring air.

Lily seldom wore makeup and never gave it a second thought…until moments like this. She felt so grubby. Odds were two-to-one that she'd managed to smear a grease stain across her chin since lunch. What a sight *that* would be for this attractive customer! Not that he'd given her a second glance.

She returned her attention to his hands as he finished fumbling with the key ring. When she extended her hand to collect the key, the Wilson guy took one look at her oil-stained fingertips, then slapped the key onto the counter. He gave her a generic nod.

No interest whatsoever. Not even the faintest semblance of it. Her heart dropped, which made her feel ridiculous for having harbored the idea that maybe…

"I'll just grab a seat and wait for it."

"Sure. We have a 60-minute guarantee."

And away he walked—with his eyes glued to the television host! Not even a final glance over his shoulder as he left.

Unbelievable. Another chapter in the story of her life. Then again, what did she expect? Damned oil-stained hands. Every guy's dream.

When she opened the heavy door to the garage, a cacophony of tools and engines greeted her. Lily tossed Wilson's work ticket form into a clear, vinyl pouch and hung it on a rack beside the door.

"Lily!" Aaron Varga shouted over the noise. He headed toward her, dressed in a matching pair of coveralls, wiping his hands on a rag. In the background, coworkers buzzed around three cars on lifts.

Lily was the solitary female on the payroll.

Aaron nodded toward the other employees, who let loose random shouts and guffaws. "The guys are all heading out for drinks after work. You coming?"

She peered back toward the waiting room, then looked into Aaron's dark eyes and nodded.

"What's next?" Aaron asked, looking over Lily's shoulder as she removed the next packet from the job rack.

"Serpentine belt replacement," she replied. With a spin of Wilson's key on her forefinger, Lily made her way toward the garage door to grab the car.

CHAPTER 2

"DUDE, YOU'RE SUCH a liar!" Dave pointed a finger at a coworker on the other side of the table. "The woman with the Corvette isn't married, and she wasn't interested in you!" For good measure, he added a coarse remark about the woman, muttered an expletive, and washed it all down with a swig of beer straight from the bottle. Lily couldn't help but notice the weird way he wrapped his lips around the mouth of the bottle when he drank, edging the bottle back and forth a tad. He never seemed to realize it.

Unfazed by his comment about the woman, Lily examined the festive pinks and greens of a piñata that hung low above her head. She tapped the object, which was shaped like a burro, and judged it empty, as she'd suspected. At a few minutes past six o'clock, it was happy hour. She huddled around a table with five other coworkers from River City Auto in the bar area of a nearby Mexican restaurant. A basket of tortilla chips, fresh from the oven, sat in their midst, along with a half-empty bowl of smoky salsa. Lily's stomach grumbled at the sight of the salted chips, which still glistened with cooking oil, but for the sake of her calorie count, she forced herself to avoid putting one into her mouth. The scent of enchiladas and refried beans permeated the room.

She poked a lime into her Corona and took a long pull from the bottle.

Beside her, Dave bobbed his head to the sound of mariachi horns that squawked from speakers overhead, then stopped to lean her way. "By the way, I saw you checking out that one guy this afternoon."

"You mean you were spying on me?"

"Hey, you can't help but notice through that giant window."

"Mind your own damn business."

"Whatever you say, Lily. I know what I saw." With that, he took another weird pull from his bottle. The other coworkers hung on to every word.

She shot Dave a disinterested glance, then eyed his lips in motion. "Your mouth seems unusually comfortable with the shape of that bottle neck, Dave. Do you usually spit or swallow?"

Laughter erupted around the table. Dave offered a chuckle too, but Lily noticed he pulled the bottle away from his mouth much quicker after his next swig.

In afterthought, she leaned against Aaron, a close friend and the only coworker who attempted to treat her like a member of the opposite sex.

Not that Dave's remark had annoyed her. She enjoyed the challenge of one-upmanship. Lily had worked with these guys for the last few years and had developed a callus toward their crude jokes and careless remarks.

On occasion, while lying awake in bed, she wondered whether the callus had grown rougher year by year. She'd considered asking somebody about it but wasn't sure she wanted to know the answer.

Oftentimes, though, when her male counterparts lapsed into pointless bouts of masculinity, Lily would withdraw into her own universe. Tonight, as the guys bantered back and forth, their voices fading into irrelevance, Lily grew distracted and let her eyes wander throughout the bar area. Her attention landed on a booth a short distance away, several feet beyond earshot, where two women huddled across from each other.

They looked about Lily's age, but the similarities ended there.

High-heeled, dressed in business attire—an utter contrast to Lily's jeans and steel-toed shoes—the young women engaged in what appeared to be a mature conversation. Each had styled her blond hair with a calculated use of hairspray, which caused the hair to glisten beneath the lights. The women appeared to know the precise point of balance when it came to makeup, their lips swathed with perfect touches of lipstick that enhanced the milky white tones in their teeth when they smiled.

Lily returned her gaze to the cactus-patterned tablecloth before her and rubbed a speck of salsa from one of its cartoonish images.

What do those women do for a living? she wondered. Based on their pressed attire, she guessed they worked in a corporate environment. They didn't look like lawyers, and given their ages, she wouldn't peg them as high-level executives. Perhaps they worked at the mall, but the stiffness of their outfits caused her to doubt that possibility. Executive assistants, maybe? Or consultants?

She fingered the back of her hair, which felt out of place. She traced a finger across her eyelashes—not a hint of mascara. She hadn't attempted to apply the stuff since she was a teenager and had felt free without it.

With a pull from her beer bottle, Lily sneaked another glance in their direction. One woman sipped a martini. The other consumed beer from a glass—an option that hadn't occurred to Lily, but must have held merit for this other woman. To Lily, it seemed a performance. A polished image for someone else's benefit.

Where do women learn these things? she mused. *From each other? I mean, really, does it make a difference?*

As if on cue, her answer arrived.

A handsome guy strolled over to the women's booth and struck up a conversation. Although she couldn't hear what he said, the man's casual hand gestures and confident tilt of the head indicated flirtation. Sure enough, the women nodded and responded with coy grins, eyeing each other to solidify their conspiracy.

Lily knew what would come next. More words would volley back and forth, a few more gestures, then the ladies would scoot over so he could slide into their booth. One woman would grin; the other would fake a smile and try to hide her jealousy that the man had chosen *her friend's* side of the table. Next, then the man would wave to a nearby waiter in a sombrero, who would nod and depart, then return with a second round of drinks.

Well, that's what she *thought* would happen.

She couldn't believe what she saw. The gestures, the smiles, everything unfolded the way she'd predicted until…

With the guy still standing at their booth, the women batted their eyes and responded with a slight shake of their heads. The women declined his offer. *Declined* it!

I guess some women can afford to be picky.

They probably got the offer all the time.

The guy offered a confident, face-saving nod. Then he turned around and sauntered away. Once he turned his back to the women, however, Lily watched him wrinkle his eyebrows, no doubt wondering how he'd morphed into the dumbest fuck in the bar. He walked right past Lily's table without so much as a glance.

Lily rustled her bottle. A thin layer of foam formed as the golden liquid sloshed inside. With an ounce left, she held no illusion that any guy in this restaurant was about to buy her another. She couldn't even remember the last time it had happened to her.

She felt a nudge against her arm, abrupt and insistent. The kind an older brother would use to pester you.

"Want another Corona, Lily?" Dave asked. His breath smelled sour.

She forced a grin but her lips felt taut. "Sure, why not?"

"That's my girl!" And with that, he planted a jovial slap on her back.

CHAPTER 3

WHEN LILY WALKED into her apartment, she heard the clanging of a pot in the kitchen. She heaved a brown paper bag higher against her hip as she let her purse drop to the floor. After happy hour, she had stopped at the grocery store to buy a gallon of fat-free milk, along with an individual-size container of grilled chicken from the deli counter for dinner.

Her roommate, Brooke, who must have heard the door shut, poked her head out of the kitchen.

"Tell me you didn't pick up dinner for yourself! I've got it covered."

"I'll save it for tomorrow night," Lily replied.

Lily made her way into the kitchen and stuck her groceries in the refrigerator, which contained little more than fresh vegetables and a bottle of V-8 juice. By no means did Lily consider herself attractive, but she and Brooke tried to keep a handle on their figures. The freezer didn't even contain a pint of decadent ice cream to carry them through unexpected heartbreak.

Not that either woman needed comfort from high-calorie dairy. Brooke never found herself on the receiving end of a breakup. Lily, on the other hand, hadn't found herself on *either* end of a breakup in several years. Her romantic life needed a defibrillator.

From her position at the stove, Brooke stirred the contents of a large pot. Steam rose toward the exhaust fan, swaying like a belly dancer.

"I'm making spaghetti for both of us," Brooke said. "Someone at work gave me a great new recipe. Light, low-fat. She heated up her leftovers at lunch today. I could smell it all the way from my desk and had to find out what it was."

Compared to the effervescence of Brooke's voice, Lily found her own rather bland. Whereas Brook drew out her syllables and spoke in a dynamic range of tones, Lily considered herself a to-the-point person with a blunt, linear quality to her voice.

Lily leaned over the pot but couldn't smell anything. She squinted.

"What did you put in it?" Lily asked.

"Well, nothing yet, silly. I'm stirring pasta in canola oil right now." With her eyes fixed upon the stove, Brooke smiled as she spoke. The girl always smiled. Brooke was an all-American type who seemed to exist in a state of perpetual cheer. Her perfect blond ponytail swung from one shoulder blade to the other as she poked at the spaghetti. Back in the 1990s, Lily used to joke that Brooke reminded her of Quinn, the little sister on the animated television show *Daria*.

Yet Lily couldn't imagine having a different roommate. When she was in first grade, she had met Brooke on the school bus, where Brooke created an ad-hoc word game for them to pass the time. Once they entered middle school, where the cool factor mattered, their bond remained intact despite Lily's lack of popularity. How they had maintained their friendship over the years, Lily couldn't explain, but they had remained the best of friends since the day they'd met.

"You're home later than usual," Brooke noted, turning toward a cutting board, where she hacked at a pile of fresh basil leaves. "Did you get stuck under a car?"

"Happy hour."

"With the guys from work?"

Lily nodded. "The royal court."

"I wouldn't call those guys princes."

"Who called them princes? Every royal court has its fools."

Brooke snickered as she scraped the basil into the pot. Lily stifled a grin, satisfied she had gotten a laugh but not wanting Brooke to know she cared either way. For whatever reason, Lily enjoyed keeping small things to herself.

"Any guys catch your eye at the bar? You realize some of them are on the lookout at happy hour, right?"

"I doubt I'm their vision of companionship."

"Oh, come on!" Brooke gave Lily a look before she started to dice a tomato. "Lily, you're beautiful. You just hide it beneath the layers."

Eager to change the subject, Lily asked, "So why are you cooking for us? Where's your boyfriend tonight?"

"Jeremy went to the hockey game with some friends of his. They bought a group of tickets. So after work, I went to the gym all alone, then the grocery store." At that, she drew her mouth into an *O* shape as if she'd just caught sight of a koala dressed in a tutu. "Do you know what that means? It means you and I almost ran into each other at the grocery store! Is that destiny or what?"

Lily reminded herself that Brooke was one of those individuals who could find the Virgin Mary's silhouette on a slice of marble rye. She shook her head and peered into the pot again. "You have enough pasta in there to last us three days."

Brooke stopped dicing and gave the mound of tomato a second glance. "You're probably right. I won't be here to eat it, though. I'm leaving tomorrow. I have to head to Minneapolis for two days."

"Meeting a client?"

"Yep. I don't mind this trip, though. It's my alcoholic-beverage account, so helping them come up with new campaign ideas is fun." She put a hand on her hip and cocked her head toward the side. "You wouldn't believe the subconscious ways guys relate products to sex."

"What happens if your client doesn't like the ideas you offer?"

Brooke shrugged. "I work with them and try to get them to come around by relating it to something they're familiar with," she said. "The client isn't always right, but you need to let them think they are."

Interesting, Lily thought.

Brooke worked as an account executive at a marketing agency. Brooke called it a *boutique agency,* which Lily interpreted as marketing lingo for *small.* But Brooke had mentioned the agency intended to expand its clientele. To Lily, it also sounded like Brooke spent a good deal of time reading celebrity gossip online.

On rare days when Lily's workload was slow, she wondered how different her life might look had she tried college and aimed for a white-collar profession like Brooke's. She had met a handful of Brooke's coworkers, who struck her as similar to the Wilson guy from the shop earlier that afternoon. A sharp contrast to the guys with whom Lily worked. The male population in Brooke's world seemed to treat Brooke with respect. Then again, Lily pictured dead-quiet hallways, where the only indication of life came from the sound of a printer warming up. At that point, she pegged a desk job as one of the quickest routes to boredom. For her, at least.

As Brooke added more spices to the pot, the entrée's aroma took form and Lily's stomach grumbled.

CHAPTER 4

FROM HIS PERSPECTIVE as he looked through the sliding glass door of his art studio, God had painted the still water of the Lake of the Ozarks against an indigo backdrop. Late evening rendered the environment too dark for Ryder to discern a tree from a slab of concrete. Inside, Ryder kept the room dark, except for a lone recessed light, under which he'd positioned his easel. The light bathed his canvas in a soothing, ivory glow.

From a stereo in the corner, an Ulrich Schnauss album coupled serene melodies with electronic sound effects that creaked and popped. Ryder escaped into the sonic atmosphere as he painted. He felt adrenaline buzz through his veins as he listened to the buoyant sounds.

In his left hand, Ryder held a plastic palette with dabs of acrylic paint in twelve colors. Along one side of the palette, he had arranged earth tones in vertical fashion. Across the top of the palette, he'd ordered his colors from warmest to coolest, cadmium red to ultramarine blue.

Twelve colors unlocked an endless spectrum of tones. From those core colors, Ryder could mix any shade he needed to apply to the canvas before him. Earlier that afternoon, he had used a pencil to sketch his initial image on the canvas.

Now he faced his favorite task. Tonight he would bring the image to life.

A night scene.

Once acrylics reach the canvas, they dry faster than oil paints. An artist has less time to modify his work or correct errors. So with each segment of his painting, Ryder contemplated his strategy in advance: Which colors would he mix to achieve a desired hue? Which techniques did he plan to use to communicate texture and light?

He began with the dark sky. He mixed two deep colors together with a palette knife, but stopped blending the paint early. That way, its individual base colors would spread in streaks across the canvas to give the sky a harsh, stormy feel. With broad strokes, Ryder used a flat brush, its bristles long and even, to fill in the top of the canvas.

Next he transitioned to some earth tones and yellows as he explored the background scene. To address various details of a café in Paris, he switched brushes along the way, using filberts for softer strokes and bright brushes to add texture to the café's brick façade. The lighted interior of the café provided a sharp contrast to the night sky.

The music took a romantic detour and seemed to draw Ryder deeper into the painting as he prepared to focus on his subjects.

A man and woman in love.

Ryder leaned closer to the canvas and applied short, delicate strokes to the woman's black dress. He most enjoyed bringing minor details to life—sequins on a dress, the delicate gold of a white wine, expressions on faces. How easy to overlook such details while walking through an ordinary day. Yet, for Ryder, those nuances captured the richness of life itself.

As he finished painting the female, applying a lighter shade to a portion of her hair to create the impression of sheen, Ryder noticed his heartbeat accelerating a tad. He caught himself squinting as he focused on the woman's face. She appeared enraptured, not with love itself, but with her status as the man's object of affection.

Ryder glanced at the clock on the desk behind him. Past midnight.

With his mouth closed, he released an inaudible sigh.

One step back. He tilted his head, examined the painting from another angle.

Heartache fluttered inside him.

CHAPTER 5

LILY SMOTHERED A yawn as she entered River City Auto through its rear door and clocked in at 5:29 a.m., a half hour before the shop would open. Her schedule varied during the week, and often she would close down the shop for the night. But not today.

Struggling to open her eyes beyond a squint, she made her way to the waiting room, flipping light switches along the way. She loved the early-morning darkness of springtime, which she glimpsed through the windows of the waiting room. While many of St. Louis's inhabitants were still in bed, she enjoyed the promise of a new day in solitude. Peace stirred in her.

Yet she craved caffeine. She dragged herself to the coffee machine and brewed a pot of coffee. She snickered at the words *Dreyfus Select* imprinted across the coffee bag. Dreyfus was the supply company that also delivered the shop's blue coveralls. In other words, the shop's customers would drink generic-brand coffee. Although the grinds smelled like dried vinegar in the bag, once brewed, the aroma stimulated her senses. From a cabinet below, she retrieved two stacks of recycled cardboard cups and set them on the small table. She shook the giant container of sugar—another product from *Dreyfus Select*—which sat beside the coffee pot and found it near empty, so she tossed it in the trash and opened a new container.

At the sound of rattling in the garage, she looked through the observation window and noticed a couple of her coworkers had wandered in early, laughing as usual. Aaron, dressed in coveralls, pushed his way through the heavy door and into the waiting room.

"Coffee!" he pleaded.

"I just brewed it," Lily said.

Aaron shuffled over, poured himself a cup, then rubbed his eyes.

"Late night?" Lily asked.

Aaron nodded. "I crawled into bed around one a.m. We were out till midnight."

"We?"

"A date. We went to that Peter Mayer concert at Blueberry Hill, then headed to a hole-in-the-wall bar. Had a great time, easy conversation. A few drinks later, I checked my watch and knew I'd be dead on my feet come sunrise."

"Who paid?"

"We bought our own tickets to the concert. I played the nice guy and bought the drinks."

Lily crossed her arms and responded with a smug grin. "Big spender. A dumpy bar? You took me to much nicer places back when we were still together."

"That's because you were a princess." Aaron wrapped his arm around Lily and gave her a playful squeeze. He always made Lily feel tender. Shouts and jests continued in the garage as more guys arrived and tossed their lunches in the refrigerator.

Aaron planted a final kiss on the top of Lily's head. They heard the shop's main door *thud* behind them and turned around in time to see a businessman back up, put his hands on his hips, then look at the sign beside the locked door. When he realized the shop wouldn't open for ten more minutes, he appeared confused.

Lily smirked. "Moron," she muttered to Aaron before unlocking the door and letting in the customer anyway.

"Thanks," said the man as he walked into the shop. "I guess I'm a little early."

"Don't worry about it," Lily said, then waved him over to the counter.

Aaron shot a wink at Lily, observed the man from head to toe, then disappeared into the garage. The shop filled with the sounds of drills firing up and the whir of a lift as it elevated a car into the air, a project held over from the previous day.

Lily estimated the customer's age at mid-thirties. His brown hair, short and styled, had strands of gray interspersed along his temples, a feature which rendered in him a hint of intrigue. His large, brown eyes commanded attention in a way that made a woman swoon. Dressed in a sport coat and a power-red tie, he looked ready to make a day's worth of decisions, the kind that involved seven figures and a dollar sign. The longer she looked at him, the more Lily found him attractive. For once, she knew her hair wasn't a mess and she didn't have any oil smudges on her face. Then again, did it matter? These guys never noticed her anyway.

"Name?"

"Evan Lancaster."

As he provided his information, Lily captured it in the computer, along with the details of his BMW, which was only two years old. What on earth could have brought this guy into an auto shop before sunrise with a car so new?

"It's the sunroof," Evan said before Lily had a chance to ask. "It won't open fully."

"A tragedy, huh?" Lily replied, then gave her remark a second thought. She peeked over her shoulder, expecting to find an offended customer, but Evan seemed to appreciate her humor.

"I don't want to risk getting stranded on the side of the road without ideal air circulation," he replied with a wink, his tongue poking against the corner of his mouth after his witty comeback.

Lily caught a glint in his eye. She returned her attention to the computer and entered the reason for his visit. She sensed him scrutinizing her as she typed. Not in a creepy way, but with kindness.

"I like to beat the rush-hour traffic."

"Huh?" Lily looked up.

Embarrassed, Evan chuckled under his breath. "That's why I'm here so early. I just like to beat the volume on the roads."

"Oh," Lily replied. "Yeah, I live right around the corner, so…" With a click of the Print button, the dot matrix fired up. She ripped the work ticket from the printer and slid it across the counter for Evan to sign. He seemed amused by her movements.

"This is going to sound odd," Evan began.

This can't be going where I think it's going, Lily thought. Granted, she seldom attracted attention from the opposite sex. But enough of her coworkers and friends had hit on her over the years, guys in search of a one-time date and a quick lay. She eyed Evan with suspicion. Apparently a BMW doesn't equal dignity.

Then again, Evan didn't strike her as a guy with low standards. No wedding band, either. Curious what he would say next, she caught his eye to invite him to say more.

"It's just…" Evan crossed his arms. He pursed his lips, then squinted at her. "Have I seen you before? You look familiar, but I can't put my finger on why."

Maybe she was wrong. He wasn't trying to hit on her after all. Of course not.

"No, I don't think so." She'd had to create a new customer record for him, which meant Evan hadn't seen her in the shop. Who was she supposed to look like, Jennifer Aniston? She extended her hand. "Key?"

Evan removed a car key and placed it into her palm. Lily slipped the key and the work ticket into a vinyl pouch.

When Evan declined to wait while they serviced his car, Lily replied, "We'll run some diagnostics on it, then call you with a price estimate. It shouldn't take more than an hour to figure it out."

Evan nodded but didn't appear ready to leave.

Lily ran her fingernail against a faux itch on her chin. Her heartbeat accelerated a notch. Why did he continue to stand there and look at her? "Was there something else you needed?"

Evan shrugged. "I was kind of hoping I could get one of those complimentary rides to work." He paused a moment, then the glint returned to his eye. "You use a BMW for those, right?"

Everything in Lily made her want to grin, but she pursed her lips and fought the urge. She scrutinized his eyes in an attempt to gauge his humor. Now she couldn't tell if flirtation was his goal. What would a guy like this see in her?

At last, she jerked her thumb toward the garage. "Our chariot's out back. Gimme a minute to grab the key and tell them I'm heading out."

CHAPTER 6

ON MOST OCCASIONS, for the sake of safety, one of Lily's coworkers handled complimentary rides to avoid putting her alone in a car with a man. Lily couldn't recall the last time she had driven north on Interstate 270 before the morning rush hour. The road seemed rather calm. Toward her right, sunlight had begun to break forth, its orange glow burning along the horizon, over which hovered a sea of light blue.

She loved to watch customers as they climbed into the shop's courtesy car, a plain, white Buick with the River City Auto logo painted on each side. Most customers expected to find the interior smudged with grease stains but discovered the shop kept it more immaculate than the cars customers brought in for service. Evan proved no different. A few minutes earlier, upon opening his door, he had given the passenger seat a cursory look before he climbed in.

Lily had snickered to herself when they'd first walked to the car. Evan had appeared unsure how to treat a lady from an auto shop and had headed toward her door to try to open it for her. From the corner of her eye, though, she had seen him dither and quickened her pace so she would reach the car before he did. He didn't need to do her any favors. This was her job.

Although the air was crisp, it felt warm enough to crack open the windows. They passed a stretch of grass along the side of the freeway, and the scent of fresh dew filled the car.

Lily wanted to talk but couldn't overcome her self-consciousness. Had a coworker occupied the passenger seat, she would come up with a snide remark for no other reason than to prod him. But a guy in a suit? What would interest him? Any other time, she would be content to keep her mouth shut unless the customer said something to her. But Evan...well, a part of her wanted to talk to him.

She tapped the steering wheel with her fingertip. She felt a buzz on the sole of her foot and reminded herself to add air to the tires.

Say something, Lily. Ask him about his job.

"So, where do you work?"

"Ross-Gurley. Ever hear of them?"

"No, I don't get out much."

"It's a medical supply company. I'm in sales."

"So you knock on people's doors and try to sell them catheters?"

"Thank God, no." Evan chuckled. "We sell to doctors, hospitals, regional suppliers. And for the record, I deal with heart-monitoring equipment. Actually, I don't make many calls anymore. I handle our largest clients but not the smaller ones."

"Why not?"

"The people in my department do most of the legwork."

"Nice. How'd you get such a sweet deal?"

Evan shifted in his seat in what appeared a touch of humility. "I'm the vice-president."

"Of the whole sales department?"

"Yeah."

Which might have meant his BMW wasn't financed. Money didn't impress Lily. She couldn't have cared less how much people earned, but now Evan started to seem more genuine than she'd first thought.

"How old are you?" Lily cringed at the question. "Sorry, I shouldn't have asked that. It's just...I always pictured vice-presidents as old guys, and you look young."

Evan took her remarks in stride. "I'm thirty-six. You're right, though: I'm young for my position. Opportunities came together. Fate, I suppose. Somewhere along the line, a director saw potential in me and decided to help me hone my skills. That happened a few years after I entered the work force, and things grew from there."

Lily clucked her tongue once, then stopped when she realized it might make her look ridiculous. "So, what are people like at your office? What do they talk about with each other in the halls?"

"Oh, the usual chitchat. News stories and sports scores. Articles they've read about the medical industry."

"Are there lot of women where you work?"

"I'd estimate about half and half. Why do you ask?"

"Just wondered." Lily paused. Conversation seemed to flow easier with him than she'd expected, albeit not too deep. Her curiosity mounted. "So if you're a guy, and you work with women, do you treat them like little sisters? Smack them on the back, that type of thing?"

"At my workplace?" Evan appeared shocked. "They'd probably sue my ass. I mean, sue my, well, you understand."

So she *was* working with jackasses. Great.

Lily wondered where guys learned how to respect women who worked with them. Was there a class for that type of thing? A few of her coworkers could secure a scholarship for themselves based on need.

"Want to turn on some music?" Evan asked.

"Sure. What do you like to listen to? Sinatra, I presume?" Just to poke him. Call it habit.

Evan lodged his tongue against his cheek. That glint, the one from the store, returned to his eyes. "No, but if that's your preference, I won't judge."

"I'm a country girl."

"As in country music?"

"You find that shocking?"

Evan stroked his chin, captured a sideways glance at her. "Not shocking, per se. I suppose I'd expected you to say something else."

"Like what?"

"Oh, I don't know. You seem like you'd enjoy indie artists."

So he thought she didn't fit in *on purpose?* She tapped the steering wheel again. Before she realized it, she had sneaked a glance at his mouth, to appraise the shape of his lips. Unfortunately, he caught her in the act and responded with a grin that spoke of compassion.

"I love Rascal Flatts," Lily said. "Something about their stuff makes me feel like there's hope in tomorrow, hope that things can always improve."

Evan nodded. "A special person like you deserves to have hope for tomorrow."

Though she didn't dare look at him now, she sensed him gazing at her, as though in anticipation of what she would say next. Not because of *what* she would say, but because he enjoyed listening to her.

Lily couldn't recall the last time a man looked at her in that way, like she possessed a charming side. Part of her wanted to discard such a notion as silly. Yet beneath her coveralls, the hairs along her arm bristled, the way they had the first time a boy had put his arm around her when she was thirteen.

Nervous, afraid she might sever the sincerity of the moment, Lily tuned the radio to a modern rock station but kept the volume low.

CHAPTER 7

As soon as Ryder peered to his left, the patron at the neighboring table shifted his eyes back to his own plate and resumed his meal.

Ryder returned his attention to his girlfriend, Carol, who sat across from him at a table for two. She poked at a salad topped with roasted red peppers and other vegetables, then took a sip of white zinfandel. Dressed in a charcoal pantsuit, she had wound her shoulder-length, brunette hair into a tight ponytail.

To Ryder, it seemed Carol hadn't spoken in five minutes.

"Is there anything I can do?" he asked.

"About?"

"You seem under pressure lately. Is it work?"

Carol nodded. "My boss is driving me insane. Remember that client I told you about, the small business in Little Rock? Their books are so far out of whack, it's taken weeks to sort them out." She sighed, then flicked a slice of asparagus over a leaf of lettuce. "Anyway, it's tax season, which means late nights coming up. Once April fifteenth rolls by, though, things will clear up."

Ryder slid his hand across the white tablecloth and drummed his fingers. Palm open, he wiggled his fingers to invite her to place her hand in his. Responding in kind, she kept her hand in his for a few seconds before she withdrew it. Carol wasn't the affectionate type and preferred not to be touched, but Ryder had hoped she'd entertain a change of heart tonight, given her state of distraction.

Then again, they had struggled in their relationship for the past couple of months. Whenever he encouraged her to open up, she remained closed. When they had first met through a mutual friend, they had shared some laughs. By the second date, she had even allowed him to kiss her. Back then, nary a day would pass without one calling the other. Not long afterward, their relationship advanced to a more committed phase.

But Ryder sensed she enjoyed the attention more than the relationship itself.

Carol jabbed the air with her fork. "Don't ever enter accounting."

"Yeah, I deal better with a different kind of figures."

She furrowed her brow a moment, until his play on words hit her. "Oh, you mean art. Painting, figures. I didn't quite know where you were headed with that one."

Carol took life so seriously, she couldn't appreciate a joke. As though you should analyze each moment in life and then find a way to streamline it. Her clothing never had a crease out of place. And she seldom smiled these days.

Ryder wished he could locate the former Carol, but once their relationship had settled in, so had she.

The truth was, they had grown bored with each other, but neither was ready to admit it. They enjoyed the confidence in knowing a romantic connection existed, however flimsy.

Waiters bustled around the small dining room. Ryder picked up the scent of fresh-baked bread, which triggered fresh interest in his entrée. He twirled more fettuccine Alfredo around his fork and consumed it.

Their waiter stopped by to refill their water glasses, then left a minor gust in his wake. With a final flicker, the flame of a candle in the center of their table died. Ryder loved the scent of a scorched candle wick. In his mind, the smoke evoked images of a cruise ship in the 1950s.

Carol tapped her fork against a red pepper. "Ugh. I hate candle smoke."

"Come on, Carol, talk to me."

"You wouldn't understand. You don't work a normal job, Ryder."

"This didn't start tonight, and we both know it. I don't think it's related to your job."

Ryder didn't take another bite. Instead, he watched her, willed her to say something. For a while, Carol said nothing. She sipped her wine again. When she lifted the next bite of lettuce to her mouth, she stopped short and set the fork on her plate with a *clink*.

"I don't want you to go to the premiere," she said.

"What? They need an answer this week. I can't let this opportunity go by the wayside."

"I wouldn't call it an opportunity, Ryder. You're an artist, a painter. Movie premieres aren't a requirement. Besides, it would take you away from your studio."

"Hold on. Suddenly, I'm not allowed to go away for a couple of days? Last week, you spent more time in Little Rock than you spent here in Missouri."

"To see a client. I agreed to travel when I took the position."

Ryder relaxed against his chair and smirked. "This has to do with Ana Ferguson, doesn't it? You can't be serious."

Carol leaned forward. "I'm not joking, Ryder. We're in a relationship. You and I, remember?"

"We also have our careers. We're 33 years old."

"I don't date people to further my career," Carol replied.

Ryder tried to read her eyes, but they appeared flat. "Look," he replied, "the premiere is nothing more than a photo op. If I can position myself as a hot property, it could attract more jobs for me. Where's the harm? Chase thinks it could pay off for me later on."

"It was Ana's idea, not his."

"Fine, but my point remains."

Ryder noticed Carol's hand at rest upon the table, her fingers still gripping her fork. Whether she would care for his reach or not, he took gentle hold of her hand and cupped it with his other hand. She released her fork.

Ryder caressed the flesh of her palm. In a low voice he said, "I've never been unfaithful to you, Carol. You know that."

Though she remained calm, Carol appeared exasperated. Sighing under her breath, she shook her head.

"This is what I don't understand," she said at last, resignation in her voice. "I know you've never screwed around on me, but your heart always seems to be somewhere else."

"You're not the only one who works day and night." Ryder increased his volume a notch. "So you're allowed to be preoccupied, but I'm not?"

"Keep your voice down!" Carol hissed in embarrassment. With a furtive scan of the room, she stiffened her neck. "And what about the woman you paint in half your work nowadays? You use the same face over and over."

"I've explained this over and over: Long ago, a face inspired me, and I based a recurring character on her."

"But you paint yourself with her in those scenes!"

"Not in all of them. Besides, lots of artists do self-portraits."

"Oh, please."

"Early in my career, someone told me my face was marketable. I decided to test it out."

Arms crossed, Carol leaned back in her chair. She pierced his eyes with hers. "Who's the woman in the paintings, Ryder?"

"I know nothing about her. I only spoke to her once, and that was years ago."

"Obviously, she stuck with you."

"Carol, you don't understand artists. She's a point of reference. A muse."

"A *muse?!*" Carol hissed.

"Yes! What's wrong with that?"

Ryder determined to keep his body rigid above the table where Carol could see, but underneath, he bounced his heel. Not even he himself could make sense of his fascination with Lily. How was he supposed to explain it to Carol? The night he had seen Lily, he had sensed something unique about her and had since chosen to honor that elusive quality. The sight of her in such a vulnerable state had left him shattered. If she ever saw his work, he hoped it would uplift her, as though he might prevent her heart from getting broken again. But he knew their paths would never cross a second time. For all he knew, she lived in Maine or Montana.

Carol placed her elbows on the table and clasped her hands. She'd painted her manicured nails with a clear polish, safe and practical. Without a word, she closed her eyes and rested her forehead against her knuckles.

He hadn't made her cry, had he? Her shoulders weren't trembling…

"I can't do this anymore," she mumbled at last.

Ryder's heartbeat accelerated. "I'm—you can't…" As he leaned toward her, a metallic taste coated his tongue.

Carol raised her eyes. He had expected to find them glazed over with tears, but instead, they looked fatigued. One heavy exhale revealed all Ryder needed to know.

"I can't do this anymore," she repeated. "You and I both know this isn't working. We're miles apart, our personalities don't click any longer. Ryder, you're a wonderful person—"

"You don't need to say this. Look, you're worn out from work. Why don't you get a good night's sleep, start fresh tomorrow, and—"

Carol splayed her fingers. Her diction precise, she continued to speak over Ryder's words, as if to freeze his protest in its tracks. "—but I…can't…do this…anymore."

Ryder stopped short.

Their eyes locked.

Numbness crept into Ryder's belly. Moisture coated the sides of his tongue the way it did whenever he went queasy. She had enunciated her words with precision to remove any misconception.

Though she had made her decision, Ryder noted compassion in her eyes. At the corner of her mouth, he caught the trace of a smile. Was it pity?

Nonetheless, Carol remained stalwart. She blinked once, the slow brand that conveyed remorse, then she laced her rejection with two painful words.

"I'm sorry."

CHAPTER 8

LILY LOVED THE jingle of car keys. She shook a set of them in her grip as she admired the fresh wax on her car, which glistened in the sunlight. A year ago, she had treated herself to a black Subaru Impreza, which contained a boxer engine, just like a Porsche. She could spend hours poring over the curves and horsepower of cars the way art enthusiasts might examine a Rembrandt. Gunning the engine of a nice car kindled in her a rush stronger than one caused by the first silky sip of espresso.

On her way up the wooden steps to her apartment that afternoon, she eyed her watch and discovered it was a little past five-thirty. Maybe she should eat that grilled chicken, the batch she had put in the fridge the other day, before it spoiled. Served cold on a homemade Caesar salad sounded like a dream.

When she reached the top of the stairs, she stopped in her tracks outside her apartment door. She thought she heard a—

Lily winced when the wooden plank creaked beneath her foot. She singled out her car key—the longest and sharpest on her key ring—and clenched it, aiming it straight in front of her. With her ear cocked toward the maroon door, she crept toward it with slow, cautious steps. Once she reached the door, she pressed her ear against its cool surface. As soon as she did, she startled at a sound that came from inside her home. An object hit the floor with a *thud*. One of Brooke's coffee table books, maybe.

But Brooke was in Minneapolis on her business trip.

So who's in my apartment right now?

Lily bit down on her lip. She felt rapid thumps of her heart as they vibrated against her rib cage. Perspiration broke out along her neck.

Careful not to make a sound, she slid her fingers around the doorknob and tried to turn it to the left.

Locked.

How stupid of her. Of course the burglar didn't want to be caught by surprise. She knew she should have bought one of those cheap burglar alarms for the door.

While Brooke would have called the police at this point, Lily had never fit the standard mold. Call it her foolish side, but she possessed a ferocious sense of independence.

According to recent rumors, a teenager had broken into cars in the parking lot to finance a drug habit. A neighbor in the next building suspected he'd targeted her car. On a couple of occasions, Lily had confronted punks like that at the shop after hours. Now, as she stood before her own front door, adrenaline surged through her veins. She was ready to kick this adolescent's ass.

Gritting her teeth, she glanced around and noticed her neighbor's son had left his baseball glove and aluminum bat outside the door.

If this punk thought he would get out of her apartment without a fight, reality was about to crack him straight in the balls.

Lily tiptoed to the neighbor's doorstep, grabbed the bat, and tiptoed back to her own apartment. Although her hand shook, she steadied herself against the door frame, unlocked the door with the slightest possible click, then tucked her keys into her pocket.

Another thump on the other side of the door. It sounded like one of Brooke's candles. No doubt about it: The intruder was in the living room.

Steeling herself, Lily sucked air into her lungs and pounced. With a twist of the doorknob, she burst into the living room and gripped the bat with both hands, high above her head.

CHAPTER 9

"GET THE HELL out of my apartment!" Lily screamed.

Another scream—female—responded in a pitch even higher than Lily's.

"Oh, shit!" A male voice, one notch above a mutter.

With the Venetian blinds shut and Lily's eyes adjusting to the sudden lack of light, Lily caught sight of two silhouettes in a scramble. She reached for the light switch.

When the light came on, her sight landed on a man's pale ass as it bucked from the sofa. A pair of boxer shorts and khaki pants, scrunched below the guy's knees, rendered him immobile in his haste. He stumbled off the sofa and onto the floor in a desperate attempt to yank his boxers over his loins.

Lily shrieked. She jumped back and covered her eyes. By the time she removed her hand, Brooke had sat up. Her roommate's plum-red face matched that of her boyfriend who, by this point, had managed to start buckling his belt. Brooke fastened the upper buttons on her top. Her skirt, one she wore to work often, had wrinkled in the heat of passion. Their perspiration had rendered the room humid. In horror, Lily sniffed the musky scent of spontaneous sex.

Lily dropped the bat, which punctuated the awkwardness of the moment with a muffled clunk. "Brooke, you said you were flying to Minneapolis this morning! What are you doing here?!"

"Geez, Lily! I got my days mixed up, that's all. I leave tomorrow."

Lily looked on as her roommate ran her hand through her hair, which was mussed in the back. It was obvious who had been on top and who hadn't. Lily couldn't determine who was more embarrassed, Brooke or Lily herself. But Brooke's boyfriend, Jeremy, appeared the winner in the humiliation contest. The guy fidgeted, couldn't seem to find a spot to rest his hands, and his eyes wandered the room before he glued them to the floor. At last, he settled one hand on his face, where he pretended to scratch an itch on his chin.

Brooke furrowed an eyebrow and shot an inquisitive look at Lily, as if *Lily* had gotten caught bumping uglies on the sofa. "I thought you'd be out for drinks with the guys after work."

Lily waved it off. "I opened the store this morning, so I got off at two-thirty. Besides, I've had my fill of asses for one day." As her mind returned to the sight of Jeremy's backside, she cringed again. "No offense, Jeremy."

"Yeah, none taken," he replied, eyes still on the floor. "Maybe you two should invest in one of those write-on, wipe-off calendars. You know, stick it on your fridge. They have 'em at the dollar store."

Oh brother.

"Great idea."

Jeremy tied his shoes and nodded toward the door. "Look, I'm gonna head on out, Brooke. Gimme a call when you reach Minneapolis."

Jeremy gave Lily a two-finger wave—he'd managed to lift his eyes to her chin level—and made a beeline for the door.

At this point, Lily couldn't wait to gloss over the scenario into which she'd stumbled, so she returned the baseball bat to the neighbor's doorstep. By the time she got back to her apartment, Brooke had pulled a mirror from her purse and started to pucker her lips, gauging how much lipstick remained on them.

The environment still felt tense. How was Lily supposed to know what she would interrupt when she arrived home? Brooke could have called her at work to warn her. Lily would have stayed away for another hour.

"Guess I ruined your before-dinner plans, huh?"

With a pop of her lips, Brooke tossed the mirror back into her purse. "No worries. He'll get over it." For a split second, her face divulged a hint of irritation about the interruption. But then Brooke handled it the way she handled other inconveniences in life: She shrugged it off. *It's over now. Time to move on.*

How could Brooke approach sex with such a casual attitude?

Lily headed toward the refrigerator to retrieve her leftovers from the prior day. Brooke hurried behind her.

"Oh, I almost forgot! You won't believe what I saw today," Brooke exclaimed. "I found your twin!"

"What are you talking about?"

"I'm serious! Wait here."

Brooke rounded the corner to her bedroom and returned with a magazine in hand, which she passed to Lily.

It was one of those pop-culture magazines that focused on fashion and movies while dabbling in tabloid territory. Lily flipped through the pages. She had always wondered where some of the photos for such magazines came from, particularly this issue's aerial shot of a large tent that housed a celebrity wedding. Did photographers hide behind bushes and sneak into helicopters to catch these people in the most private or humiliating situations possible?

On one page, Lily pointed to a picture of an actress caught by surprise with her tongue sticking halfway out of her mouth. She waved it at Brooke. "You should frame this one."

"Whatever." Brooke grabbed the magazine, located her intended page near the end, and folded the magazine along its spine. "I was paging through magazines to get ideas on ad themes we could use for a client of mine. On the phone today, the client mentioned an ad on page 58 of this issue. Said she really likes it. So I turned to it—and *this* is what I saw."

Lily examined the slick, glossy page, an advertisement for a brand of wine manufactured in Napa Valley. Instead of a photo, the ad featured a full-page replication of a painting. But the painting looked lifelike, as if the artist had taken a photograph and re-created it on canvas. In the scene, a man and woman—in their twenties, by Lily's estimation—flirted at a nice restaurant. Manhattan, perhaps. A Saturday night on the town. The man wore a dark sport coat and a shirt with no tie, and had his arm around the waist of the woman, who wore a gorgeous red dress. The couple appeared rapt in each other's eyes. Lily sensed a magnetic draw between them.

They looked as if the man had uttered a witty remark and now took delight in his date's coy reaction. The woman leaned toward him, her body language inviting more of his attention. The couple held aloft glasses of white wine as they chatted. Mere afterthoughts, those glasses of wine. Yet apparently, the beverage had inspired this moment of romance.

Lily considered the man handsome with his firm jaw and wavy, brown hair. In fact, he had one of those faces which could, with one glance, render you at ease. She sensed instant comfort in his presence. He also had the sort of appearance that made you feel as if you had met him before.

And Brooke was right. The woman looked exactly like Lily. Her hair color, complexion, nuances in her face and fingers—Lily recognized them all.

Brook leaned over her shoulder. "See what I mean?"

"Yeah…" Stunned, Lily examined the woman closer but couldn't find the words to speak. An honest-to-goodness lookalike! Yet somehow, that red dress and fancy environment had transformed her into a different person altogether. The change had escorted her into another world!

Even though this woman was a fictional character, Lily tried to imagine her background and what she did for a living. The superficial differences between Lily and this woman were obvious, but Lily knew something else must have come into play between a couple like this. What did this woman have that Lily didn't? What would draw this particular man to this particular woman?

A hint of jealousy stabbed Lily's heart, but she shoved the feeling aside.

Before she knew it, Lily pictured *herself* in the woman's place—which wasn't difficult, given the similarities.

She imagined the floral scent of that wine…

The brush of the red dress against her thighs…

His arm around her waist…

What am I doing?!

Lily snapped the magazine shut and tossed it on the dining room table.

CHAPTER 10

TWENTY-FOUR HOURS AFTER Carol ended their relationship, Ryder remained dismayed and needed to remind himself that, yes, she had dumped him. Granted, for quite a while, he had sensed he and Carol might part ways. Averted gazes, avoidance of certain topics of discussion—warning signs had sneaked into the corners of their romance and worked their way toward the center. Relational glaucoma. So, Ryder had to admit, Carol's ultimate revelation hadn't come as a total shock.

What he found odd was the blend of feelings that arose in the wake of their dissolution. He'd anticipated disappointment from rejection which, indeed, was present. But at the same time, he also felt a wave of relief. He perceived a slight sense of loss, a minor wound in his heart, but that was the extent of his emotional reaction. He hadn't shed a tear over the breakup.

Yet his frustration remained real.

A photo of Carol sat at the corner of the desk in his studio. Ryder turned it face down.

Relationships. They always fell apart. For him, at least. And though he had never discussed it with anyone, he had grown suspicious that maybe, on a subconscious level, he *sabotaged* them.

Maybe he didn't *want* his relationships to work out. Was that possible? With each trial, maybe he believed something better was on its way.

Something that might involve…what? He had no idea. But whatever it was, he clung to it.

Yes, with the end of each relationship in the past, hope bubbled within him.

In the meantime, the dream would continue to unfold on canvas.

Sitting at his desk, Ryder sketched out a concept for an upcoming advertisement for an Alaskan cruise ship. An array of books filled with pictures of the state's shoreline lay scattered across his desk, along with a brochure from the cruise company. He filled in the background with a mountain scene based on a photo he'd found in one of the books.

He had never visited Alaska, but now he wanted to go.

In the forefront of the scene, he sketched the ship's white railing and exterior. Then he sketched himself leaning against the railing, looking deep into the blue eyes he remembered so well. Would an Alaskan cruise pique Lily's interest? Or did she hate the cold?

He wished he could ask her.

But that would never happen, would it?

When his thoughts returned to Carol, Ryder gritted his teeth and resolved to focus on the project before him. With feathered strokes, he added shadowy edges to his subjects' shoulders.

A knock on a glass pane interrupted his concentration. Before he had a chance to respond, Chase let himself into the studio through the sliding door. As Ryder's business manager, Chase paid regular visits to the studio, so Ryder left the door unlocked during the day. That way, he wouldn't need to stop working to let his friend into his home.

After years of effort by Ryder and Chase, a steady flow of projects started to roll in. At that point, Ryder hired Chase, an Internet marketer, in an official capacity, albeit part-time. After all, Chase had believed in Ryder from day one and had performed the role on a gratis basis. When it came to promotional efforts or the securing of clients, Ryder couldn't imagine himself trusting anyone more than Chase. And now that a small degree of fame had launched Ryder into the limelight, Chase had entered continual brainstorm mode. Sometimes the guy called Ryder in the middle of the night with new ideas. Oftentimes, Ryder was wide awake and working to meet deadlines when those late-night calls arrived.

"Brought you lunch." Chase plopped a submarine sandwich onto Ryder's desk.

At the scent of oil and vinegar, Ryder's stomach grumbled, but he forced himself to keep moving forward.

"How's my favorite artist?"

Ryder didn't break his gaze from the sketch. "Hanging in there. Thanks for the sandwich."

"Which project are you working on? The tanning salon chain?"

"Cruise ship."

"Think you'll have that concept sketch done today?"

"I'll scan it and send the file to the client this afternoon."

Chase sauntered to the other side of the desk, leaned over Ryder's shoulder, and peeked at the sketch. "Same girl?"

Ryder nodded.

"Who is she?"

"I don't know." Technically, that was the truth. He didn't know her last name or anything about her.

"If she's real—"

"Everyone has a lookalike. Don't worry, I've taken a lot of artistic liberty. Legally, I'm safe."

Chase shrugged. "The public seems to like it. Believe it or not, when I'm on the phone with clients, some of them bring her up." Chase sat down and crossed one leg over the other. "I can probably secure you more jobs if I guarantee your famous couple will make an appearance in the client's ad. Would you mind?"

Ryder suppressed a grin. "Go for it."

"Remember the company that just bought the painting of your famous couple for a poster and postcard? They'd like to buy another. Do you happen to have any on standby?"

"I'll email samples to you. I finished two more last week."

"Do you ever sleep?"

"Not last week."

Chase furrowed his brow. "Don't burn yourself out, okay?"

"You know me better than that. Besides, you're the one with the track record for making 2 a.m. phone calls."

"Hey, you laugh, but one of these days, I'll have a million-dollar idea for you," Chase said. "And for the record, I *wake up* with those 2 a.m. visions. You're the one pulling all-nighters to complete some of these projects. Make sure you don't sacrifice your health."

When Ryder reached a stopping point, he tore open the foil sandwich wrapper and bit into the spicy Italian sub. Still warm from the toaster oven, the first taste of capicola, salami and melted pepper-jack cheese—his favorite combination from a nearby deli—made his mouth water.

"Speaking of all-nighters," said Chase, "you must've been in quite a trance last night. You never replied to my text message."

Ryder's stomach clenched. He swallowed his bite. "Carol and I went to dinner."

"At least *one* of us is in a nice, healthy relationship."

"We broke up."

Chase froze in place, then eyed Ryder as if unsure what to say. "Sorry to hear that, man. Are you okay?"

"I can't say I'm torn up over it." Ryder ran his finger along the bread's flaky surface. "As you know, she had a few concerns about my career. I can't say I didn't see this coming; I just expected it later rather than sooner."

"Remember that old song, 'Islands in the Stream'? What a load of crap that was, huh? As if love is all palm trees and twang," Chase snorted. "A stroke of marketing genius, though. I mean, Kenny and Dolly? I'm sure people ate that shit for breakfast back in the day."

Chase knew the right things to say in moments like these. Stupid as it might sound, the thought of Kenny Rogers and Dolly Parton lifted Ryder's spirits. He hoped people wouldn't poke fun at *his* art thirty years from now.

"Carol and I had a decent run," Ryder said. "Eight months together." It was the longest Ryder had ever stayed in a relationship. He didn't know whether to celebrate or groan.

"Would you mind if I say something honest, even if it doesn't reflect well on Carol?"

"Okay…"

"The woman is dull. Besides, she isn't your type," Chase said. "Carol lives and breathes numbers. She probably has dirty dreams about the number 8 and its gentle, hourglass figure."

"Let's talk about something else."

Chase shrugged. "Works for me. Now that you're a bachelor again, you can say yes to that film premiere."

Although the notion of attending a premiere sounded exciting, Ryder felt a bit like a pawn in the scenario, a lifeless mannequin.

"Ana Ferguson could have her pick from a slew of young actors. Each one would fall over himself to escort her on the red carpet," Ryder pointed out. "I'm just the guy who designed the movie poster."

"But she *loved* that poster. Seriously! She told her manager it was sexy." Chase grabbed Ryder by the shoulders and looked directly at him. "Ana's stock is rising in Hollywood these days. Picture it: You attend the premiere together, and the public thinks, hmm...*maybe* there's a flame between the two of you. Rumors start to buzz, but they turn out false. She stays in the spotlight and signs another movie contract. You look honest because you never claimed the rumor was true—and suddenly, you become the elusive bachelor every girl wants but can't capture."

"And you're sure it will cause more demand for my work?"

"It's a no-brainer! Remember, this represents another step in a long-term strategy. People already know you're the subject in many of your own paintings. That was brilliant, by the way—I wish I could claim credit for it. You're recognizable. You have people talking. If they associate you with a celebrity or two, you could become a household name." When he didn't receive a response, Chase tapped his foot. "It's in two weeks, so I need to give her manager an answer ASAP."

The concept seemed so impersonal to Ryder. He wasn't a shallow individual. Yet he knew enough to seize an opportunity when it arrived.

Chase backtracked a step, spread his arms, and awaited an answer. "Well? What's it gonna be?"

Ryder exhaled.

"Okay," he said. "Count me in."

CHAPTER 11

A FEW DAYS later, after waving good-bye to a mid-morning customer, Lily punched some final details into the computer behind the cash register. At the squeal of a tow truck's brakes, she glanced at the bank of windows along the side of the shop. The truck driver had called a few minutes earlier with notice that he would deliver a vehicle that had died on the shoulder of the interstate. Lily's manager had promised the staff would give the car a thorough examination. So Lily had expected the vehicle.

Lily *hadn't* expected the vehicle's *owner.*

Stunned, she stared out the window as Dave jogged outside to meet the truck driver and provide instructions as the tow truck idled behind them. Then Dave gestured with his thumb toward the rear of the building, whereupon the driver climbed back into his truck and shifted into reverse. Meanwhile, Dave approached the car's owner to collect more information.

Evan Lancaster tugged at his tie in obvious embarrassment at having to return to the shop for his second visit in a week. Rolling his eyes once, Evan appeared to find humor in what had happened—that is, as much humor as you can find when your vehicle dies. Dave gestured to the waiting room.

Lily jerked her attention back to the computer monitor and pretended to look busy, as if she hadn't spent the last minute admiring how gorgeous Evan was. She scrambled to open a customer record—*any* record—an empty record, perfect!—and clicked away at random keys on the keyboard. By the time she heard the door jingle, she had entered *FOIJJJAD8834N8H4DSF* into the First Name field and hit the Tab key.

Her heartbeat accelerated.

From the corner of her eye, she watched Evan's hand place a cell phone on the counter in front of her. She clicked the Cancel button to close the record without saving the changes. Steadying herself, she looked up and attempted her best expression of surprise.

"You're back?"

Evan nodded toward the tire display and its mascot made of black rubber. "What can I say? That tire man turns me on."

Before she could help herself, Lily let out a chuckle and drew a hand against her mouth to silence herself. "Well, who says there isn't a silver lining to everything?"

Despite his humor, Evan looked a bit flustered, like someone who had finished a series of ad-hoc phone calls and signed an expensive towing bill. Lily saw it daily.

She opened Evan's customer record.

Risking a quick glance at him, she tried to conceal her delight—and her hope that he might need…

"I take it you'll need another ride?"

"Yes, please. If you don't mind." Evan drummed his fingers on the counter. "I think I got a lemon of a car. It's not old. I shouldn't have issues with it yet, should I?"

"No problems before? What happened today?"

"I don't know. The engine shut down on the interstate. I was in the far-right lane, so I coasted to the shoulder as the car decelerated." He grinned. "Grandma Moses nearly rear-ended me."

Lily entered the details into the record. "We'll check it out. I have a few ideas, but it's all guesswork until we look under the hood and start troubleshooting."

A smile brought new life to his hazel eyes. "Okay, just for fun, suppose you needed to take a guess. What do you suspect might have gone wrong with the car?"

Lily pondered a moment. "The vehicle wouldn't start at all once it stopped?"

"No."

"Not even a clicking noise when you turned your key in the ignition?"

"My key wouldn't even budge when I tried to turn it."

"Once you rolled to a stop, did you put the car in Park?"

"I don't think so." He paused. "So, what's your preliminary diagnosis, doctor?"

She'd seen this happen before, too, and almost hated to admit her suspicion. For *his* sake.

"Well, like I said, we'll run some diagnostics on it. But it's a newer car, so…"

Evan leaned forward.

"…it sounds like you couldn't turn the key because you still had your car in Drive. The system won't let you start it unless you have the car in Park."

Maybe she shouldn't have told him that. Now she didn't know how to spare him further embarrassment. Poor guy. She had to try, at least.

"But you also said the engine shut down while you were driving," she added. "So even if you *had* put your car in Park and turned the key, I'd guess you would've heard a clicking noise, but the engine still wouldn't have started. If that's the case, we'll get it fixed pretty fast."

"How much is this going to cost me?"

"If it's what I think is wrong, no charge. It'll be on the house."

"Why?"

"I'd wager it's a loose wire between the ignition and the starter. We'd tighten the connection and you'd be good to go."

Evan's jaw dropped. He shook his head. "Seems impossible. There's no way it can be that simple—I mean, the car *shut down on the highway.* If you're right, I owe you one hell of a dinner."

The door to the garage burst open.

"Sir?" Dave called out.

Evan looked his way.

"We have your car in the garage. No big deal—just a loose wire between the ignition and the starter. We'll tighten the connection and you're good to go." A thumbs-up from Dave. Then the door slammed shut again.

Evan looked dumfounded.

The silence made Lily feel awkward, so she said, "By the way, don't feel stupid about not putting the car in Park. At least the car was on level ground and didn't roll downhill."

Evan blushed. "Geez..."

She couldn't help but feel bad for him. She hadn't meant to make him look foolish. "Don't worry, you're not the first. Happens every week."

"I guess my secret's out: I'm not much of a car guru," Evan shrugged.

Lily glanced at her handsome customer, dressed in his suit and tie worthy of a *GQ* magazine cover. His gelled hair, his unbitten fingernails—*manicured?*

"I think your secret was out the moment you gelled your hair and put on that tie. Sorry."

With a self-deprecating laugh, Evan said, "Yeah, well, I may not know much about cars, but I *can* tell you this: It's the best time of year to stock up on those hospital gowns that tie in the back."

"Wisdom for the ages. Socrates would be jealous."

"I must admit, I'm impressed with how you had the issue pegged right away. Seems like I owe you something."

"Tell you what," Lily said, "I'll spare you the embarrassment of buying me dinner. Just tell your girlfriend I said hi."

Evan hesitated a moment, then said, "Oh, there's no girlfriend in the picture right now."

"Seriously, you don't—"

"You won the bet. I think I owe you."

Lily caught a glint in Evan's eye. Sure, he was beautiful, but he seemed way out of her league. She'd feel too ridiculous walking into his kind of place, whatever that was. Expensive, probably. She could only imagine.

"Well, technically it wasn't a bet," she said, "and technically, I'm not much of a Champagne Chateau kind of girl..."

Lily blinked to make sure she saw what she thought she saw. Was that disappointment in his eyes? Had he asked her out—as in, *asked her out?*

She wanted to say yes. She opened her mouth to say the word, but then her stomach sank. What would a guy like Evan see in her? Guys didn't ask Lily Machara out. They didn't find her attractive. Once Evan got to know her better, she would disappoint him, and she didn't want to end up hurt.

So when she opened her mouth to speak, she took the safest route for her: humor.

"But hey, look on the bright side," she said. "You could loosen that wire in your car and try your luck again—maybe break down in front of a spa or something. Destiny, the woman of your dreams, and all that."

She offered him a smile. Then she felt her eyes moisten.

"Yeah, maybe." He forced a halfhearted chortle, tried to maintain his composure, but Lily could see he was now eager to escape. He slid his cell phone from the counter and gave her a wave. "See you next week, right?" he said with a wink before heading toward the door.

Call it a nervous response, but Lily felt her mouth open and heard her own voice before she could stop herself.

"Yes," she said a bit too loud.

A customer in the waiting area turned her head at the sudden burst of noise.

So did Evan.

How embarrassing! Lily scrambled to organize her thoughts as Evan turned around.

When he'd eased back to the counter, Lily said in a hushed tone, "I mean, yes, dinner sounds nice. A...yeah, a date would be fine."

Evan's eyes softened, his countenance kind.

Lily felt warm all over.

CHAPTER 12

TWO HOURS LATER, when Lily headed outside for lunch, her arms prickled in the sunlight. As March matured, the air felt balmier by the day. Three of her coworkers had already gathered around an employee picnic table behind the garage. Someone had collected orders and grabbed to-go burgers from a fast-food joint a few doors down. What Lily wouldn't have given for a double cheeseburger! But her slim figure was the one thing she believed she had going for her.

The guys laughed and took verbal jabs at each other, something about the previous night's happy hour and a woman who had stopped by their table for a drink.

Wonders never cease, Lily mused.

"Puh-lease!" she heard somebody shout. "Dude, you couldn't land that woman if you were the last man on earth!"

"If we could get Aaron hooked up with one of those ladies that practically throw their phone numbers at him, we'd have a miracle on our hands. What's up with that, man?"

Lily tossed her brown bag on the table and took a seat beside her friend Aaron. She nudged him as she took a bite of her sandwich—cucumber on whole wheat, a smidgen of light cream cheese, sprinkled with dill.

The guys stopped chattering.

"We were wondering when you'd get out here, Lily!" shouted Dave.

He tossed a magazine her way, its pages in a flutter frenzy, one of the shop's many subscriptions. Lily recognized it. It was the same issue Brooke had shown her the day before.

"Have you seen page 58?" Dave leaned forward on his elbows. "Is there something you're not telling us?"

Chuckles all around.

"Yeah, yeah," she muttered.

At first, Lily ignored the magazine. Then, with half-interest, she found page 58 and gave the glossy advertisement a once-over.

"Posing for ads in your spare time?" Aaron jostled her finger.

Lily tossed the magazine back on the table. "Apparently, I'm in the wrong business. Didn't realize I was such a model. Maybe I should move my ass to Monaco, huh?"

"You *eat* like a model," Dave volleyed. "All that rabbit-food shit you bring for lunch."

"What can I say? I'm a dainty freakin' lady. Didn't you know you're in the presence of a lady?"

The guys loved that one, based on the boom of laughter the remark triggered. Afterward, they moved on to car chatter.

Grinning, Aaron murmured, "You're a piece of work."

"What, you too? Don't mess with my cucumbers."

"Never!" He paused. "So, you and that BMW guy seemed to be hitting it off this morning."

Lily feigned innocence. "What are you talking about?"

"He was totally flirting with you in there. I noticed it when I picked up a work ticket behind the window." He jiggled her hand. "I saw that sparkle he had when he talked to you!"

"It was nothing. Evan's just some guy who sells medical supplies. Says he's a vice-president, so I guess he's got his life figured out."

"Evan?"

Lily sneaked a quick glimpse of her other tablemates to make sure they couldn't overhear this discussion. That was the last thing she needed. As it turned out, she had no reason to concern herself with them, lost as they were in their own self-absorbed worlds of women and pointless banter.

When she returned her focus to Aaron, she realized he hadn't stopped staring at her. He looked amused.

Leaning his head closer to hers, he asked, "Okay, what *really* happened with that guy?"

Lily couldn't help but beam. She hoped she wouldn't end up getting her heart broken.

"Come on," Aaron coaxed.

"Fine!" Lily sighed. "He asked me out."

"And?"

Lily hesitated a moment.

"And…I said yes."

"Well, well." He pursed his lips. "At least you have good taste, right?"

She gave him a playful slug to the arm.

"Leave me alone."

CHAPTER 13

BY SEVEN O'CLOCK on Saturday night, Lily regretted her decision to let Evan take her out.

He had given her a quick call Friday afternoon to make sure she hadn't changed her mind and, once again, she had blurted her response before she'd thought it through.

"Yeah, of course," she had replied. But now, she wished she had backed out.

This sudden case of cold feet had nothing to do with Evan. Rather, Lily wasn't used to the scrambling around, the second-guessing, the nervousness that preceded dates. After surviving for so long without a date, she'd forgotten how it all felt; but tonight, it returned in a tidal wave of nausea.

Of course Brooke was nowhere to be found when Lily needed her. She and Jeremy had headed out an hour ago. Brooke knew how to prepare for these things. The girl would know how Lily should fix her hair, what she should wear, and whatever other details that wouldn't occur to Lily until a humiliating circumstance reared its head. Then again, Lily hadn't mentioned this date to Brooke. After envisioning her roommate's slew of questions upon learning Lily had actual romantic plans for Saturday night, Lily had figured the commotion would only increase the apprehension. Nonetheless, she knew Brooke would have postponed her own plans to help Lily prepare.

But that didn't matter now. Lily remained alone.

She had hoped some old Taylor Swift music in the background would help calm her, but instead, the noise increased her tension. She shut it off and headed back into the bathroom.

She didn't make much of an attempt at makeup for fear of how it might turn out. She had applied a decent foundation—she knew how to do that from watching her roommate—but nothing fancy. To take advantage of her slim figure, she'd squeezed into a tight-fitting, dark green dress she had purchased years ago when Brooke had convinced her to go clubbing together. Lily smoothed out the dress and scrutinized herself in the mirror. Not one to study fashion magazines, she had no idea if the dress was still in style, but she had to admit, it blended well with her porcelain skin.

Where was he taking her tonight, anyway? She wished she'd thought to ask. And what would they talk about once they got there?

Oh, geez.

No. Don't think about that now.

She picked up her brush and ran it through her hair, which she had already done so many times she'd lost count. Her fingernails, coated with red nail polish, reflected the row of decorative light bulbs in the bathroom. As she set down the brush, she noticed a few strands of hair had escaped from it and landed on her shoulder.

No!

One by one, she peeled them off and let them flutter into the wastebasket.

The truth, Lily had to admit, was this: She didn't feel pretty.

And she was afraid Evan would figure it out before the evening ended.

She felt her stomach fluids slosh around. She wanted to vomit.

A knock at the door startled her.

She grabbed a small, digital clock from the counter and gawked at what she discovered. It was already 7:29. He was a minute early.

"Just a minute! I'll be right there!" she shouted as she poked her head through the bathroom door. Grabbing her mouthwash from the cabinet, she took a swig before darting to the front door.

With a deep breath, she smoothed her dress one last time and exhaled. Her pulse slowed. Then she flung the door open.

Evan looked gorgeous. His dark blue shirt brought out the rich tone in his skin. Before he had a chance to respond, she searched his eyes to catch whether his unfiltered reaction exhibited disappointment or delight. If he was disappointed, he hid it well. Hands behind his back, he appeared relaxed.

Then he greeted her with a broad smile.

"You look beautiful," he said.

Lily couldn't think of what to say next. Unconvinced whether she should believe the compliment, she offered a little shrug and peered into his eyes again.

Evan withdrew one arm from behind his back and handed her a Dean Martin CD. She had to giggle. The CD reminded her of the day they'd met, and the smart-aleck guess she had made about his taste in music while she'd given him a ride to work.

"For the girl who likes the Rat Pack," Evan said with a wink.

Lily recognized the jest and had to match him. She couldn't help herself.

"I don't think so. Nice try."

"Oh, right!" Evan snapped his fingers and withdrew his other hand to reveal another CD.

And with this gift, he had her.

"I doubt you buy CDs anymore, but the digital route would have blown the surprise." His grin possessed a blend of confidence and pleasure. "You said you like Rascal Flatts, right?"

Before she caught her unconscious reaction, she ran her hand along the front of her neck as she stared at the cover of the band's latest album. She tugged at the necklace Brooke had re-gifted her years ago.

Not only had Evan listened to her…he'd remembered.

CHAPTER 14

EVAN TOOK HER to a Mediterranean-themed restaurant. A nice one.

A *very* nice one.

She sneaked a glance at the couple who sat at the neighboring table, a man and woman who, by Lily's estimation, were triple her own age.

Her nervousness had resumed the moment they entered the place. She felt underdressed, undercosmeticized, under*something.*

Why did he bring me here? Lily wondered. *I told him I'm not into these places.*

But Evan seemed comfortable, and he didn't appear embarrassed to have her with him. Maybe the rationale behind her self-doubt was a figment of her imagination. When the hostess had led Lily and Evan to their table, Evan had held out Lily's chair and scooted her in. From that point, she had followed his cues. Her white napkin had sat atop the table in a starched swirl of elegance. She'd set it on her lap the way Evan had—she'd expected that—but she'd noticed he didn't fold the napkin in half before doing so. He'd set it flat upon his lap. She'd asked why, and he'd mentioned he sees people treat it both ways during dinner, whichever size covers your lap.

She peered past a pair of candles at the center of the table.

"How often do you come to this place?" Lily asked, a covert attempt to find out how frequently he dated.

"I take a lot of business associates here."

"Job perks, huh?"

"For a foodie like me? Definitely."

Lily picked up her menu and figured she could use it as an excuse to duck conversation for a few minutes. As it turned out, her concentration on the menu wouldn't be an excuse. With dark brown print against a dark tan background, she could barely read it in the dim room. She angled it toward the candlelight, which helped. She'd never been more grateful for descriptions on a menu, because based on the entrée names, she couldn't tell what the hell half of them were. Paella, calvados, gnocchi—who knew what she was about to put into her mouth! Whatever it was, she hoped it wouldn't give her the shits. Perhaps she should play it safe and order one of the pasta dishes…

With another glance to her left, she noticed an older woman had lowered the menu to her lap and now perused it with a tiny flashlight she'd smuggled in her purse. Lily was tempted to borrow it.

"What do you recommend?" Lily asked Evan, her eyes back on the menu.

"The salmon is delicious," he said.

Lily located it on the menu. Grilled and served on a bed of asparagus. Okay, she could handle that. Her appetite rumbled to life.

With that settled, she placed the menu on the table, handling it as though it were a piece of delicate china. When she looked up, she found Evan staring at her, but in a pleasurable way. His subdued, confident air complemented his handsome face. The man seemed to fall silent at the right moments, almost by design. Maybe it was a byproduct of his job; she had heard salespeople remain silent and wait for the other party to speak so the salesperson can gauge areas of uncertainty or openness. When Evan *did* speak, he gave the impression of choosing his words with forethought, but not in a way that would take advantage of her vulnerable heart.

At a loss for words herself, Lily was about to say the first thing that came to mind when their waiter, dressed in a black tie and a shirt as starchy as Lily's napkin, arrived to take their orders. Evan also recommended the lobster bisque, which she agreed to try.

On any other occasion, Lily wouldn't have wanted suggestions on what to eat. But Evan didn't strike her as the domineering type. Years ago, she'd had her fill of that type of man and had no desire to repeat her mistake. Rather, Evan delighted in seeing her enjoy every ounce of their evening together, like he wanted to take care of her. She had to admit, it was a nice change from the guys who tended to cross her path.

Once Evan ordered a bottle of pinot noir, the suggested pairing with Lily's grilled salmon, the waiter sealed the order with half a bow and departed. Lily sipped her water, then decided she couldn't sit there the rest of the evening and say nothing. Seldom did she have the opportunity to take a stab at mature conversation.

Her plan was to ask questions and let him do the bulk of the talking.

"You mentioned you're a vice-president where you work," she said. "So if you don't handle many sales yourself, how do you make them happen?"

"I lead a team of people in my department. We divide the United States into regions, and people are responsible for each of them."

"And St. Louis falls into what region?"

"Missouri, Iowa, Arkansas and Illinois."

Lily couldn't fathom her work stretching that far. "They must spend all their time on the road."

"They travel a lot, yes. They also work the phones here and try to set up appointments. If they have an appointment with a client in Little Rock, they might contact other prospective clients in the area to line up several visits in one trip. That way, they can consolidate their travel."

"And meanwhile, you stay home and monitor them?"

"I work directly with a handful of major clients, plus I look at our upcoming products and determine strategies for selling them."

Lily was surprised at how simple it had become to ease deeper into conversation with Evan. Although some aspects of their date struck her as superficial, she discovered she could play the part rather well. From time to time, though Evan might have noticed her unfamiliarity or a wrong gesture, the evening blossomed by the minute.

She scoped out her environment again, took note of the tables and cozy, circular booths along the periphery, their cushions covered in a tapestry pattern of burgundy, turquoise and autumn yellow. Greek music played overhead. Ivory-colored stone accented the columns and walls. In one corner of the restaurant, she noticed a bar area beneath a canopy of polished wooden beams.

A waitress walked past them, steam rising from the tray in her hand. Lily inhaled the sharp scent and tracked the waitress to a nearby table, where patrons admired what looked like lamb dishes. Lily returned her attention to Evan.

When a wine steward arrived with their pinot noir, he poured a dash into Evan's glass and halted. As if on cue, Evan lifted the glass to his nose, inhaled, then sipped from it. He nodded to the steward, who proceeded to fill the remainder of Evan's glass and Lily's, as well. Lily kept a close eye on their behavior, their nonverbal communication, and pegged this as a code of conduct in a nice restaurant.

Amused, she looked forward to whatever little games might come next.

And to her astonishment, she grew more relaxed in her surroundings.

CHAPTER 15

"DID YOU ENJOY the restaurant?" Evan asked in the car later that evening. "I hope it didn't make you uncomfortable."

"It was nice. I'd never been there before." She'd savored each bite of her salmon, which she'd found tender and glazed to perfection. She'd left a few bites on her plate, but only to avoid a stomachache. "Maybe next time, we could go someplace, um, simpler."

"Next time?" Evan grinned, a glint in his eye. "I'm looking forward to it already."

At a few minutes past nine o'clock, streetlights and business signage lit the busy suburban street with electric fire. Lily eased against her seat, though it still seemed strange sitting in a BMW beside a man she hardly knew.

He was interested in a *second* date? In truth, she wasn't sure where she stood on the matter and wasn't ready to talk about it further. A touch of nervousness returned, albeit lighter than before. She decided to change the subject—something, anything, fast.

At the next intersection, a half-mile ahead, a billboard hovered. The billboard was the electronic type that changed its image several times per minute. As Evan and Lily approached, it promoted a local television news team.

"It's nice not to see those peeling signs anymore," Lily said, nodding at the advertisement. "That's modern technology for you."

She turned her head and peered through the passenger window at a retail store. When they reached the intersection, Evan braked for a red light, which reflected in Lily's window.

His voice startled her.

"*Now* I know why you looked so familiar when we met!"

"Huh?" She turned back toward him.

"Up there." He pointed to the billboard.

Lily leaned forward for a better view. The news anchors had disappeared, and a new image had replaced them.

Her jaw dropped.

Before her eyes was a picture of her lookalike, along with her familiar male companion.

Same couple from the magazine. This advertisement, however, touted a national corporation that sold concert tickets for a variety of venues in major markets.

Hand in hand, the couple walked out of a concert hall. In the image, the woman, in contrast to Lily, had applied her makeup better and appeared confident in the tasteful black dress she wore for the evening. Lily deduced the couple had attended a symphony together.

She had to consider this a coincidence. But it grew odder by the day.

Though she didn't tell Evan, Lily had seen her lookalike in *three other images* since Brooke first showed her the magazine.

Evan chuckled.

"Remember when I first walked into the auto shop? I recognized you but couldn't put my finger on why," he said with a sideways glance. "See? You're famous and you didn't even know it!"

Too engrossed in the couple to respond, Lily watched as the image dissolved to a school of fish, an advertisement for the local zoo.

When the traffic light turned green, Evan eased the car forward and shot her a wink.

"I'll bet you thought it was my standard pickup line."

CHAPTER 16

A DARK APARTMENT greeted her when she returned home. Alone.

Fearful Evan might try to kiss her good-night, she'd lost no time unbuckling her seatbelt and opening the car door once he'd reached the parking lot. On one hand, she would have welcomed the gesture; on the other hand, she couldn't bring herself to trust. She'd remembered to thank him and had told him she'd had a wonderful time. Although she'd invited him in, she'd done so as an afterthought, to which he had responded with a polite decline. No surprise there, given how fast she'd tried to escape his car. But he'd promised to call, if that was okay with her.

She'd said that would be fine.

Lily flipped the light switch and set down her purse. Brooke had left a note on the counter mentioning she'd stopped in after dinner and would spend the night at Jeremy's place, so don't wait up.

Have fun hanging out with Aaron, her note said. Brooke had assumed Lily would spend her Saturday evening at her friend's place, as she often did.

If only you knew.

So Lily had the apartment to herself tonight. She considered giving Aaron a call but, on second thought, decided against it. Maybe she would fall asleep to a good movie instead.

Her mind returned to the billboard and the other artwork she'd seen the past week. Regardless of the scene, the female subject looked so comfortable in her life, in her surroundings, in the presence of her significant other.

And in each scene, the man found the woman desirable. He didn't hide his affection. In one image, Lily had seen herself—or rather, her lookalike—wrapped in the man's embrace.

To have a man's arms wrapped around her.

Lily tried to recall the sensation.

Exhausted, she padded to her bedroom closet and hung her dress toward the back. The March nights carried a slight chill, so she changed into a cozy sweatshirt and sweatpants, relieved Evan couldn't see her now. Or her lookalike, for that matter.

At the bathroom sink, Lily ran the water and was about to remove her makeup when she stopped short. She turned off the faucet and inspected her hair in the mirror, then scrutinized her face. She studied her deep, blue eyes. She fingered her chin, her lips...all in search of what someone might consider attractive.

Lily wondered how it might feel for a man to look at her and find her beautiful. To say to her, *You're stunning.*

Her cheeks, her neckline. She considered every inch.

Without a sound in the apartment, Lily grew absorbed in what she saw.

She yearned to feel loved. A longing so strong, tonight it brought a film of tears to her eyes.

She removed her clothes, article by article, and stared at her slim figure in the mirror.

What was it like to be beautiful? How would it feel to trade places with her lookalike?

Lily couldn't recall the last time a man had touched her, made her feel attractive or secure.

She closed her eyes and felt the sting of tears. With delicate strokes, she ran her fingers along her bare shoulders, her arms, the upper portion of her chest two inches below her neckline.

She imagined the sensation of a man's caress, a strong arm wrapped around her.

Then she eased her eyes open and beheld her figure in the mirror once again. Her chest possessed what Brooke would refer to as an athletic build. Pivoting at the waist, Lily noted the appealing curves of her buttocks, the blush of pink upon her delicate skin.

And she had to admit, she did have cute toes.

The tears stopped. Lily blotted her eyes with a hand towel.

Even though she didn't expect Brooke to return home until morning, Lily grew self-conscious as her eyes darted to the bathroom door, which stood wide open. How humiliating should Brooke and Jeremy have a change of plans and walk in as Lily, disrobed, stared at herself in the mirror!

She got dressed again, turned the water back on, and made another attempt at removing her makeup. The last time she'd applied it to her face and scrubbed it off, the routine had left her cheeks chapped. Her skin wasn't accustomed to such abuse. She expected the same result this time around.

Yet, something inside her told her tonight had been worth the effort.

Maybe she would pour herself a glass of wine and listen to the Rascal Flatts CD, the one Evan had given her earlier. Heck, she might even try the Dean Martin one. She hadn't had the heart to admit to Evan that she'd gone digital and abandoned CDs ten years ago.

Evan.

Logic told her Evan had potential. And he'd left no doubt about his interest in her.

Maybe her heart would catch up with his.

CHAPTER 17

"LILY! VISITOR!" SHOUTED a coworker from the entrance to the waiting room.

Lily eyed the clock. Shortly past eleven on Monday morning. She finished checking the charge on a car's battery, craned her neck toward the waiting-room window, and saw Evan standing at the counter. Lily gulped. On Saturday night, she'd entered Evan's world, if only for one evening. She had no desire to remind him of hers. It seemed deficient by comparison. A fresh wave of self-consciousness swept in.

Not to mention the fact that she hadn't returned his call yesterday.

She'd *wanted* to return his call but wasn't accustomed to attention from the opposite sex.

Lily bit her lip. When was the last time a guy visited her at work?

Come to think of it, this was a first for her.

She wiped her hands on a rag, steeled herself, then headed for the door.

Evan's face beamed when she stepped behind the counter. Lily, ashamed because they both knew she was the reason their communication had sputtered, found it difficult to hold his gaze, but she forced a smile anyway.

"Hope you don't mind my stopping by." Evan shoved his hands into his pockets. "I'm on my way to a lunch meeting and can't stay long, but Monday didn't seem complete without seeing you."

How sweet. Lily considered herself savvy at detecting insincerity. She searched for some clue that he kept this line on standby for all the women he dated, but she couldn't locate one. He meant what he said.

"I got your voice message yesterday. Sorry I didn't call you back. I didn't hear it ring," she fibbed, "then when I realized you'd called, it was too late at night to call you back." The truth was, she'd lost confidence in her ability to carry on a conversation and couldn't face him the day after their date. Worse, she feared Evan would figure out she didn't compare to the other women he'd dated in the past, whoever they were. So when Lily's phone had rung and Evan's name had appeared on the caller ID, she'd yielded to insecurity and let the phone continue to ring.

"Hey, it happens," Evan responded with a smile, then blinked once. His blink took a split second too long, and Lily knew he had seen through her fib. He was a salesman, after all. He probably knew her motives better than she did.

Maybe she could salvage the moment. "Thank you again for Saturday night. I had a nice time."

He shrugged as if to say it was no big deal.

"I'm sure you found a way to occupy your Sunday without my providing a song-and-dance routine," she added.

He squinted in an *Ah, touché!* sort of way. "Song and dance? You're a Broadway star too? Impressive." With a grin of nonchalance, he added, "I have to admit, Sunday without Lily was uneventful. Then again, you gave me a chance to get some work ready for Monday morning, so maybe I owe you my gratitude."

"More work? On a Sunday? Don't you take a day off?"

"Habit."

A whoosh of cacophony announced Aaron's arrival from the garage. The door sucked itself shut behind him. On his way to the computer behind the counter, he recognized Lily's visitor and did a double-take. When Evan spotted him, Aaron diverted his glance and started punching keys.

"Anyway, I'm dominating your time and should head to my meeting." Cognizant of Aaron's presence, Evan lowered his voice a notch. "Can I call you again?"

"Sure." Lily thought for a moment, then added, "And next time, I'll even answer the phone instead of making you talk to my voice greeting."

"No need for that. I think I've developed a crush on your recorded self."

She laughed as he headed out the door, then stopped herself when she realized a customer might overhear her from across the room.

Once the door closed, Aaron eased alongside her and shuffled some papers on the counter.

"Apparently, I'm not the only one you avoided calling yesterday," he said. "Looks like you two had a good time on Saturday night."

"It went fine. One of those Euro places. I'd never been there."

"And?"

"The salmon was awesome."

"And…"

Lily shrugged. "He's a nice guy." She waited a beat for Aaron to respond, but he didn't budge. Instead, he stared right through her nonchalance. Lily sighed. "I don't know what's wrong, okay? It's just…my heart wasn't in it. I've been racking my brain since I met him, trying to figure out why. My mind tells me I'd be crazy not to pursue this. Maybe because a guy like him has never shown interest in me before."

"Do *you* even know what you're looking for?"

Lily laid her hands on Aaron's cheeks, gave them a playful squeeze with her thumbs. "Someone sweet. A guy like you."

"Well, not *exactly* like me. Besides, we already tried it years ago, and it didn't turn out as we'd hoped, did it?"

They leaned into each other until their foreheads touched. Their eyes locked. After a beat, Aaron pulled himself away and sauntered back toward the garage. Grasping the door handle, he stopped short, snapped his fingers, and turned around.

"Oh crap, I almost forgot! I brought something for you." He jogged back to the counter, where he retrieved some sheets of paper from a drawer. "I found these on the Internet last night."

Aaron had printed the pages in color on an inkjet printer. They looked like news articles.

"What's this?" Lily waved the pages before she had a chance to peruse them.

"You know all that art you keep finding yourself in? I found out who the guy is, the one in all the pictures *with* you."

Puzzled, Lily read the headline of the first article, scanned its first few paragraphs, then paged through the remainder of it.

And almost collapsed at what she saw.

CHAPTER 18

"I CAN'T BELIEVE it!" Brooke squealed with excitement several hours later. "Do you realize how lucky you are?!"

"*Lucky?* My face is plastered all over the country!" After arriving home, Lily had read the articles over and over but still couldn't shake the astonishment.

Brooke seemed to ignore Lily's comment and continued to stare at the article on top. Lily watched her roommate's eyes scan each page, up and down. Jeremy read over her shoulder, his lips moving in silence, a grin plastered across his face. He looked like he was about to burst out laughing. Lily wanted to slap him.

Brooke appeared awestruck. She shook her head. "I think it's beautiful. Any girl would be flattered by this. He must adore you."

"Adore me? He doesn't even know me! I've never met him."

Brooke lifted the printout closer to her eyes and scrutinized a line. "It says he lives in southern Missouri, in the Ozarks. That's not too far away. Maybe you ran into him somewhere."

"Yeah, at an art show. My usual hangout," Lily replied, laying her sarcasm as thick as she could.

Brooke kneaded the budding muffin top above Jeremy's waist and asked him, "What do you think, babe? How does something like this happen?"

"How should I know?" he snorted.

"You're a guy. You'd know better than we would. What makes you notice a girl?"

"Testosterone."

"No, I mean, what makes you check her out?"

"I refuse to answer that. You'll force me into celibacy for a month."

"I will not!" Brooke rolled her eyes. "You could help Lily with some of your insight."

"Don't do me any favors," Lily muttered. "I'm begging you."

Jeremy stabbed himself with a thumb. "You don't want to see what lies underneath this dude's layers."

"Are you kidding?" Lily shot him a dismissive look. "I saw your bare ass in motion a few days ago. You've got nothing left to hide."

"Come on," Brooke coaxed. "Spill it."

Jeremy sighed. "Guys check every woman out. We're designed that way, the whole visual thing—Mars, Venus and whatnot."

"Forget it." Lily rapped her finger against her lookalike's picture. "The whole thing is too damn ridiculous. This isn't who I am."

"Of course it's who you are!" Brooke insisted.

"Look at how she's dressed. I'd never wear that." Lily could sense her resistance softening, but she refused to admit it. Not in front of Jeremy. "She's beautiful."

"And *he's* gorgeous," Brooke added.

Jeremy took a step back and spread his arms. "Excuse me?"

Brooke paid him no attention. She remained glued to the article, which, according to the printout's footer, had come from an entertainment website. " 'By no means is Ryder Flynn a stranger to the world of commercial art,' " she read aloud. " 'The artist began his freelance career more than a decade ago. Now, at the age of 33, he finds himself in the Hollywood spotlight due to his work on high-profile movie posters in the last year. An eligible bachelor, Flynn has become the object of affection for a quorum of leading ladies and female recording artists. As of late, actress Ana Ferguson is rumored to have her eyes on him.' "

At that, Lily rolled her eyes.

Brooke read on. " 'Yet, for all the pomp and circumstance, one can attribute Flynn's meteoric rise to fame to his aura of mystique. Frequently, the artist inserts himself—and a recurring female companion—into his own pieces. As Flynn paints the couple in more and more of his own work, fans across the nation wonder: *Who is the mystery woman in his paintings?* Flynn denies the woman exists, referring to her as a character, a figment of his imagination. But his continued denials fail to quell growing speculation. Real or imaginary, an anonymous woman has the public riveted. In the twenty-first century, Ryder Flynn has introduced us to a new maiden of mystery, a modern Mona Lisa.' " Brooke crossed her arms and raised an eyebrow.

"How stupid," Lily said.

"See? For years, I've told you how beautiful you are," Brooke said. She tossed her hand in the air. "But no, don't believe me. Let a nationally renowned artist make you famous—and you *still* refuse to believe it!"

Jeremy lodged his tongue against the inside of his cheek. He shot Lily a nod of confirmation. "Beautiful inside and out."

"Don't pull an Oprah on me," Lily shot back.

Jeremy thrust his hands toward her, palms out. "Hold on. Before you insult me, I'm going to say something nice, and I think Brooke would know I'm not hitting on you, just being the man here."

Lily felt her blood pressure rise. What humiliating observation would he subject her to now?

He continued, "I'll admit, I've noticed a...uh, let's call it an *attractiveness*...about you. As a female."

Lily stared at him and waited for more.

Jeremy shoved one hand into his pocket. "On occasion. Not always, but sometimes—I mean, when the lighting is right."

God love Jeremy. Lily searched for a compliment somewhere in that verbal mess.

Brooke, on the other hand, rested her head upon his shoulder. Jeremy wrapped an arm around his girlfriend.

"That was a sweet thing to say," Brooke said. "A little treasure wrapped inside something unexpected. Like a seed inside an avocado."

"Yeah, Jeremy. So unlike you, but thanks, I guess."

Still in Jeremy's arms and in obvious enjoyment, Brooke shuffled printouts and scanned the next article. "What's this?" she murmured. Upon reading the first few lines, she said, "Hey, this article came from a website for the art industry. It says Ryder Flynn will be a panel guest at an artists' conference, April 28-30, in Cleveland, Ohio." She looked closer. "They're holding it at some place called the Royal Flower Hotel."

Lily's attention perked up. She grabbed the article and read the details firsthand. "I know that hotel. It's downtown. Years ago, my cousin held her wedding reception there. Giant flowers printed all over the carpet in the lobby."

"Maybe you met him there."

"What, you think he followed me to Ohio for my cousin's wedding? Besides, the other article says he didn't hit the big time until now. What kind of traveling would he have done as a starving artist? Besides, that hotel isn't exactly cheap."

"Good point." A quick pause, then Brooke, her eyes sparkling, seized Lily by the shoulders. "You should go introduce yourself to him at the conference!"

"What? Hell, no!"

"You totally should! Now's your chance, since you know where he'll be that weekend."

"I'm not so sure about that," Jeremy interjected. When Lily turned toward him, he added, "Men don't like women appearing out of nowhere, unless she shows up at a bachelor party wearing a thong."

Lily grunted. "You're disgusting."

Brooke smacked him. "You earned those sweetheart points a minute ago. Why didn't you quit while you were ahead?"

"Sorry, it came out wrong. I'm used to telling it to Lily like it is. What I meant is, men don't like women taking them off guard."

Brooke shot him a look of suspicion. "In most cases, you're probably right. But this is romantic. He's *searching* for her, whether he knows it or not."

Jeremy laughed. "That's an assumption on your part."

"No, it's intuition. A woman thing." Brooke handed the remaining sheets to Lily and said, "You have nothing to lose."

"Except my dignity. No way."

"Fine." Brooke tugged at Jeremy's shirt. "I'm going to start dinner."

Jeremy trailed behind her. Lily heard the suction of the refrigerator door opening, followed by the clink of a beer bottle as someone retrieved it from a shelf. Then she heard a muffled comment from Brooke, followed by what sounded like a muffled excuse from Jeremy for drinking Lily's beer.

Lily folded the printouts in half and ran her finger along the crease. Slapping the stack against her palm, she eyed the kitchen entrance to make sure Jeremy and his mouth wouldn't notice her. Then she carried the papers to her bedroom and shoved them into a dresser drawer.

For some reason, she couldn't bring herself to discard them.

CHAPTER 19

FROM BEHIND THE tinted windows of the limousine, a nervous Ryder's stomach performed somersaults at what he saw. Camera flashes glittered amid the horde of reporters and spectators.

Even on a Thursday night, onlookers filled the sidewalks and leaned on the temporary, waist-high railings that cordoned off one section of the street. Ryder chuckled at how his once-in-a-lifetime event appeared commonplace for the Los Angeles general public. A few evenings earlier, someone told him, a similar event had occurred at another venue in town.

Ana Ferguson squeezed his hand as the limousine eased to a stop in front of Grauman's Chinese Theatre on Hollywood Boulevard. He had seen photographs of the building, but, prior to tonight, he had never beheld the real thing.

Before their arrival at the theater, Ana had introduced him to an exclusive restaurant in West Hollywood, where, while dining on the most mouth-watering pork tenderloin he'd ever tasted, they'd shared casual conversation. All smiles and minimal substance. Yet he'd found her company delightful. After dinner, as they meandered to the limousine, she had flirted with him for the benefit of the paparazzi, to which he'd responded in kind. She'd also warned him in advance that a reporter might ask him a few questions once he hit the red carpet.

Ryder was about to experience his first film premiere.

Ana flashed one more perfect smile his way. Her teeth, which were so white, their tone couldn't be natural, gleamed beneath the limousine's inner lighting. Each curl of her shoulder-length, chestnut hair looked perfect, courtesy of an expensive stylist she visited with regularity. Ryder wouldn't have pegged Ana as older than twenty-four.

The limo door jolted as somebody opened it from the outside—their cue to enter the frenzy. Ana emerged first. Joining her outside, Ryder offered her his arm, which she took as fans cheered and reporters shouted for the couple's attention. Ana nodded to a few anonymous faces. A stunning vision in her blue dress, Ana pivoted and waved to her admirers. Arm in arm, Ryder and his date made their way along the red carpet.

He inhaled the mid-April air and marveled at its balmy tinge. Already perspiring underneath the black tuxedo he had rented for this event, the lingering sunlight and dozens of bright lights heated him to a degree of minor discomfort, but he didn't care. Nervousness subsided. Ryder basked in the ambience. He yearned for a canvas on which he could capture the scene but would have to settle for a mental snapshot.

Meanwhile, back home, thunderstorms had brought a downpour of rain and a tornado watch, according to a recent text message from Chase. Quite a contrast to Ryder's current backdrop.

Cameras continued to snap among members of the press who lined the carpet behind more metal railings, the kind that reminded him of his childhood, when he'd wait in line for a ride at the amusement park. He doubted he would find a wad of bubble gum stuck to the railing beside him tonight, though.

The theatre loomed ahead in a semi-circular arrangement. Its pointed architecture reminded Ryder of the time he'd spent in Asia as a teenager. He felt at home. A pair of Chinese lion statues stood guard before two pillars, daring moviegoers to walk through the main entrance. Even from this distance, he noticed small ripples in the pavement up ahead—hand and foot imprints from celebrities past and present. He'd once seen a photo of Cary Grant autographing his own slab.

A voice interrupted his fascination.

"...one of the film's stars, Ana Ferguson."

Ryder and Ana had progressed a few yards before he tore his eyes from the theatre and focused on a woman with shoulder-length brunette hair, small hoop earrings, and a microphone. He recognized her as an entertainment reporter from a syndicated television show.

"Ana, your performance in *Love Story Accidental* has gotten a lot of buzz prior to tonight's premiere. After a string of suspense films, you changed course and went with a romantic comedy. Is there a particular goal you hoped to achieve?"

"Well, as an actress, you want to broaden your horizons. Sometimes a part of you wants to step outside the image you're known for and take on new challenges," Ana replied. "Plus, I couldn't pass up the chance to work with Michael Bay. He's known for action films, so he's taken a chance of his own by directing this."

The reporter nodded. "In the film, you play Melanie Worthington, a dog catcher with champagne-and-caviar dreams." A quick wink. "Not an *autobiographical* film, I take it?"

On cue, Ana offered a lighthearted laugh. "No, but a role dear to my heart."

"Fair enough." A chuckle. At that point, the reporter leaned toward Ryder. "I see you attended tonight's premiere with Ryder Flynn, who painted the poster for the film."

Ryder squared his shoulders. He still couldn't understand why an artist would capture anyone's interest, but he was willing to play along for as long as they were.

"Ryder, you've painted posters for several films this year," the reporter said. Her eyes glimmered with gossip. "You've already established a notable career as an artist. However, the film posters have launched you as a hot commodity in Hollywood—not to mention one of Tinseltown's most eligible bachelors. Does this take you by surprise?"

"Yes, a *pleasant* surprise." He felt his face blush. To this day, he hadn't grown accustomed to the attention. "I must admit, during my years as a starving artist, I hadn't envisioned a movie premiere in my future."

"As viewers watch footage of tonight's red-carpet event, they'll see you here with Ana and wonder if you're Hollywood's latest couple. Any rumors you'd like to put to rest?"

"Ana's a talented actress and we enjoy each other's company." Chase had coached him to say that, and back in the limousine, Ana had agreed.

"So, nothing to admit tonight?"

"I'm afraid not."

"Your work outside the film world has received growing attention, too. There's a lot of intrigue surrounding your decision to put *yourself* into many of your projects, along with, shall we say, a leading lady of your own. Any comment on who your female lead is, the one who appears with you?"

That question caught him off guard. Ryder felt a muscle flinch in his abdomen. As his heart hammered, he tried his best to maintain his composure. "I suppose, with the billions of people in the world, it's bound to look like *somebody* out there. It's an inspiring face that stays with me. People enjoy her presence in my work, so I just give the public what it wants."

Ryder felt Ana nudge the underside of his arm, which he interpreted as a hint to move on. And gladly so. He'd expected Ana to be the press's sole target tonight.

So with a nod to the reporter, Ryder led Ana farther along the red carpet as another limousine pulled in front of the theatre.

CHAPTER 20

RYDER LOVED THE way a brush felt when he stroked it across a canvas.

Norah Jones crooned from the stereo. Chase sat at the desk in Ryder's studio and finished some paperwork. Beside him, Ryder's most recent project, the cover art for a rock band's latest album, dried on top of the desk.

Ryder had awakened in the middle of the night, an idea for a painting taunting him, one which featured Lily and him. For fear his inspiration might depart before morning, he had crawled out of bed and wound his way through the darkness to his studio, where he'd sketched his idea upon a canvas. Now, as he took a break from his paid work, he added some initial color to his latest personal project.

Years ago, Chase admitted he had misjudged an artist's palette as an impromptu mess with colors splattered everywhere. To his surprise, Ryder had informed him that artists kept their palettes well organized. Ryder preferred to run his colors, from warm to cool, across the top of the palette. He kept his earth tones along the bottom and used the middle of the palette to mix hues. By keeping his palette in this constant arrangement, he could keep his eyes on the painting before him and touch the paints by instinct.

Ryder stared closer at the painting of Lily and him in a floral garden. He had already added shades of green foliage along its left and right sides. With quick dabs, he filled in the greenery with shades of pinks and purples, flowers in bloom. It seemed so real. He could envision Lily at his side, feel the warmth of her hand in his as they strolled through a garden like the one in his painting. A warm June evening, one hour before sunset.

On the canvas, the wisp of Lily's smile enraptured him. With each painting, Ryder endeavored to communicate her inherent value, a gift from his heart to hers.

As he elongated his strokes and added more color to the background, he glanced again at Lily and him. He would paint his subjects last. At the moment, they remained a sketch in harsh black and white.

What if Ryder were to tell anyone the truth about the woman in the paintings? Would it strike them as pathetic? Not even Chase knew Ryder had fallen for her. Chase had chalked it up to infatuation and saw it in light of its marketing potential, nothing more.

Love at first sight? Does anybody believe in that?

The concept had infused countless fairy tales, songs and films. But could it happen in real life?

Ryder's cheeks grew warm. He wondered about Lily. As memories fade with time, so her visage had begun to dim in his mind. It pricked his heart. To the best of his ability, though, he had used his art to keep her facial nuances at the forefront of his mind. He didn't want to lose her.

She looked so sweet and gentle. He wondered about her interests and her sense of humor. What about her weekends? Did she prefer to remain at home and read, or did she thrive on night life?

And what did she do for a living? Perhaps she taught kindergarten, helped kids learn to read and count. Or maybe she worked in an office environment or in customer service. Surely she interacted with people, at least the way he envisioned her.

Ryder couldn't help but smile at the possibilities. What he wouldn't give to talk to her once more! He'd waited six years.

A few months ago, while in Cleveland on a business trip, he'd returned to the hotel where he and Lily had first met—if he could call it meeting. He'd known he wouldn't see her there again but had hoped, by some miracle, he could defy logic.

She hadn't appeared.

Although he'd give anything to find her, he wouldn't know where to begin. She could live anywhere in the country—Chicago, Orlando, Seattle. *North Dakota,* for all he knew. He didn't even know her last name.

As he pondered Lily further, Ryder realized he'd never given this much thought to the other women in his life since he'd met her. Carol represented little more than his latest romantic fiasco. He'd cared for her. He'd cared for every woman who had preceded her, but he couldn't find a way to commit his whole heart to a relationship. Upon sensing this, Ryder would, without fail, attempt to distance himself from the risk by losing himself in his work. To make matters worse, Ryder had, after meeting Lily, constructed a love-at-first-sight ideal to which no other woman could measure up.

Did that render him a romantic or just an old-fashioned loser?

He continued to dab at the painting.

His best paintings came from his heart. Shouldn't his relationships follow suit? Didn't he owe a woman that much?

Imagination was uncomplicated. It was so much simpler than reality. Yet it was also abstract, unattainable…and lonely. An emotional ghost.

In a way Ryder couldn't explain—a hybrid of sentimental longing and an artist's bipolar complexity—his heart rested with the young woman he had met six years ago in a Cleveland hotel. Ever since that Saturday night, Ryder had sensed their encounter was destiny, but he couldn't prove it and had no way of finding out.

But as long as he painted her image, the memory remained alive. Tangible. It offered him hope.

Chase's voice jerked Ryder back to the present.

"Do you think this album art will dry by tomorrow?" Chase rubbed an unpainted edge of the canvas.

Ryder nodded. "It's acrylic."

Chase rose from his chair, stretched, then shoved his paperwork into a manila folder. He sauntered over to where Ryder worked.

"I can't comprehend how you come up with these ideas," Chase said. With a glance over Ryder's shoulder, he asked, "Business or pleasure?"

"This one's for fun." Ryder set his brush in a jar of water. He selected a wider brush and added earth tones along the bottom of the canvas.

Chase crossed his arms and studied the work in progress. "Everyone wants to know about her. They're chattering all over the Internet."

"You promised you'd never tell."

"And I won't. Besides, as long as people wonder, it keeps you the hot topic. It's like women are *drawn* to you now. They want you but can't have you—because *she* stands in their way."

"I don't care about the spotlight," Ryder said, his eyes riveted to his work. "Those women aren't my type anyway. I'm looking for more than that."

Chase waved his index finger at the painting. "You mean, like her?"

Ryder paused. The look in Chase's eyes—pointed, bemused—revealed he struggled to comprehend Ryder's plight—or, for that matter, why Ryder even considered it important. Chase had never lacked a woman on his arm, nor did long-term commitment to one interest him. Granted, Chase's intentions were honorable, but when it came to Lily, Ryder could have explained his dilemma in Swahili and it wouldn't have made any less sense to Chase.

Ryder mixed a light brown on his palette and continued applying wispy strokes to the canvas.

Chase muffled his voice. "Look, man, the chances of you running into her again have gotta be a million to one." He squinted, stroking his chin with his thumb and forefinger like a Harvard philosophy professor. "Then again…"

"What?"

"Well, she could be closer than you think."

"Meaning?"

"The whole who-is-the-girl situation. When mysteries like this charm the public, revelations have a way of rising to the surface, don't they? The press wants to know who this girl is, or *if* she exists."

"What does the press have to do with it?"

"Consider this: How many marriages come to ruin because they played out in front of the cameras? I don't want to be negative, but even if some reporter managed to track down this girl, the circumstances of *how* she surfaces—well, it might be too much pressure for her. It's possible you could end up living without her anyway."

Ryder bit the inside of his cheek.

Chase patted his business partner on the back. "Think about it."

With that, Chase gathered his folder, zipped his messenger bag, and headed out the sliding glass door.

Ryder, his heart still drawn to the painting of Lily and him, lifted his eyes toward the windows and studied the lake in the distance.

He exhaled.

"I'm *already* living without her."

CHAPTER 21

LILY COULD ALMOST picture the airy notes as they slithered from the bell of the musician's tenor saxophone, melodic felines nuzzling tables and chairs.

Evan had taken Lily to a winery on a Saturday afternoon. Though only a twenty-minute drive from the western suburbs of St. Louis, its location struck her as rural. After sampling a few wines, they had agreed on a white zinfandel and made their way through the building's back door to a multilevel deck. They had arrived before the afternoon crowd poured in, so they had settled into a small table on the uppermost tier, a prime spot about thirty feet from where a modern jazz quartet now played.

Evan eased back in his chair and studied the musicians. Lily followed his gaze toward the ensemble, where a keyboardist, a bass player, and a drummer accompanied the saxophonist. The music sounded carefree and she enjoyed it, but several minutes into the song, she could no longer identify a melody. As far as she could tell, the band members concocted the song as they went along, which, at first, had intrigued her. Now, however, their creative process had begun to get on her nerves. No longer could she tell what the hell was going on. Nonetheless, she wanted Evan to think she'd enjoyed the afternoon, so she continued to smile and wondered if she'd kept that packet of Tylenol in her purse.

Lily couldn't reconcile her feelings toward Evan. She'd expected to have grown more open toward him after several weeks. Sure, she found him comfortable. Evan went out of his way to try to make her feel special. But he couldn't seem to reach her. Without a doubt, he respected her. They hadn't slept together, and on their third date, she had allowed him to attempt a first kiss. When he did, however, nothing ignited within her as she'd hoped. Or *thought* she'd hoped.

Now the bass player assumed the lead role in the quartet and steered the song along a new curve, like he'd turned a corner and ushered Lily into a different neighborhood. She perked up and listened with renewed vigor. The notes were deep and buoyant, like popcorn popping inside a tuba, the low tone of an informant whose digitized voice might appear in a television news interview.

Lily *wanted* to muster attraction toward Evan. If this romance—or whatever it was—didn't bloom, who knew how many years might pass before she would capture another man's interest? In fact, as she lay in bed at night, she pictured Evan's face, tried to imagine herself happy in his embrace. She visualized them leaning toward each other for a kiss but ended the mental sequence before their lips met. Should it feel this forced? How long should she wait for enthusiasm to manifest before calling it quits? Yet, day by day, she determined to maintain hope.

The quartet started a new song. Even now, as the rhythm and melody began to grow on her, she felt bad: Evan had tried to arrange a pressure-free date for her, an environment she would enjoy. And that touched her. So why did she feel on edge?

Perhaps because, judging from his state of behavior, Evan appeared to enjoy this afternoon more than she did. He bobbed his head to the music. His shoulders swayed in subconscious reaction to what he heard.

She tried some Brie on a cracker, sipped wine from a plastic cup. While Lily possessed limited knowledge of wines and even less about cheese, Evan had impressed her with his insight into both—as well as which cheeses complemented particular wines and why. Lily, on the other hand, had browsed the entire wine selection before she'd figured out the winery had arranged its bottles from sweet to dry. When she and Evan browsed for cheese, he had pointed toward the Brie, to which she had replied, "You mean the white one?"

Evan seemed to enjoy her personality. On occasion, he snickered at her comments, some of which she didn't *intend* as funny. But since he always treated her with respect, she decided not to correct him.

As the ensemble switched to a mellow number, Lily's mind wandered to the woman in Ryder Flynn's artwork. *She* would enjoy the ambience here. *She'd* enjoy traveling from one wine to the next, discussing aromas and tannins. A woman like that would be an ideal match for Evan. But Lily?

Lily understood cars, but not this.

That's it! she thought. That was why she continued to feel uncomfortable here and anywhere else Evan took her. Lily felt like a trespasser in his world, as if he'd invited her to his own private island in the Bahamas. A guest but not a resident.

Still, she could see herself enjoying this setting. Eventually.

Lily settled back into her seat and allowed the alcohol to ooze through her bloodstream.

Why not enjoy the afternoon? A light breeze tickled her earlobes with its cool tinge.

And who wouldn't enjoy this view? To her right, Lily peered beyond the deck's wooden railing and into the distance. She could see for miles from this height. A lonesome, rural road meandered across a rolling Missouri hillside. Hickory and oak trees, their green leaves tinted gold in the sunlight, speckled the peaks and valleys. She inhaled the scent of foliage, lush from the prior day's rain shower. Lily envisioned how breathtaking this view must appear during autumn as the leaves changed color.

Two hundred feet above the ground. Nothing could touch her here.

Her mind drifted to the billboard Evan had pointed out on their first date, the ad where Lily and her male companion walked hand in hand after a symphony performance. When she'd first seen her male counterpart in the art, she hadn't considered whether he was the artist himself. Not until Aaron's discovery.

The more she saw herself in those images, the more she believed it was possible to sample that woman's culture. And she had to admit, Ryder's handsome features rendered the dream more savory.

Ryder Flynn.

He had touched upon a quality in Lily that she herself couldn't identify. Yet the woman in his art embodied it.

An artists' conference in Cleveland next weekend…

Ryder's work personified tenderness. The way he reached toward the woman, held her, valued her, caused dawn to break in Lily's chest. She wondered where he lived and how he—

"Improvisation is a common technique."

His words startled her from her trance. She cut her eyes from a solitary car that puttered along the rural road below and peered at Evan, who now leaned toward her, his arm at rest along the back of her chair.

"Technique?" Lily repeated. It was the first thing she could think to say, lest she look like an idiot for not paying attention.

Evan gestured in the direction of the saxophonist, who had resumed the lead. "He's creating his part on the fly. But if you listen closely, you'll detect the original melody hidden deep down, no matter how different his improvisation sounds."

"I never realized that."

Evan regarded her a moment. "You're deep in thought." With a gentle brush of his finger above her right eye, he added, "Your eyebrow gets a cute little arch when your mind is churning."

"Just looking at the hills below." How long had she zoned out? She folded her hands in her lap and feigned interest in the music at hand. "I always wondered where jazz came from."

"It has a fascinating history. Once the United States abolished slavery, some of the newly freed people migrated to large cities, where they wove their own traditional music into city culture. Jazz evolved from there." He grinned. "Fascinating, isn't it? Even from a blight as horrible as slavery emerged something exquisite."

Lily tried to pay attention. Honestly, she did. But her thoughts returned to Ryder.

She ached inside. Her heart felt sore.

CHAPTER 22

LILY LISTENED TO cabbage soup simmer on Tuesday evening. She inhaled the steam that drifted from the pot, a tantalizing scent upon its wisps. She had found the recipe online, along with a guarantee that it would keep a woman's waist trim. Granted, Lily didn't need to lose weight, but Brooke would be thrilled with the low-calorie dinner. The two-gallon pot would last the roommates several days. As she stirred the contents, she kept an eye on a small television at the corner of the counter. The program's host interviewed a guest who had restored a classic car.

At the sound of the apartment door bursting open, Lily dropped the ladle, which clanged against the pot. Brooke darted around the corner and stood at the entryway to the kitchen, holding a large poster with its backside facing Lily. Lily saw only the dull tan of the cardboard slab upon which the poster was shrink-wrapped. Brooke's forehead glistened with perspiration, her face flushed. She must have sprinted across the parking lot, then dashed up the stairs two at a time.

"You're not going to believe this!" Brooke shook the poster, an awkward shake given its bulk. When she swallowed, her throat sounded parched. "I stopped by the mall to buy a gift for Carla and Doug's housewarming party later this month. I started at the place that sells engraved knickknacks, but nothing captured my interest, so I headed to an artsy shop on the second floor. Maybe I'd find a nice print and frame it, right? Well, I flipped through posters with nature scenes, didn't find anything, and moved on to the next rack to see they had something romantic—you know, with people in it. Silhouettes or something."

Amused at Brooke's attempt to catch her breath, Lily handed her a glass of water and continued to stir the soup. "You look like you stopped by Sears and tested the treadmills for an hour while you were there."

Brooke gulped the water and set the glass on the counter with her free hand. "Anyway, I fingered through those posters, one by one, scenes of couples in romantic destinations and backgrounds. Halfway through the stack, I found *this!*"

When Brooke revealed the poster, Lily's mouth dropped open. By this point, the car show sounded like nothing more than excessive noise. She turned off the television and clamped the lid on the pot of soup.

It was a print of a painting, so Lily assumed hundreds, maybe thousands, of copies existed across the country.

Yet *another* portrayal of Lily and the artist—but this one surpassed all the others she had seen.

It depicted a calm evening. By Lily's estimation, the artist had set the scene around nine o'clock. It looked like a full-color image in various shades of blue and gray, as if Lily were viewing it through a blue filter. From high above, a bright bluish-white moon glowed, imparting a cascade of light upon the subjects' faces and bodies. Apart from that natural illumination, the artist had painted the subjects and background in shades of dark and darker, the way a person or object would appear walking past you on the street. Just a hint of moonlight to accent their figures. The scene took place outdoors, but Lily couldn't make out the environment well enough to decipher its location. In the background, she noticed an ocean, along with the silhouette of a palm tree. The place looked secluded. An island in the Caribbean, perhaps.

The couple embraced in the moonlight. The painting depicted them from their waists up.

A romantic scene. Given the other works in which Lily had spotted herself, this one wouldn't have caught her by surprise—if the couple had worn clothing.

In the painting, Lily's back faced the viewer, her head tilted at an angle to give the viewer a glimpse of her face as she and the artist shared a tender, prolonged kiss.

Lily considered the painting tasteful, especially since it depicted nothing below the waist. She could tell the artist's motive had emerged from his heart rather than his loins. Nonetheless, she had to steady herself against the kitchen counter as she examined her bare back.

If she and this artist were in a relationship, she would have found this sort of painting flattering.

In truth, she felt flattered already. Even now, the more engrossed in the painting she became, the more the image grew on her.

Then reality shook her. She remembered Brooke still held the poster, waiting for her reaction. At that point, embarrassment settled in, and Lily felt a burst of anger detonate inside her. Anger at herself for feeling flattered by this…this…romantic painting or whatever it was. Lily returned to the soup on the stove before she revealed any further interest. She would study the poster later, when Brooke wasn't home.

Brooke sighed. She turned the poster back toward herself and gave it another look. "This is so romantic. You're his muse, Lily!"

"I don't want to be his muse!"

Unable to concentrate on the soup, which now bubbled on the stove, Lily shut off the burner. The more she thought about the poster, the tighter she clenched her teeth. Her pulse raced. The heat from the stove now made the kitchen's temperature unbearable to her. Watching the soup boil had made her blood boil more.

She couldn't stand still. Lily slammed the ladle onto the counter.

"That's it," she said. "I'm going to Cleveland."

"The conference? This weekend?"

"You bet your ass."

CHAPTER 23

ON FRIDAY AFTERNOON, Lily's heart palpitated as she raced from one end of her bedroom to the other, grabbing items to pack and tossing them on her bed. She didn't need to hurry; her plane wouldn't depart until the following morning. But Lily recognized her stress behavior when it surfaced—and the mess on her bed was evidence of either stress or neurosis.

Ever since she'd seen the moonlight poster on Tuesday, the image had remained burned into her memory. Her mind bounced between anger at being depicted in the nude and another sensation she couldn't shake: Lily took *pleasure* in the fact that the artist saw her as beautiful and had painted her in such a complimentary way. Then she grew irritated at herself for feeling flattered.

To make the conundrum worse, another emotional dichotomy preceded her arrival in Cleveland. On one hand, Lily found Ryder Flynn attractive and wanted to meet him. On the other hand, she wanted to look him in the eye and ambush him with a string of choice profanities for invading her privacy.

Lily didn't know which one would surface when she found him.

If she found him.

But she couldn't concentrate on that at the moment. Before she made this insane trip, she had to find something decent to wear. As she ravaged her wardrobe, her stomach felt like a load of laundry in its spin cycle.

Brooke dodged articles of clothing that flew her way. She had camped out on Lily's bed, lying on her back beside an open suitcase, and stared slack-jawed, as if her Mona Lisa roommate had overturned Da Vinci's favorite can of paint.

"It's only an overnight trip," Brooke said. "Aren't you going overboard packing all these clothes?"

"I'm keeping my options open."

With a shrug, Brooke's face resumed its usual beam of enthusiasm. "Do you want me to go with you?"

"No," Lily said. "I need to do this alone."

Heading back into her walk-in closet, Lily considered reaching for the green dress she had worn on her first date with Evan but decided against it. Not in front of Brooke, anyway. She didn't want her roommate to get more excited than she already was. Not while Lily felt queasy.

Brooke looked like she itched to dive in and help pack. Then, sure enough, she sat up, grabbed a top, and went to work. Piece by piece, she folded the clothes and arranged them in the suitcase. When she caught a pair of faded jeans Lily had tossed in the air, she began to fold them, but stopped midway. Her brow furrowed.

"Are you sure you want to bring *these?*"

Lily poked her head out of the closet to find Brooke waving the jeans in one hand.

"What's wrong with them?"

"Well, it's not what *she* would wear."

"Who?"

"You." Brooke shook her head. "I mean, the you in his art."

Lily rolled her eyes. "Tell me you didn't just say that."

"Come on," Brooke whimpered. "You're not even giving yourself a chance. You should have fun with this!"

"What!" Lily stomped out of the closet. *"Fun?* Did you not see me naked on that poster?"

"Okay, if you're not aiming for fun, then what *do* you hope to accomplish during this little jaunt?"

Lily snorted. "I don't know. I'll figure it out when I get there."

Brooke propped her chin on the palm of her hand. Her eyes took on a dreamy look. "What if he turns out to be cuter than in the artwork? What if you end up attracted to him?"

"Not gonna happen. I should sue his ass."

"Let's look at it from another angle: Ryder Flynn is standing in the hotel lobby, sipping a glass of *Dom Pérignon.* He's engaged in a conversation with another artist about Van Gogh, Dali and Da Vinci. Meanwhile, his thoughts turn to his own Mona Lisa—a beautiful Mona Lisa, not the dog-faced one Da Vinci painted. No, Ryder Flynn's Mona Lisa has hair that shimmers in the moonlight. *His* Mona Lisa has a gorgeous smile when she lets it burst through. *His* Mona Lisa looks sexy in her sleek, black dress. He takes another sip of his champagne. Then, lo and behold, before him stands his Mona Lisa…in faded blue jeans."

Lily heard a sad trombone triad punctuate that last remark.

She didn't realize how enraptured she'd become with Brooke's description until it arrived at its abrupt end. Lily shook herself from the fantasy.

Brooke hopped from the bed. Grabbing Lily by the shoulders, she stared straight at her until Lily looked her in the eyes.

"You deserve some adventure," Brooke said, her voice low and sincere. "For once in your life, you should allow yourself to live a dream."

At that, Lily's heart eased.

Without another word, the roommates stared at each other for a beat. The next thing they knew, they erupted into snickers, the kind twin sisters would share. Brooke released Lily's shoulders and folded her arms across her chest, renewed vibrancy in her eyes.

"I can teach you makeup. Let me make you beautiful, just this once." Brooke crumpled her lips and offered her finest puppy-dog pout. "Please?"

She looked like a ten-year-old.

With her resistance on the decline, Lily's shoulders sagged. She tossed her head back and sighed, blew a puff of air toward the little speckles on the ceiling.

When she returned her attention to Brooke, she found her still staring at her, waiting for an answer.

Lily came to the realization of what she was about to do this weekend. Who knew what lurked on the other side of this mysterious door?

On second thought, she *wanted* to discover what awaited her on the other side.

She held Brooke's gaze.

Indecision tugged. Lily bit her lip.

PART TWO

LITTLE WHITE LIES

CHAPTER 24

HER PLANE TOUCHED down at Cleveland Hopkins International Airport around four o'clock Saturday afternoon. Deep down, though she wanted to confront Ryder Flynn, she hid an inexplicable fear of rejection and wanted to spend as little time in town as possible. Her flight home would depart the next day. Less than twenty-four hours for this adventure.

Brooke had arranged a rental car by redeeming some customer-loyalty points. To help keep costs down, Lily checked into a suburban motel, a twenty-minute drive from the freeway. On her way there, she stopped by a drive-thru and forced a few chicken nuggets into her belly.

As Lily dragged her suitcase down the hall, she concluded Brooke was correct: Lily, in her anxiety, had packed in excess for such a brief jaunt. She had no idea what to anticipate. Even if the weekend went well, what would he do? Ask her out on a date?

She didn't realize how much she appreciated Brooke's ordinary noises until now. The atmosphere was too silent, too still. Lily turned on the television to fill the room with sound as she mustered her courage.

An hour later, with no other plans to stop her, she drove downtown, her stomach a nervous wreck, a jungle gym with a spoiled brat kicking the framework.

Lily parked her car in the underground garage at the Royal Flower Hotel and stepped out. Stale exhaust fumes lingered in the recycled air. From somewhere in the distance, she heard tires squeak as a vehicle rounded a corner. Looking down at her feet, she discovered why such noise made sense: The steel-gray floors of the garage were so smooth and tidy, they looked polished.

On her way to the elevator, she retrieved her phone and thumbed her way to the conference website. According to the schedule, a networking reception was underway in the hotel atrium. Ryder's panel session had occurred earlier, which Lily had avoided on purpose. She wanted herself surrounded by people so she could talk to him without attracting attention. A casual conversation. Nothing unusual.

As the minutes passed, her anger seemed to subside. Was she *eager* to say hello?

With a beep, the elevator doors opened and Lily entered the lobby. Upon stepping out, the first thing she recognized was the pattern of giant roses on the carpet. It summoned memories of her last visit to this hotel six years ago. Lily and her relatives had stayed here when her cousin, who no longer lived in Ohio, got married. The wedding ceremony had taken place at a local church, followed by a reception in one of the ballrooms in this hotel. Lily remembered the stupid chiffon bridesmaid dress she'd had to wear. And the black-suited loser she had met at the reception—the one who had come across as so kind at first but, as it turned out, had sought nothing more than an easy lay. When she'd refused, he had stormed off and left her alone somewhere around here. Beyond that point, she recalled nothing—until the horrible headache that had welcomed her the next morning.

She'd had too much to drink that night. She had felt so out of place, she'd started with a cocktail and kept them coming. How she'd ended up in her own hotel room by morning, she would never know. A relative claimed she heard a knock at the door, and when she opened it, she found Lily nestled on the floor. Lily assumed a bellhop had returned her on a luggage cart—a flat-hat knight and his brass horse on tiny wheels.

Tonight wouldn't end that way.

When Lily reached the atrium, she couldn't help but gasp at its beauty. The glass roof loomed four stories above her head. A solitary elevator, a glass icicle framed in brass, rose and descended on one side of the red-carpeted room. The tiers above, where the elevator stopped, featured conference rooms and a quaint restaurant which, Lily assumed, charged twenty bucks for a Caesar salad. From its perch on the second floor, the restaurant overlooked a large fountain surrounded by an assortment of greenery and large river rocks. The sound of the water's steady splash soothed Lily's nerves.

She'd had no trouble entering the reception. With all the entrances to this room by elevator, stairs, and its main doorway, no one could prevent individuals from coming and going. If someone asked why she wasn't wearing a convention lanyard, she would tell them she'd left it in her room.

Sure enough, the attendees had stuck to the business-casual dress code as dictated in the schedule. What some called casual, Lily considered dressing up. She could never understand guys who dressed in khaki pants to relax, but to each his own.

Lily had dressed the part—in Brooke's attire. She tugged at her stylish, white top and the dark skirt that reached down to her knees. She felt self-conscious with her calves exposed. She lounged around in shorts at home, but she usually wore jeans—or, while working, coveralls—in public. Nonetheless, she reassured herself no one would notice her since all the other women in the room had shown up in similar attire. Lily wore her hair up, the way she did at work, yet tonight it felt nicer, like it complemented her outfit. She'd kept her makeup to a minimum but had taken Brooke's advice on which colors to apply. It felt caked on her face. And although the departure from her usual appearance left her feeling out of her element, she also noticed a boost in her confidence. She fit in, if only on a visual level.

Had she walked into this room without foreknowledge, Lily never would have pegged these people as artists. Scoping out the crowd, she noted a professional ambience had soaked the room.

How would he respond when she approached him? Maybe she had made a mistake by coming here…

She still had time. Her options remained open. She could turn around and head back to her motel, and Ryder Flynn would never know she had stepped within a hundred miles of his conference.

No, she refused to back down. Besides, she was curious about him. And though she wouldn't admit it to Brooke or anyone else, Ryder's smile lingered in her mind.

He could be anywhere in this room.

At that realization, tension seized her belly. With each passing minute came the awareness that she had come closer to meeting him.

If she could find him.

Lily sneaked a glass of wine, a blush, from the complimentary assortment on the table beside her. She felt a bit guilty about it since she hadn't paid for her attendance, but she was desperate to calm her nerves. This time around, she promised herself, she would stop after one drink.

She meandered among the guests, holding her wine glass close to her chest in hopes of hiding the absence of a conference lanyard. As she eased along the periphery of the room, she perused a variety of paintings on easels. Beneath each painting hung a small placard to identify its artist. Lily recognized names from the schedule she had found online. They were featured speakers and panel participants.

"Ryder…"

She caught his name in mid-sentence, spoken from somewhere to her right, toward the middle of the atrium. With a casual glance, Lily tried to pinpoint who had said it.

"Tell you what, let me introduce you to Ryder. Maybe he's heard of that agent. I never have."

There! In the corner of her eye, she caught sight of a young guy with ash-blond hair. He patted another guest on the back and led him halfway across the room. Lily followed the pair from twenty feet away. Lifting her free hand, she covered her face by pretending to scratch her forehead.

And viewed Ryder Flynn through the crevice between her fingers.

CHAPTER 25

SHE DIDN'T RECOGNIZE him at first. An array of chandeliers cast a cozy dimness throughout the room and a shadow across his face. But when Ryder Flynn turned in her direction, the shadow disappeared, and his countenance struck her as familiar. She had laid eyes on it more times than she could count. Yet, for Lily, seeing his face tonight—in person—sealed the reality of her circumstances. Standing in such close proximity to him made her feel like a stalker, even though *she* was the victim of his imagination.

"If you've crossed paths with Chase, I feel sorry for you," joshed the artist as he pointed to the ash-blond guy. "He's trouble."

Lily almost gasped but caught herself and remained discreet as she pivoted on her heels, certain he hadn't seen her. With her back to the artist and his acquaintances, she uncovered her eyes and took a gulp from her wine glass.

Now what? she wondered. Judging from the way her stomach fluids sloshed inside her, she'd sputter through any attempt at words. Her nerve, not to mention her confidence, dispersed, the way dead foliage scatters in the wind.

Maybe this was a big mistake.

No, she couldn't go through with it after all.

Undecided, Lily sighed, then she scanned the lobby entrance on the other side of the room, where she noticed an individual who squinted at her from a distance, as if he knew her.

Probably from that damn artwork, Lily almost muttered to herself.

As she prepared to make a beeline for the hotel lobby, she looked beside her, where more paintings sat upon easels—and found herself staring into her own face.

A huge print of Lily and Ryder, sitting amid a crowd at Wrigley Field as they clinked two amber-colored, longneck bottles. A beer manufacturer's logo was centered below the couple.

A bullhorn would have called less attention to her!

The sight of herself decked out in the Chicago Cubs' team colors, fawning over Ryder Flynn with a carefree laugh, was enough to piss her off.

She felt beads of sweat break out across her brow.

Great, she thought. *What will* that *do to my makeup?*

She couldn't shake her nervousness. And why? Ryder was the one who should be nervous. *He* was the one who had taken artistic liberty with her image.

Then again, she'd heard everyone has a twin. What if it wasn't Lily in the art? That would explain the difference in attire and flair, not to mention why the woman in the art was so gorgeous.

Why hadn't she thought about this *before* she trekked all the way to Cleveland?

What if he—

"Excuse me," came a gentle male voice from behind Lily. "This will sound strange, but—"

When she spun around, Ryder halted mid-sentence. Lily's knees locked. Rigid, she watched as shock registered on his face. Her heartbeat went into staccato.

Ryder's eyes grew wide, his mouth frozen in the shape of an *O,* as if he couldn't locate his voice. When he spoke again, he sounded like he had awakened her with a kiss, a happy ending straight out of a fairy tale.

"It *is* you..." he whispered.

CHAPTER 26

HE LOOKED LIKE he wanted to reach for her cheek, to convince himself she was real, but he restrained himself. The murmur of conversation in the atrium seemed to grow louder in Lily's ears as she stared into Ryder Flynn's face. She willed herself to respond but found herself paralyzed with anger and fear.

Dreamlike, Ryder shook his head as though time had paused for him. He squinted his eyes, yet kept his gaze fixed upon her in astonishment. "I…I saw you from across the room and—"

Reflex. That was the only way Lily could explain her response.

She didn't know how it happened. She didn't have a chance to think about it. A fiery sensation rushed through her veins.

Once she made contact, the palm of her hand reddened as if she had massaged a hot stove.

And Ryder had a face to match. In fact, she couldn't help but stare at the flaming handprint she'd left on his cheek. It seemed to shine—the portion she could see, at least. Ryder winced in pain and began to rub the point of impact. Lily could only imagine the burning sensation. It probably stung as much as her hand did now.

Although she'd faced the temptation many times, she'd never slapped a guy in the face.

Speechless, Ryder stared into her eyes, probably scared of whatever reaction he might trigger with another word.

Lily recoiled once she realized the entire room had gone still. Echoes had stopped bouncing against the walls. With a groan, she forced herself to eye her surroundings and, sure enough, everyone had stopped to stare at the famous couple.

A whisper ignited somewhere in the background. From the far side of the atrium, she heard someone snicker.

Lily pierced Ryder's eyes with her own.

"Next time, keep my clothes on!" she hissed through clenched teeth.

Unsure what to do next, she lingered, yet couldn't stare at him any longer. Humiliated, she suspected her face and neck matched the shade of her palm, which still throbbed from its collision with Ryder's face. Lily drew her hand to her eyes in an attempt to shield herself from the onlookers who continued to gape at her. Her sole comfort rested in the fact that she would never see these people after tonight.

Turning to dart away, she took one step forward and slammed into a table of hors d'oeuvres. Its contents remained intact, but the table rattled and the platters clanged atop it, sending fresh echoes throughout the atrium.

Of course. What else could go wrong?

Furious, Lily stormed toward the lobby entrance. Conference attendees parted before her. A few individuals chanced a glimpse as she passed. However, most attendees, in a clear state of awkwardness, stared at the floor, pretending not to notice as she stormed past them. As if anyone could have missed the epic encounter between the artist and his muse, or whatever she was. *If* she was. Shit. Her mind ran in circles.

With her eyes glued to the floor, she bumped into an older man and whispered an apology, but continued to forge ahead. At last, she reached the lobby. She wanted to head straight for her car and leave a pair of steaming skid marks in her wake, but

Ryder would catch her while she waited at the elevator. At this point, facing him again was rock bottom on her bucket list. She hesitated a moment to think.

Ryder's voice trailed behind her.

"Wait!"

Against her better judgment, she peered over her shoulder, catching sight of Ryder as he reached the rose carpet and scanned the onlookers for her.

Their eyes locked. Lily gasped.

Hotel guests turned to watch the commotion. Ryder shouted again.

"Excuse me, Miss…uh, Miss!"

Lily noticed a set of automatic revolving doors at the hotel entrance and bolted for them.

"Miss—uh, Lily! Come back!" Ryder pushed his way through the crowded lobby.

Lily never realized how slowly automatic doors moved until tonight. Afraid Ryder would catch up to her, she squeezed through her first narrow opportunity to save a few seconds. Once outside, a gust of air, chilled by Lake Erie after dark, blasted her face.

How far could she get? Her shoes had heels, but they were short. The stupid things would keep her from moving fast, but she could clunk along at a decent clip.

One quick glance to her right. Pedestrians dotted the sidewalk.

Lily took off running.

CHAPTER 27

WITH CHASE FOLLOWING close behind, Ryder fought his way through the revolving doors and willed himself to find her as he scoped both directions of the sidewalk outside. He'd seen her dart out these doors. At last, he caught sight of her as she ran beneath a streetlight, one block south. Ryder took off in her direction, running as fast as he could. Thank God his black dress shoes had rubber soles.

"Ryder, where are you going?" Chase called from behind. "Hey, Ryder, are you coming back?" He stopped at the hotel entrance in time to see Ryder darting down the sidewalk.

From over his shoulder, Ryder saw Chase toss up his arms and head back into the hotel.

Ryder cupped his hands around his mouth.

"Lily! Wait up!"

From his limited vantage point in the darkness, he noticed Lily stopped running at the sound of her name. He took advantage of the opportunity and sprinted down the sidewalk, dodging pedestrians and pushing aside others, leaving a string of apologies in his wake.

She turned and took off again. Was she running even faster?

Nonetheless, he gained ground and, as he began to close the gap between them, he assumed she, too, had worn nice shoes which slowed her down. For the first time in his life, he found a reason to thank God for heels on women's shoes.

Finally, he watched Lily go limp and lean against a brick building, awash in a streetlight's fluorescent glow. She must have stopped to catch her breath.

Though his lungs burned in the crisp air, he sprinted faster, before she would have a chance to bolt again. He hadn't run this fast since his high school P.E. class.

When Ryder caught up with Lily, he found her flushed and out of breath. They panted in syncopation. Hands on his knees, he bent at the waist and attempted to inhale deeper. Neither individual said a word. Though Lily had worn her auburn hair up, strands had come loose and now swayed in the breeze. Her gasping mouth, her rose-red face—she was more beautiful that he'd remembered.

She slapped him on the cheek again. *The same cheek!*

"Wait! Stop doing that!" he shouted. To his surprise, his face remained tender from her previous slap. Did she grip copper pipes for a living?

Once their breathing patterns recovered, Lily put her hands on her hips and stared at him.

"Well?" she said.

Ryder caught her eye and returned her stare. As often as he'd dreamed of crossing her path again, he'd never believed it would happen.

"It's really you," he said.

"You keep saying that!"

"I'm sorry, it's just—" He peered over Lily's shoulder and discovered another four-star hotel a few blocks south. He nodded toward it. "Listen, there's another hotel down that way, isolated from all the conference people. I'm sure it has a restaurant. Can we talk?"

Lily examined the flow of headlights and taillights, peppermint dots of white and red that glowed in the darkness. Vehicles eased past in a low, perpetual hum. Ryder prayed she wouldn't dart into the street and hail a cab. Then again, the way this evening had unfolded, he couldn't count out anything.

Desperation set in. After all these years, she had walked back into his life. He couldn't say good-bye without at least learning who she was. He'd made that mistake six years ago.

Lily didn't answer him. Instead, she bit her lip and set her sights on a passing car. Perhaps he still had a chance to convince her. After all, now that she had caught her breath, she hadn't broken into another marathon.

He tilted his head down and met her at eye level.

"At the very least, it seems I owe you dessert," he added.

Ryder watched Lily's jaw grow firm. Though her mouth remained closed, he could tell she had started to grit her teeth. Finally, her hands fell from her hips as she exhaled in resignation.

Her countenance softened as she gazed into his eyes.

"Fine, might as well."

CHAPTER 28

LILY AND RYDER had tucked themselves into a booth on the far side of the dining room. At a few minutes past eight o'clock that night, the dim restaurant, located in a hotel several blocks away from the site of Ryder's conference, had emptied except for a trio of patrons at a distant table. Awash in antique tones of tan and brown, the restaurant had adopted a metropolitan train-station motif.

They had decided on coffee and cheesecake, the restaurant's self-proclaimed specialties, which boasted ten flavors of each. Ryder had finished half of his slice, layers of cheesecake amid alternating layers of red velvet cake, topped with cream cheese frosting. He had offered Lily a bite but she'd refused. Her own slice carried the rich flavor of a vanilla latte. As delicious as it was, Lily hadn't taken more than a few nibbles. She couldn't summon her appetite. With each sip of her cappuccino, though, her anxiety melted further. The heat soothed her belly.

She couldn't get over how strange it felt to look into Ryder's familiar face. Having seen herself in various scenes with him, one would expect her to know him better, but their conversation—or lack thereof—since entering the restaurant proved they were strangers. Neither had said much. When their coffee arrived, Lily felt so relieved, the server might as well have been a paramedic offering resuscitation. Each time Lily tilted her cup for a sip, she kept it against her lips long after the liquid had entered her mouth. In total, the strategy had bought her an extra minute or two.

Did Ryder feel this awkward? When they'd first arrived, she could tell he had trouble looking her in the eye, a guilty child who had siphoned a dollar from his dad's bundle of cash. Yet his tentativeness appeared to fade as the minutes lapsed.

And now, as he sat across from her, he continued to stare. He swallowed another bite of his cheesecake and peered into her face, searching.

"Is something wrong?" Lily asked.

Ryder didn't break his focus. He sat mesmerized. "I've painted you for years, but I know nothing about you except your name."

She squirmed. "You don't need to stare."

Ryder shook himself from his haze. "Sorry, I don't mean to make you nervous. It's just...I never thought our paths would cross."

"Do you always put strange women in your paintings?"

That remark caused Ryder to shift in his seat.

Lily stifled a grin. Good. For once, *he* was embarrassed.

"I might owe you an apology," Ryder said. "I didn't mean to invade your privacy with that painting you referred to earlier, the one in the moonlight. Maybe I got carried away. When inspiration hits, I tend to follow blindly."

"So what about the paintings I *didn't* refer to? More inspiration?"

"You found those too, huh?" Ryder blushed. "I can't put my finger on what it is, but whenever you come to mind—"

"It makes you want to paint?"

He shook his head. "No, bigger than that. It makes me want to strive harder," he said. "Each time I finish painting your image, no matter how well it turns out, I feel like I've fallen short. So I try again and again, with the hope that maybe, this time, I'll finally get it right."

That melted her defenses.

And he hadn't even intended to schmooze her.

"Get *what* right?" she prompted.

"Your essence, I suppose."

"My essence *eludes* you?" she teased.

"I've tried to capture it in my work by putting you in different scenes: a baseball game here, a winery there. But it's not about location. It's about who you are on the inside, and like I said, I don't know much about you."

Except her name.

That's right, her name!

"How do you know my name?"

Ryder settled back against his booth and crossed his arms. He grinned. "You don't remember, do you," he observed, as if marveling at her curiosity.

"I beg your pardon?"

"Don't you remember the hotel down the street, the Royal Flower, where they're holding the conference?"

Remember? Odd choice of words. Lily chalked it up to coincidence.

"As a matter of fact, I stayed there once," she responded with a shrug. "My cousin lived in Cleveland years ago. She held her wedding reception at that hotel."

Ryder leaned toward her again, rested his elbows on the table and his chin upon his hands. "And you had a little bit to drink while you were there?"

Lily snickered. "To put it mildly. I don't remember much about that night. It went from good to bad, then got worse from there." Given the fact that Lily confided in few people, she surprised herself when she began to open up to Ryder. Then again, after seeing herself in those paintings with him, one side of her felt at ease in his presence. And the way he stared at her suggested he wanted to hear what she had to say. Fearful of getting hurt, though, she forced herself to remain on guard. "The truth is, I was quite drunk. I don't remember how I got back to my room that night."

Ryder shifted in his seat again. He furrowed his eyebrows as if measuring what to say next. A moment later, his pupils fluttered wider. His countenance softened.

Unblinking, Ryder held her gaze and whispered, "I do."

Another enigmatic response. At a loss for how to decipher it, Lily set her coffee cup down. "Excuse me?"

"I brought you back." When Lily offered no response, Ryder added, "That night. I gave the receptionist your first name, explained the circumstances. She told me your room number, and I carried you back to your room."

His remark hurled her into a daze. Too stunned to speak, Lily caught herself shaking her head. She studied his face and searched for a lame punch line, waiting for him to burst out in laughter. This was how the guys at work behaved before following up with a comment that turned her into the butt of the joke. But when she pored over Ryder's expression, all she found was sincerity.

Ryder must have sensed her confusion. A smile broke through at one corner of his mouth as he spoke. His voice, a blend of comfort and security, soothed her like bath salts and bubbles.

"A peach-colored dress," Ryder continued. "You had worn your hair up for the evening, a little like tonight. And you looked so sad." He didn't appear to know what to do with his hands. He slid them along the table in her direction but stopped short, tapping his fingertips upon the surface instead. It looked like he had wanted to reach out, then reconsidered. Perhaps he realized, as Lily had, that whatever connection they shared had occurred on an artist's canvas, not in real life.

"I stayed at the hotel that same night," he explained. "They'd held an art show in the ballroom next to your reception, and I was one of the artists. I noticed you in the lobby. You looked vibrant. So full of life." As Ryder continued, however, his expression grew somber. "After the show, I headed out for drinks with a friend. When I returned to the hotel and waited for the elevator to arrive, I heard someone sobbing. Whoever the person was, I wanted to make sure they were okay. So I searched for where the sobbing came from and wound up looking in a dark room—a storage room or office. And there you were. Weeping, crumpled on the floor like a broken flower."

In a subconscious reaction, Lily drew her hand to her mouth and ran a fingertip along her upper lip. When she realized what she had done, she placed her hand flat upon the table, determined to keep her guard up. Though her pulse increased, she fought to maintain her composure.

"I could tell you'd had a little too much to drink," Ryder said. "You'd weep for a while, then giggle, then weep again. Without intending to, you had drawn me in. Although I never expected to see you again, your face became etched in my mind that night. After seeing you so happy earlier, I couldn't help but wonder who had broken your heart." Ryder shrugged, and even in the dimness of the restaurant, Lily could see his cheeks redden. "The sight of you in such brokenness—it didn't seem right. I never wanted to see you in that state again, so without knowing you, I painted you in the state you deserved: happy, content." He hesitated for a beat. "And beautiful."

His words softened Lily's heart. A tear formed in her eye as she tried to recall the event Ryder mentioned, one episode in an endless series of disappointments. Such road signs dotted the course of her life's highway. As she examined the horizon, she could see those markers in the distance: *HEARTACHE CITY - 2 MILES AHEAD.* Callus had layered upon callus until, at last, they had shielded her heart from love.

Lily detested vulnerability, at least in herself. On the night of her cousin's wedding, the guy she had met at the reception had taken advantage of her, treated her like an empty gum wrapper. For once in her life, she had felt beautiful—but it had turned out to be a mirage. Nothing more.

In her hardened state the last several years, she had observed men's behaviors and had grown adept at perceiving superficiality. Phoniness, sex starvation, insincerity—she could identify such attributes without wasting much time.

But Ryder Flynn was different.

He didn't strike her as a creep. When Ryder gazed at her, she didn't detect a narrow edge to his eyes or ferocity lurking behind his irises. Was it possible he wanted nothing except an opportunity to get to know her? The *real* her?

He seemed...well, *genuine.*

Tonight, as she considered the tenderness with which he had described her, the painted images of Ryder and Lily flashed across her mind's eye. The truth settled in: He didn't actually *know* her.

Ryder clung to the same image Lily had concocted for that jerk at the wedding reception. The bubbly, fun image. That was the image Ryder portrayed in his art.

That was the Lily which Ryder found attractive. Not that she could blame him. After all, Lily herself preferred Ryder's version of her rather than the cold truth.

A crescent wrench sank to the pit of her heart. Once Ryder discovered the real Lily Machara—who she was and what she did for a living—how could it not come across as a letdown?

She didn't want to tell him any little white lies about herself. But Ryder seemed enthralled with the image he'd created. Hands down, it was more exciting than the truth. Her life in St. Louis appeared downright paltry compared to his.

Lily Machara, who spoke her mind and had grown immune to what others thought of her, now cared about Ryder Flynn's opinion. Whatever existed between them, she couldn't describe, but Lily knew this: She didn't want to let it go.

CHAPTER 29

RYDER WAS SURE he had gone too far and exposed his heart too early. But as an artist coping with reality, he had a tough time finding the proper balance. The goal of an artist is to dig down and bring motives to light, to capture emotion. But while a painting captured and communicated life, it remained stationary on a canvas. It didn't tap its foot with impatience while it awaited your response. It didn't pressure you into reflex decisions.

Ryder knew women longed for emotional depth. He could hear it in their conversations and in the songs they sang. Romance novels, even those with vampire protagonists, boiled down to honest emotion. And Ryder had mastered the process of channeling those yearnings into his paintings.

Personal relationships, on the other hand, were a separate matter altogether. When he allowed himself to let his guard down, Ryder possessed a talent for being too straightforward. In fact, his honesty seemed to drive a wedge between women and himself.

In other words, he had a knack for making them nervous and putting them to flight.

And given the way Lily fidgeted with her hands, he couldn't help but suspect he'd unsettled her tonight. Perhaps they never should have talked. He had borne his heart in the few things he'd said to her, but for all he knew, he sounded like a nutcase.

Perhaps he could salvage this conversation by searching for common ground.

"So, anyway, you know what I do for a living," he said. "What do you do?"

Lily perked up in her seat. "I'm a—"

She halted in mid-sentence. Her eyes darted from his and settled somewhere beyond his shoulder. He peeked behind himself to find the source of her distraction but noticed nothing out of the ordinary. By the time he returned his attention to her, she had recovered.

"I—I'm in marketing," Lily replied.

"Really?" Ryder straightened his posture. That sounded promising. "In that case, our careers share some common ground. Marketing, artwork—they both focus on an audience."

"The client isn't always right, but sometimes you need to let them think they are," she said, then lodged her tongue against the inside of her cheek.

"Exactly!"

Ryder asked a few specific questions about marketing, but Lily seemed on edge answering them. Maybe he'd delved too deep for their first conversation. But it was all he knew to ask her. Her remark about customers had come so fast, as if by reflex, that he thought he'd hit fertile ground. But her next answers came across as tentative, maybe even self-conscious. He wanted to switch to a more comfortable subject, but didn't know her well enough to know what to ask. And he hesitated to ask whether any of his paintings were an accurate reflection of her life. For all he knew, she might take off running again.

Although he had just met her—or met her *again*—he sensed kindness about her. Sincerity. He picked up on it in the way she glanced at him, as though she longed for affirmation. Her demeanor, her subconscious manner of leaning toward him, suggested that perhaps she didn't perceive him as a jerk after all.

Sticking with the same topic of conversation, he dialed it back to respect her comfort zone. Should he aim for flirtation-lite? She didn't appear to mind.

"So if you're a marketing person," Ryder said, "then I'd guess you're from…New York?"

Lily shook her head.

"Chicago?"

"Nope?"

"Somewhere in North America?"

"You're getting warmer," she replied.

She lodged her tongue against the inside of her cheek again, in front of her lower jaw. She'd given him a clever reply and she knew it. Ryder found it attractive.

He clasped his hands upon the table and leaned toward her.

She responded in suit.

"I'm from St. Louis," she said at last. "Born and raised."

Without intending to, Ryder chuckled. "You're kidding."

"What's so funny about it?"

"Missouri?"

"I know it's not as glitzy as Manhattan, but—"

"No, it's not that," Ryder said. "I'm from Missouri too. I live southwest of St. Louis, in the Ozarks."

Lily's countenance eased. "Must be nice having Lake of the Ozarks nearby in the summer. Do you live far from it?"

"*On* it is more accurate."

"You live on a boat?"

"Okay, my *boat* lives on the lake," he chuckled. "I have a house on the shore. The water is about 40 feet from my back door. Right against my backyard."

"I would've pictured an artist living in New York," Lily joshed. "You've shattered my illusions."

"Sorry about that," Ryder replied with a wink. "But that means we live only a couple of hours from each other—and you know what they say about the path of fate."

"What do they say?"

"They say fate travels Interstate 70, to Highway 54." Almost a straight shot from her city to his town. "But sometimes it takes I-44."

"Whatever."

There! Did she just stifle another grin?

How many times had Ryder traveled the route from the Ozarks to St. Louis? All these years he'd clung to her memory, and for all he knew, he might have driven past her as she sipped cappuccino at Kaldi's Coffeehouse!

Marveling at how they could have gone six years without meeting closer to home, his mind returned to the location at hand.

"So if you live in St. Louis and I live two hours away," Ryder said, "why did we travel to Cleveland to meet each other twice? Wouldn't it have been easier to meet halfway, back home?"

"I think fate enjoys turning my life into comedy," Lily replied.

"But you figured out I'd be in Cleveland this weekend."

"A friend of mine found an article about the art show online."

He'd forgotten how much information floated around cyberspace. "Few people know I live at the lake. It's my refuge, my place of tranquility. I don't talk about it during interviews."

"People haven't tracked down the famous artist yet, huh?"

"My studio is in my home, so people in my industry know I live there. But given the fact I'm not George Clooney, I doubt anyone cares enough to track me down at home." He took another sip of his black coffee and decided to risk another tease. "Art shows, on the other hand, are a different matter. Who knows who will track me down *there,* right?" He shot her a wink.

Lily lifted a hand to her head and hid her eyes behind it, tilted her head downward. "I can't believe I did that. I can't believe I'm here. I'm in *Ohio* right now." She removed her hand and glanced up at him, an expression of horror on her face. "This must look crazy to you. I'm not a psycho. I swear I've never done this before. This isn't me."

"What do you mean?"

"I'm not the type of person who leaves town on a whim to chase down some guy." She let out a heavy breath. "You must think I'm ridiculous for finding you."

Ryder's chest felt aglow. He traced a tiny circle on the table with his finger, then their gazes connected again.

"I wish you had found me six years ago."

The words oozed from his mouth like caramel. If other customers remained in the restaurant, he'd forgotten about them. Ryder wanted to savor the moment as he waded into the ocean of Lily's cobalt-blue eyes.

After all these years, she had found him.

And he wouldn't have altered a single detail.

CHAPTER 30

WHEN LILY RETURNED home, it was almost one in the morning. Thunderstorms and a tornado warning in the St. Louis metro area had delayed her departure from Cleveland by several hours. By the time she arrived at her apartment, Brooke was already in bed.

Exhausted, Lily kicked off her shoes in her bedroom, brushed her teeth, and crawled into bed in the same clothes she'd worn on the airplane. She fell asleep within minutes.

Lily's manager hadn't scheduled her to work on Monday. Aaron had stopped by her apartment once his workday ended. She'd given him a few details about her weekend, but kept much of it to herself. Sitting side by side on the sofa, he filled her in on his day at the shop.

When Brooke arrived home a short while later, neither Lily nor Aaron had a chance to utter hello. As soon as Brooke dropped her purse on the counter, she prodded for details. "I want to know everything! What happened with Loverboy?"

"I don't—"

"Wait!" Brooke halted her with the palm of her hand. "Occasions like this warrant a glass of wine."

With that, Brooke disappeared into the kitchen. When she returned with a blush for herself and longnecks for Lily and Aaron, she settled beside them on the sofa. Lily now found herself stuck on the middle cushion, surrounded by two friends gawking at her, expecting particulars.

Aaron lifted his bottle in the fashion of a toast and said, "I want to hear the in-depth version too. Start talking."

"Fine." Lily rolled her eyes. "What do you want to know?"

"Did you wear the dress I lent you?"

"Of course."

"And?"

Lily threw herself back against the sofa, crossed her arms over her chest. "I got to town, headed for my motel—"

"Yeah, yeah." Brooke twirled her index finger to hurry her along. "Fast forward to the pertinent stuff."

Granted, Lily didn't date much, but this current spotlight illuminated that fact. She hated being the center of attention. That was Brooke's calling.

Eyes wide, Brooke set her glass on the coffee table. "Did you find him? Of course you did. I can tell—you're being evasive."

"I found him at the art show."

"How'd you confront him?" asked Aaron. He leaned forward and rubbed his palms together, a hunter waiting for the kill.

Lily had tried to forget about that weekend's initial encounter with Ryder. Still horrified at how she had greeted him, she shrank in her seat and relented. *Get it over with, Lily.* "It wasn't a confrontation so much as an accident."

"Huh?"

"When I got to the show, there was a reception going on in the atrium. I wore Brooke's dress to it."

At that, Brooke beamed and took a triumphant sip from her glass.

"The room was crowded with conference people," Lily continued, "so it took me a while to find him, but there he was, mingling with people."

"And?"

"I wimped out."

"Why would you give up after traveling all those miles?" Aaron asked.

"I realized it was possible he'd modeled the woman in the art after somebody else. How humiliating would it be to make a presumption and get it wrong? So I turned around and eyed my escape route. That's when he tapped me on the shoulder and—"

"Ryder?" Brooke covered Lily's hand with hers. "How did he know it was you?"

"He must have seen me from across the room. Anyway, I turned around—"

"Stop! How did he react when you turned around? Did he smile? Did he look deep into your eyes?"

"I couldn't quite tell."

"Why not?"

"I kind of...slapped him."

"You what?!" Brooke and Aaron gasped in unison.

"I couldn't help it! All this rage built up inside me when I saw his face, and my mind went back to that poster that had me, you know—*without any clothes on."* Lily couldn't help but whisper that last phrase, as if the FBI had bugged her apartment. "It was one of those impulse responses. How would *you* have reacted?"

"Don't go there," Aaron joshed.

"Anyway," Lily continued, "once my hand hit his face, I hauled ass out the front door and sprinted down the street, but you've seen how well *Brooke* runs in *her own* heels."

"Don't tell me you broke my shoe," Brooke said.

"Everything's fine," Lily replied. "I was ready to ditch my rental car at the art show and catch a cab back to the motel, but he caught up with me before I could get the hell out of sight."

Brooke perked up. She crumpled her lips. Her facial expression melted the way it did when Jeremy gave her a dozen roses for Valentine's Day. Ryder had scored points with the roommate.

"He pursued you!" Brooke waved her fingers to summon forth more. "What happened next?"

Lily sighed, took a long pull on her beer to stall for time. "We went to a restaurant at another hotel for coffee and cheesecake."

"Cheesecake?" Brooke cooed, her voice easygoing and tender, the way she'd speak to a puppy.

Under normal conditions, answering questions about dates didn't suit Lily, which was why she hadn't told Brooke about her first date with Evan. For Lily, circumstances in life could be classified as black or white, hot or cold, manual or automatic. She didn't waste time with unnecessary particulars or shades of gray. But now, a subtle rush made its way along her flesh as she spun this tale for her rapt audience. To Lily's surprise, she enjoyed recounting the aspects of her Saturday night once Ryder had entered the picture.

Aaron shook his head in disbelief. "Gourmet coffee?"

Lily rolled her eyes. "I discovered I like cappuccino."

"Look who's getting adventurous!"

"Half the drink names were in Italian. I picked something I'd heard of before."

"What kind of cheesecake?" Brooke chimed in again.

"Vanilla latte. Apparently, I must like lattes too."

Brooke's eyebrows shot up. "Ryder Flynn has convinced Lily Machara to expand her horizons and try new things. Hmm."

"Whatever."

"So what did you talk about?"

With that question, Lily felt her stomach constrict. "General stuff. Jobs, art, where we live."

"Was he surprised to hear what you do for a living?" Aaron asked. "You always love to watch people react to that."

Once Lily's conversation with Ryder turned away from the topic of her career, they hadn't revisited it. As far as Ryder knew, Lily had a career in marketing. Brooke's job was the first position that had crossed her mind. Lily had hated to tell a white lie, but her conversation with Ryder had turned out so well, she'd found herself not wanting their evening to end on a bad note because of one little unimportant fact. Ryder hadn't turned out to be a creep. She had discovered a gentle soul. She *liked* the man she had gotten to know. For once, to her astonishment, a decent, handsome man seemed attracted to her on a romantic level. And unlike with Evan, a man for whom she couldn't muster reciprocal interest, Lily had discovered a mutual attraction to Ryder.

She decided to cover herself for now. Keep it simple, stupid. "We focused on *his* job—you know, the fact that he put me in his paintings."

"So there's no doubt about it? He confirmed it?" Aaron asked.

Lily nodded. "Remember when I told you my family's wedding reception took place at the same hotel as this conference? Well, Ryder was there the night of her reception, too."

Brooke blinked, her mouth agape. "Years ago?"

"That's where he saw me the first time. That's how I'd gotten back to my room when I was drunk out of my skull. Somehow, later that night, *he* found me and brought me to my room." Lily felt her mouth flirt with a smile. "He says he never forgot about me. After all this time."

Brooke sank back into the corner of the sofa with one hand upon her heart. Her blond hair splayed across her chest.

Aaron wrapped his arm around Lily. "Lily has herself a brand new beau."

"See?" Brooke nodded to him. "I told you, Aaron. You should have held on to her. Now she's taken!"

Though that bittersweet memory prodded the surface of her heart, Lily suppressed it.

"And it turns out he lives in the Ozarks, right on the lake," Lily said.

Aaron patted her arm. "So what's next?"

Brooke shot up in her seat, her spine ramrod straight. "Yeah, are you going to see him again? You live so close to each other."

Lily couldn't help but chuckle. Hard to believe she was one step ahead of Brooke.

"This weekend," Lily said. "We're getting together again on Saturday." She paused, then added, "A little closer to home this time."

CHAPTER 31

LONG ROWS OF attached shops stood guard along each side of Main Street. Their brick edifices ranged from whitewashed to *au naturel.* Although Hannibal, Missouri, stretches about 15 square miles, several blocks along Main Street form the core of its historic district. Author Mark Twain, the town's native son, had set several of his novels in his hometown. To this day, the town preserves landmarks that served as points of inspiration for some of Twain's creations.

When Lily and Ryder had arrived a couple of hours earlier, they had walked to the northern end of Main Street and climbed concrete steps to a lighthouse that overlooked the Mississippi River. Afterward, they had decided on lunch at LulaBelle's, a mom-and-pop restaurant beside a gravel parking lot. Lily couldn't get over how much gravel remained scattered around the area. She marveled at the town's tranquility. It possessed a naiveté, one which suggested the buildings and land hadn't received news of their legendary status. Since seeing each other would require a drive regardless of where they met, Ryder had suggested the town as a fun alternative to an official date.

"Do you come to Hannibal often?" he asked her.

"Once," Lily replied. "My dad took me here as a kid, but I haven't visited since."

Ryder nodded. "I get out this way on occasion, for inspiration. I consider how Mark Twain centered so much of his work around this place, and it makes me want to connect with whatever he found here."

After lunch, Lily and Ryder window-shopped up and down Main Street. They stopped at a place called Antique Row, its old-fashioned sign bolted to its exterior. From beneath the shop's blue-and-white striped awning, she peeked at a variety of knickknacks that sat behind the storefront window. Lily wondered if the same knickknacks sat in that window ten years ago.

A warm breeze and clear, blue sky beckoned tourists, who filled the sidewalks on this Saturday in early May.

It had taken Lily less than two hours to drive north from St. Louis to Hannibal. For Ryder, the drive had taken closer to three hours from his home in the Ozarks, which hadn't occurred to Lily at the time. When Ryder had suggested meeting at the town, Lily had agreed without a second thought. It gave her another chance to see him. And on a more important note, neutral territory assured her that Ryder wouldn't pressure her to return to his place that night.

Several miles from Hannibal, she had stopped at a visitor's center off the highway to gather ideas for fun spots in town. When Lily had first walked into the visitor's center, the employee had given her a double-take, the kind that indicates you recognize somebody but don't want to ask for confirmation. Anytime that occurred, Lily wondered if a nearby billboard had Ryder's and her faces plastered on it.

The afternoon felt so casual, and Ryder possessed such an inviting air, that Lily felt more comfortable talking to him as the day progressed.

"So, if you're an artist, are you also a ladies' man?" she joshed. "Do women show up at your doorstep and clamor for a date?"

He chuckled. "Truth?"

"Of course. I'm all about the romance."

Ryder waved off the notion with a halfhearted gesture. "Sure, a few individuals have made interesting, shall we say, *advances* toward me. Nothing I've given in to, though."

"Celebrities, from what I've read."

"A few celebrities, an art school student, some magazine readers." He shot Lily an amused look. "A librarian."

"Were they stalkers?"

"Thankfully, no. I'll admit, though, I do get a little paranoid about it sometimes."

"Who were your most outlandish admirers?"

Ryder thought for a moment, then replied, "A couple of bored, unfaithful wives. One was a Congressman's wife, who will remain anonymous. But like I said, I never gave in to the temptations." Ryder kicked a stray piece of gravel into the road. His voice grew softer. "The truth is, I'm not too successful when it comes to romance. And the spotlight that people have placed on me—well, it sort of happened. It's not my favorite part of my career, in spite of how it might appear to a lot of folks."

That last remark, the honesty of it, stirred Lily's heart. She didn't want to dig further. For a moment, she wondered if she had gone too far with her questions already, but Ryder seemed comfortable with them.

Lily sensed in Ryder a wandering soul, restless, hungry for a place to settle. When it came to his fame, he seemed to feel out of his element, like he hadn't found a place where he fit.

Much like Lily herself.

They turned a corner and meandered along a side street, its first block paved with red brick. Soon they reached a narrow, rectangular building, which looked like someone had turned the historic structure sideways and planted the front door on its side. Atop the white siding sat a sign that read, *J.M. Clemens, Justice of the Peace.* Mark Twain's birth name was Samuel Clemens, and his father was a judge.

But the house next door caught Lily's attention when she noticed its sign.

"It's Becky Thatcher's house!" Lily said as she grabbed Ryder's arm by accident and tugged him along. They passed a white-washed fence and jogged up wooden stairs to a small front porch.

The plain house had tan siding and dark brown shutters. At the front door, the character Becky Thatcher—or what looked like her image painted on a piece of plywood—served as sentry. Lily had to snigger when she caught sight of a modern-day security camera hanging from one corner of the 19th Century home.

They found the front door locked, but Lily and Ryder peeked through windows. Inside the house sat antique furnishings arranged in a layout befitting Twain's era.

Lily wondered if Ryder felt the way this house might, with its unending parade of people staring in from the outside. A life on display. She wondered how it must feel for people to project an image upon you, an expectation or belief about who you are. Meanwhile, a small voice—the true you—whispers, gasping for air as it struggles to find its way to the surface.

Then again, for the past couple of months, courtesy of Ryder's art, Lily had stared into an alternate version of her own life. And she had to admit, she found its layout appealing. The furniture of her life seemed to fit in Ryder's paintings. She had a place. Yet, in reality, Lily had yet to find a place of her own.

CHAPTER 32

HOPPING INTO RYDER'S car, they headed south on Route 79. While chatting with the owner of a soda fountain on Main Street, the woman had given them directions to a small clearing with a decent view of the Mississippi River. Once they reached their destination, Ryder parked his car on the shoulder of the road and they sauntered toward the river. They took a seat on an aluminum bench located on a patch of grass fifty feet from the road.

A warm breeze tickled Lily's chin. She felt her hair rustle. With her eyes on the river, she pretended to focus straight ahead but remained attentive of Ryder in her peripheral vision.

To her surprise, Lily found herself wishing Ryder would put his arm around her. How would that feel? But she feigned engrossment in the muddy water ahead, which lapped beneath a handful of cumulus clouds in an otherwise crystalline sky.

"I've concluded that our circumstances aren't quite fair," Ryder said as he leaned his head toward Lily's but kept his eyes on the water. A riverboat filled with tourists eased upstream. It left behind such a minor wake, Lily considered the term *wake* a technicality. In fact, the boat moved at such a slow pace, the lazy water didn't appear to notice.

"Unfair? Why?"

"You seem to know about me from articles you've read, but I don't know much about you."

Self-consciousness shot up Lily's spine and transformed it into a copper pipe. "What do you want to know?"

Ryder shifted in his seat as if indecisive on whether to tread further. "I never asked if you were in a relationship. The fact you met me here today must work in my favor, though."

"I'm swinging single, as they say." Granted, she and Evan had seen each other for the past month or two, but neither considered it a relationship. For that matter, Evan had never brought it up. Their dating remained casual.

"So you're a heartbreaker?" Ryder shot her a mischievous smirk.

"I'm about as unlucky with romance as you claim to be."

"Ouch. That's not good. It's also hard for me to believe."

"Tell that to the guys who cross my path." Lily crossed her arms and felt more secure. "Put it this way: When men look at me, they don't see the woman in your art. They see *me.*" When Ryder's expression morphed into confusion, Lily, eager to change the subject, asked, "Why does this town inspire you?"

Ryder stretched his arm along the length of the bench, the opposite side from where Lily sat. "The simplicity of yesteryear, I guess. Years ago, I used to walk down Main Street, and it reminded me that Mark Twain walked along the same street. Following his footsteps triggered an artistic connection with him." Ryder raised his hand to shield his eyes from the sunshine. "That sounds weird, doesn't it!"

"Not if it helps you do your job."

"I imagined him growing up in this area, starting his career. I figured if he could end up spending his life doing something he loved, then one day, maybe I could too."

A couple in their sixties walked in front of them. Lily pegged them as locals enjoying an afternoon stroll.

The woman, a touch overweight with salt-and-pepper hair, paused and stared at Lily and Ryder. The woman looked stunned. The rail-thin man—her husband, Lily assumed—

stopped beside the woman and appeared to wonder why time had reached a standstill.

"Excuse me," said the woman in a hushed tone, "I apologize for staring, but you two look so familiar. I haven't seen you in town, have I?"

"No ma'am," Ryder replied. "But don't feel bad. We get that a lot."

The woman nodded, then offered a wave as she and her partner moved along.

Ryder sneaked a glance at Lily. They erupted into mischievous snickers.

Lily heard a cell phone buzz and, by instinct, shot her hand to her back pocket before she noticed Ryder retrieving his phone from his own pocket. Eyeing the display, he furled his eyebrows and shook his head. He appeared regretful when he returned the phone to his pocket.

"Sorry to be rude. I have that annoying habit of checking my phone whenever it announces itself."

"Who was it?" Lily asked, nonchalant—then realized it was rude of her to ask. She wanted to slug herself in the arm.

Ryder snorted. "Brenna Shire."

"The singer?"

Ryder nodded. No big deal. "Got a text message from her. I get them sometimes. Women who want to meet me next time I'm in L.A., but I usually decline. I don't know how they get my number."

"Why would you say no?"

"I only agree if it involves a prearranged event. Platonic stuff, though gossipers try to spin it otherwise." Sheepish, he added, "I can't help it. I'm a private person."

"That's what I find curious about you. If you don't like the spotlight, why do you go to places you know are crawling with attention? Why be seen with famous people if you know your face will get plastered across the Internet?"

"Maybe it's fear of not having enough jobs. A remnant from my days as a starving artist when nobody wanted my work. I grew resilient from that season, scraping dimes together to make ends meet, but I wouldn't want to relive it."

"And celebrity status protects you from that?"

"Call it a lucky break. I painted a movie poster a few years ago, which turned into a breakthrough in my career. It also created the perception that Ryder Flynn is tied to Hollywood. If you're tied to Hollywood and people want to know about you, it makes you a hot property. And as long as you're a hot property, jobs pour in. So I play the part to stay in demand—but it's not truly me."

Lily watched as Ryder, heavy in concentration, traced the shiny ridges of the bench with his finger. With a deep breath, she caught a trace of his natural scent as his skin warmed in the spring air. She wanted to reach for his hand but held herself back.

Lily understood creating images. After all, she still hadn't told him about *her* career. Oh, how she wanted to. Ryder embodied velvet strength draped in kindness. Maybe he wouldn't look down on her career, but she couldn't risk losing him.

One day, she would, she promised herself. But not today.

For the first time in years, destiny had drawn her to someone with whom her heart connected. Rejections from decent, genuine guys lay strewn in her past, shrapnel scattered across an emotional battlefield.

"I must sound like I don't have my life figured out," Ryder said. "Do I make any sense?"

More than you can imagine. "Yeah," Lily whispered, "you do."

Ryder gave her arm a gentle nudge. "So, what about you?"

Lily struggled for words. "Me? Oh, I wouldn't know anything about fame."

Ryder gave her a humorous look. "But maybe you've experienced a version of it in some way. You've never been the center of attention?"

"Not really. Well, not until *you* made me the center of attention in those paintings."

Ryder turned toward her. He rested his arm behind her. "No school plays? No team trophies?" He appeared doubtful as he tapped his index finger against his chin. "No honor roll? Nothing?"

"Nope."

Lily paused. She sensed a piece of her heart sink but held her countenance steady, returning her gaze to the water. The steamboat had drifted out of sight.

She tossed her hands in the air and attempted a humorous tone of voice to hide the sudden sting she felt. "See? I told you." She turned to face him. "I'm nothing special."

Ryder leaned closer. His eyes danced with sincerity as they pored over hers. His compassion drew her soul toward his.

"I beg to differ," he whispered.

Silent and still, they gazed into each other's eyes.

CHAPTER 33

THAT NIGHT, LILY drove straight home and discovered she had the apartment to herself. Before departing Hannibal, she and Ryder had enjoyed an early dinner at a restaurant in the heart of Sawyer's Creek, a collection of tourist shops on Route 79. They had dined at a table overlooking the Mississippi River, then poked through a year-round Christmas shop for fun.

Afterward, they had parted ways, disappointed their time together had come to an end.

During Lily's drive home, both Brooke and Aaron had left voice messages to ask how her date—or whatever it was—had gone. Lily hadn't answered the phone. She had yet to make sense of what had happened that day. But as she considered the ease with which she and Ryder had bonded, she wondered whether her life was on the verge of a dramatic shift.

Now, at a little past ten-thirty, she plunked down on her bed and reached for a car magazine she'd left on the nightstand. After flipping through a few of its slick pages, she set it aside, unable to concentrate.

Lily rolled onto her back and stared at the tiny bumps on the ceiling She studied the golden glow cast by a lamp beside the bed.

Her breathing pattern slowed as she relived her day with Ryder. She called to mind his eyes, the color of milk chocolate, and the way his sandy-brown hair had fluttered in the breeze as he'd gazed at her. Her thoughts turned to his posture, which dripped with confidence, and the decisive stride with which he walked, as if he would reach his life's destination by sunset. Ryder didn't seem to place expectations upon her. Lily could relax around him and didn't feel like he would judge her behavior or reactions. She drew comfort from the fact that she could be herself around him—aside from that little white lie about her job.

Was it harmful to let him see her the way he wanted to see her? It was only outward, after all. He seemed to know and savor who she was on the inside. Wasn't that what mattered?

When Ryder Flynn whispered her name or escaped into her eyes, Lily almost believed in herself.

Next, she turned her thoughts to Evan. She felt awful comparing him to Ryder, but she couldn't deny the contrast in how she felt around each man. Each was gentle and kind, driven in his career. Each man sought to ensure Lily felt comfortable—even special—in his presence.

With Ryder, everything unfolded in such a natural way, it felt effortless, the oozing of melted butter. On the other hand, when she spent time with Evan, she felt nervous. And no matter how often she and Evan got together, from the first minute to the last, her tension seldom let up.

Lily sighed.

She glanced at the clock, which now read 11:02. A sweet pang settled into her belly.

She *missed* Ryder.

Four hours had passed since they had said good-bye, yet she yearned to see him again.

A few more minutes passed. One final glimpse at the clock before she tucked herself into bed for the night.

And to think, in the hotel atrium a week ago, she'd seethed at the sight of him.

Maybe one phone call wouldn't hurt…

She fought the temptation. How desperate could she be! How pitiful would it look for her to pick up her phone this late on a Saturday night—after they had spent the whole day together! It might suffocate him or scare him off, and she would chase away the one promising thing to emerge in her love life. She didn't want that rejection. But she couldn't bear to lay there thinking about him.

Brooke would know what to do. She'd had plenty of experience with this. But Lily? Talk about clueless. Lily squeezed her eyes shut.

Her cell phone vibrated on the nightstand.

Great, she thought. *Now Brooke couldn't wait any longer.* By this time, she must have figured out that Lily had ignored her voice message. She had sneaked away from Jeremy and into a restroom so she could hear the details about Lily's infamous date.

Lily didn't bother to open her eyes as she grabbed the phone. "Hello?"

"Hi Lily."

A male voice. Lily's eyes shot open.

CHAPTER 34

"I HOPE IT'S not too late," Ryder said.

"No, not at all." Lily shook the fuzziness from her brain and tried to disguise the exhilaration in her voice. "I'm hanging out at home, tired after the drive and being in the sun all day."

"Me too. I walked in the door a while ago and thought I'd give you a call."

She wasn't used to hearing his voice on the phone. She perked up, fluffed a pillow, and sat up against it. Lily drew her knees to her chest, wrapping one arm around her knees as she held the phone with her free hand.

"Did you forget something?" she asked, hoping she was wrong. Maybe humor would work. "Did I take your Becky Thatcher shot glass home with me by accident?"

She swore she could hear that faint grin of his, the one that suggested he delighted in her presence even more than her words. He spoke above a whisper. "No, I—well, I just didn't want to go to sleep without hearing your voice once more."

Lily melted at that.

In spite of her best effort to resist a smile, it seeped through her armor anyway. Lily tried to convince herself this wasn't happening, that a quick pop would sound, the bubble would burst, and the dream would end.

But she couldn't.

They talked for two hours before turning out their lights.

CHAPTER 35

When Monday morning arrived, Lily continued to soar on an emotional high. Despite the hours they had spent together in Hannibal, she considered Ryder's Saturday-night phone call the highlight of her weekend. Invigorated with excitement, she had kept herself awake in her bed for another hour after their phone call had ended, recounting every detail.

Ryder made her feel desirable.

On second thought, it was more than that.

He made her feel valued.

Lily pushed through the bulky door and entered the garage at the auto shop. With her mind fixed on Ryder, it took her a moment to notice the cacophony of drills and other machinery. The scent of rubber emanated from a stack of new tires that had arrived minutes earlier. She dropped the newest vinyl pouch into the queue bin and grabbed the door handle to return to the waiting room.

"Good weekend for you, eh?" Dave approached from behind, a cordless drill tucked in his armpit, before she had a chance to yank open the door. Dave wiped his hands on his coveralls and grabbed the next job order from the bin.

Lily maintained a poker face. "If you say so."

She hadn't told a soul at the auto shop except Aaron, who would have kept the news to himself. A bead of perspiration wiggled down her temple. Not even a pair of king-sized fans and open garage doors could disperse the heat she felt at this moment.

Dave shot her a look of amusement. "You know what I mean," he teased, then opened the pouch and perused the job order. "I ran into your roommate at the gas station. She told me you had a date with that artist guy."

Great. Leave it to Brooke.

Since Lily hadn't made full sense of her weekend or what it meant for the future, she wasn't ready to delve into its details. Not with Dave, of all people. Couldn't he let her savor the memory for a few days before giving her the third degree?

"So it's true?" he pressed.

"Yeah, what about it?" Lily studied her palm and noticed she had picked up a fresh oil smudge. She wiped it on a rag and returned it to the pocket of her coveralls.

"Sounds intriguing."

"It wasn't a date. We met up, that's all."

"Oh, okay, I get it." With that, Dave winked, then pointed at her with a clichéd, smoking-gun gesture and clucked his tongue.

Jackass. Why did he need to ruin this for her?

Lily threw her hands on her hips. "What's *that* supposed to mean?"

"Well, I'm sure more went on than just"—Dave curled his fingers into quotation marks—"meeting up." Another clichéd gesture. *Come on, Dave, go for a third!*

"So you're saying I'm a slut?"

"Naw, you're cool. And I'm sure *he's* cool, too."

"Do you have a point, or are you babbling to hear yourself talk?"

He snorted. "Come on, the dude's an *artist!* He hangs out with famous babes and movie people. Besides that, he's a *guy.* You think he's interested in your delicate *smile?*"

That got her burning inside. Lily folded her arms across her chest. She wanted to punch Dave in the teeth but gritted her own instead.

"Are you jealous?" she said, a challenge more than an inquiry, like a cat pawing a toy.

"No, I'm curious."

"Curious? Maybe *you* should date him, then."

"Fine. If you don't want to talk about it, I'll leave you to your thoughts." With a finger tap to the job-order pouch he'd picked up, he added, "I'll move along to this tire rotation." He squeezed the trigger of his electric drill and gave it a playful whir.

"Careful, Dave. Don't screw yourself." She pursed her lips at that remark. He made it so easy.

On his way toward the exit to retrieve the vehicle for the job, he stopped, turned back around. "By the way, someone came here looking for you on Saturday."

"Evan?"

"Oh, is that the name of that customer you've been dating? Sorry, I can't keep up with all your admirers." He waved at her in jest. "No, it was a woman. Reporter or something."

A reporter? What the hell would a reporter want with her?

CHAPTER 36

"BAKER TENNIS RACKETS?" Chase asked as he stared at his tablet.

"I don't think so," Ryder replied.

Chase nodded, then swiped the tablet to switch to the next record.

Ryder tried to concentrate on the job offers Chase rattled off but found it difficult to concentrate. His mind returned to Lily, as it had throughout the day. From time to time, Ryder still shook his head in disbelief, trying to convince himself that he hadn't gotten trapped in a dream.

No, Lily was real. And she was really in his life. After six years of waiting and expecting to wait an eternity longer, the pieces of his life seemed to have fallen into place. Maybe.

Lily seemed to struggle with insecurity of some sort. She tried to hide it when they were together, but his instinct picked up on it in the way she spoke. And she didn't seem to grasp the beauty he saw in her. Lily wore an impervious exterior, the kind with which you would surround yourself to avoid getting hurt. *That* was something he could relate to.

But as the weekend progressed, as they sat together and talked, she grew more comfortable around him. The more relaxed she grew, the more she allowed her words to flow forth, speaking from her heart, unlike the night she'd tracked him down, when she had kept her sentences clipped. It's harder for someone to find a chink in your armor when you're cagey.

Last Saturday night, as he'd sat at his kitchen table with a cup of decaffeinated coffee in one hand and his phone in the other, he could have listened to her voice for hours. And he did.

Six years ago, he had sensed a depth about her but had lacked the chance to unearth it. As the years passed, Lily's visage was the only thing to which he could cling, so he'd pictured her in a variety of scenarios to try to decipher who she was. Without facts to hinder him, he'd grown attracted to the notion of who she *could* be.

But now, after spending two weekends with her, he found himself attracted, day by day, to the true Lily. With each layer she allowed him to peel away, he wanted to learn more. He wanted to study her countenance as she spoke of a childhood memory, to listen to the phrases she used, to absorb every tangible detail she invited him to explore.

And today he missed her.

"I've got a fast-food chain here," Chase said.

Ryder's daydream dispersed. "Nope."

"A resort in Antigua?"

"Now you're talking!"

Chase chuckled and started to tap an email message on his own device. "As you'll recall, there was a day when you couldn't be so picky about which jobs you'd accept."

"The luxury of choices is much better."

Not long ago, Chase had rented a two-room office for himself in a small retail building. Once Ryder's career gained steam, Chase branched out further and managed other individuals in southern Missouri, from artists to dancers to lounge crooners. But while Chase's client repertoire and commission earnings had grown, Ryder remained, by far, his most-sought client.

"You might want to think about the tennis offer, though," Chase said. "Sports could be lucrative."

"I'll think about it." Ryder opened the calendar app on his tablet. "Did any interview requests arrive?"

"The *Seattle Times* earlier today. They've asked for a phone interview with you later this week, Thursday if possible. Would that work for you?"

Ryder still found it amusing that people considered him the least bit interesting. "No complaints from me. How about late morning?"

"I'll see what I can do. They want to do a feature article. Do you have any personal ties to the state of Washington?"

"No."

Chase shrugged. "I didn't think so, but it never hurts to see if we can tie a local angle to it." With a few more taps and swipes, Chase closed the application, cracked his knuckles, and leaned back in his chair. "So what's she like?"

"Who?" Ryder set his own tablet aside.

Chase gave him an *Oh-come-on* look. "The girl," he said. "The one you drove all the way to Hannibal to see again."

This was one reason Ryder enjoyed having an old friend as his manager. One minute they talked business. Then, without hesitation, Chase would morph into Ryder's buddy, and they would shoot the breeze as if catching up on their college lives during semester break—including the latest on the dating front.

"She's fun," Ryder replied. "Deep. Deeper than she comes across when you first talk to her."

"If memory serves, you didn't have a chance to say a word to her in Cleveland before she smacked you upside the head. You don't look like you suffered any injuries this time, though."

"I'm intact, ready for the newspaper interview you've got for me."

"You told me she lives in St. Louis," Chase said. "Does she have family there?"

"Her dad, but that's all. We didn't talk much about our hometowns."

"So what *did* you talk about?"

Ryder tapped a finger on his knee and leaned back in his chair, searched for an answer. In truth, he wanted to treasure his time with Lily in private. "We talked about life. What we like, what we don't like."

"Ordinary stuff?"

Ryder shrugged. "We had fun and listened to what each other had to say. She asked about life-of-an-artist things, and the spotlight."

"Are you gonna see her again? Are you into her?"

"You're creeping me out, man."

"Just being nosey."

Ryder's muscles relaxed as he imagined Lily sitting beside him, taking in the expanse of the Mississippi River. "I'm not sure how she feels, but yeah, I think there's potential for Lily and me."

Chase rested his elbows on his desk and steepled his hands beneath his chin. He let out a long exhale. "I'm thinking outside the box as your manager, but there's a lot of opportunity if we keep you a hot property, play the celebrity angle for all it's worth. I wonder if putting this girl—"

"Lily."

"Right. Maybe putting this Lily into so much of your art will distract from your spotlight."

"Lily has nothing to do with my spotlight. The spotlight happened because of the break we got with the movie poster."

"Sure, but they're starting to take a closer look at your past work and your life. Think about it: It might start to work against you if people see you as attached to Lily instead of maintaining your eligible-bachelor persona. If they see you as taken, the luxury of picking which jobs you want could dry up."

"That wasn't a problem when I was with Carol."

"Carol didn't make cameo appearances—uh, I mean, *alleged* cameos—in your work."

"Chase, a couple of articles appeared speculating about the girl in the art. That doesn't constitute a national obsession."

"I've already gotten calls about it. They started after you and Lily ran into each other at the conference in Cleveland. I didn't tell you before, in case it died down. But today alone I got"—Chase pulled his cell phone from his pocket and scrolled, counting under his breath—"eleven voice messages from reporters and gossipmongers. Rumors appear to be circulating that you've been spotted with the girl in your art, the Mona Lisa or whatever they're calling her."

"I think you're making a bigger deal out of this than it is. Did we experience some growth because of the Hollywood thing? Sure. But that raised awareness of my product and caused potential clients to take a look at the quality I offer. The tennis company didn't ask me to paint an ad for them because of the red carpet on Hollywood Boulevard, Chase. Their ad stands on its own."

Chase kept his eyes on Ryder in an intent stare that seemed to last a full minute. Then he leaned forward, planted his palms flat on Ryder's desk.

"Does she know what she's jumping into by getting involved with you?" Chase asked, his face sincere.

Ryder didn't want to think about the possibility of letting Lily go. Not after his dream had become tangible.

He gave Chase's question a shrug. "Like I said, I don't think it'll be a major issue. Besides, she got a kick out of it when a couple of people recognized us in Hannibal. She finds it fun."

"Yeah, but if these rumors intensify, people will start to dig. They'll try to track her down, find out who she is, search for embarrassing details strewn in her past. Does she know what she's getting into with that?"

A smile flickered at the corner of Ryder's mouth.

"Don't worry about her," Ryder said. Embers of resolve glowed inside him. "I'll shield her from it."

CHAPTER 37

LILY HAD NEVER acclimated herself to the humidity of Missouri summers. It was the middle of June, and she noticed her breathing had grown shallower. With an enormous lake adding to its moisture, the air felt even thicker as it coursed through Lily's lungs.

When she'd reached Osage Beach that Saturday afternoon, Ryder had met her for cappuccinos at a Starbucks on Highway 54, the main artery in town. For the last month, they had met on alternating Saturdays at neutral locations somewhere in the state, such as Kansas City or Columbia. They hadn't met last Saturday, and Lily had missed him so much, she'd wanted to drive to where they last met time, just to feel closer to him.

But today was different. It marked their first Saturday on home turf—Ryder's home turf. As she followed him to his house, she vibrated with nervous anticipation. He had told her not to worry about how she looked. He'd advised her to dress for comfort in case they decided to spend the afternoon on his boat. Although she had tossed a nicer change of clothes in the back seat in case they went out for dinner, she'd worn a T-shirt and jeans for her road trip. To her relief, Ryder had shown up at Starbucks dressed the same way.

Lily parked in front of Ryder's house. She gasped as she took in the home's backdrop, which included a view of the lake and hills in the distance.

"It's gorgeous."

"My home's located in a cove, so despite all the out-of-towners who come here in the summer, it offers a degree of privacy," Ryder explained. His eyes studied his house as if he noticed a new feature. "The previous owners rented it out to vacationers."

Hand in hand, they wandered up the asphalt driveway toward the single-story home, which had an edifice of light gray stone.

"How long have you lived here?"

"Almost five years. Once I felt confident about jobs coming in, I bought it. The owners didn't want to maintain a second property, and the troubled housing market helped make its price more affordable."

"Why did you decide to buy a home *here?* I mean, you could live in some artsy area like San Francisco or New York."

Ryder swept his hand toward the neighboring homes, which sat several acres away on each side. "The seclusion inspires me, and so does the lake in back. The backyard runs right up against the water. I'll show you later."

When they entered the home, Lily realized the stone edifice had made the house appear smaller than it was. The front door opened into a quaint entryway with a simple chandelier that hung overhead and made Lily feel cozy at the sight. As a guest in Ryder's home, she removed her shoes out of habit, and Ryder followed suit.

Barefoot, they padded down a narrow hallway, past a dining room with sleek, modern furniture the color of mahogany. Lily peeked into a kitchen triple the size of her own and imagined how Brooke would squeal at the sight.

But the room at the back of the house took Lily's breath away. Back and forth, over and over, she scanned the room in awe before she could utter a word. The entire far wall contained accents of gray stone similar to the house's exterior. And the room was spacious—no, *enormous* was more like it. She wondered if her entire apartment would fit inside.

"Do all the houses have a den this huge?"

Ryder's grin suggested he had anticipated her question. "When I bought the place, this area was three separate rooms—the den, a small bedroom, and a living room. I knocked out the walls and turned it into my studio."

That explained the fireplace on one side of the room.

Ryder wrapped his arm around her shoulder, which she had grown to enjoy. If any anxiety had lingered after she'd stepped foot on his home turf, his touch swept it away.

"The lake is out that way." Ryder pointed toward the sliding-glass doors at the back of the room. He led her to the doors and she peered outside. Sure enough, grass stretched about thirty feet before it reached the water. At the edge, she noticed a pontoon boat docked. A smattering of trees dotted the cove and complemented its air of privacy, but in the distance, Lily saw motorboats ease across the water, with individuals on inner tubes or water skis following behind.

Lily turned around, then took in the breadth of Ryder's studio from the opposite angle. "So this is where the artist works his magic," she whispered to herself.

Beside the sliding-glass door sat rows of bookshelves, each packed with books arranged in subject order. Some were filled with sketches and photos from other artists and photographers—flowers, car designs through the decades, human anatomy. She could understand an artist owning such materials. Other books, however, were dense with prose. Their subjects covered an impressive range of topics, from Presidents of the United States to historical eras to novels. She flipped through a biography of Martin Luther King, Jr.

"You read a lot?" she asked.

"Research materials," Ryder replied. "The novels help me visualize compelling scenarios. But the nonfiction books are for my higher-brow projects. Sometimes I get a chance to make a social statement rather than to advertise something. Before I sketch out a concept, I'll read up on the topic to learn the history behind it." He nodded at the book in Lily's hand. "Once, I painted a mural that documented the key events during the Civil Rights Movement, so I read up on Martin Luther King and our society at the time."

On a desk at the center of the room, Lily noticed pencils, brushes, colored pencils, and an array of colors beyond her imagination. At the sight of such a spectrum, she realized when she saw blue, Ryder saw a specific shade of blue. She pictured the largest box of crayons she had owned as a child, then multiplied all those colors by ten.

That's how Ryder Flynn must view the world, she figured.

She strolled along one side of the room, in the vicinity of the fireplace, where several framed paintings hung on the wall. Some were original paintings, others prints behind thin glass. Ryder's signature appeared in the lower-right corner of each. She recognized a print of the movie poster that had rocketed Ryder to fame. The other paintings were fragments of advertisements she recalled seeing in magazines and other places. One painting featured an orange-haired clown that had become the focal point of an ad for a national pizza chain.

Halfway down the wall, she found various prints of Ryder and her. Some were new to her. Others she had seen before, like the wine advertisement, which depicted Lily and Ryder dining at a glamorous restaurant in New York.

Ryder took a long look at one of the paintings. "Now that I've gotten to know you, I've realized how unfair this was. I should probably compensate you for using your image in these."

At this point, Lily no longer cared. "It's a compliment. I'm honored." When she noticed he bit his lower lip in uncertainty, she decided to ease the tension by teasing him. "You didn't frame the picture of us in the moonlight—the one that yanked me to your show in Cleveland."

"I didn't want to get slapped again."

When she reached the corner of the room, she found a collection of original paintings that didn't appear to fit in with his other work. They didn't look like magazine or movie art. Instead, they seemed a bit muted, focused on nature rather than people. Each one possessed what Lily considered an Oriental tinge.

Unable to determine the location of these paintings, Lily wrinkled her nose and turned toward Ryder, who crossed his arms casually and strode up alongside her.

Before she could resist, she found herself drawn to the paintings and leaned closer to examine their aspects and hues. She could tell a part of Ryder resided in these works.

Lily felt the edge of her heart soften.

"These are beautiful," she said. "You paid attention to every little detail. How did you come up with the idea to paint them?"

"I saw them firsthand when I was a teenager."

Lily guessed some of them depicted a Japanese garden. "Are these in a park somewhere?"

Ryder shot her a knowing grin. "Just your average, everyday sights."

Lily chuckled. "Average where?"

"Thailand."

CHAPTER 38

LILY FELT HER jaw slacken but kept it from dropping. "You went to Thailand?" She returned her eyes to a painting of a purple flower with ruffled petals and yellow highlights and found herself absorbed again. "How'd that come about? I mean, most people don't wake up one day and decide to go to Asia."

"A friend of mine grew up in America but has relatives who live in Thailand. Lots of aunts and uncles over there, so he and his parents made the trip every couple of years. One summer, when we were fourteen, he invited me to tag along. I couldn't miss an opportunity like that, so my parents allowed me to go. We stayed a whole month."

"These paintings aren't like your others, though," Lily said. "Everything I'd seen until today were real-looking images with people in them. But these are—I don't know to describe it. Softer."

Ryder nodded. "Thailand is my favorite place on earth. Even though I hadn't begun my professional career when I visited, it captured my heart and triggered those instincts that define you as an artist. By painting images of it from time to time, I suppose it keeps the memory alive in my heart."

"The way you kept me alive in your heart?"

"I suppose you're right," Ryder chuckled to himself. "But you're more intriguing than Asia."

"What made you respond to Thailand that way? Why wouldn't you respond that way to, say, Chicago?"

"I discovered a tenderness about the culture. The Thai people tend to be family-oriented. My own family wasn't close, and my parents fought on a regular basis. Thailand represented a place of peace for me. The people there possess contentment about their places in life. So in my teens, when my parents' arguments got heavy, I'd retreat into my art—a return to that place of contentment—to find tranquility and beauty."

Ryder paused a moment, and Lily could see the yearning in his eyes as he stared at the flower. For a moment, he looked as though, in his mind, he had escaped the studio. Amid the intermittent silence, Lily could hear herself breathe until Ryder spoke again.

"That's a Thai orchid." Ryder tapped his finger against the side of the frame. "Here in America, orchids are difficult to find, but they're abundant in Thailand. They're so common there, people use them as a garnish on their plates." He waved his finger over the purple petals. "The nation is filled with color. It's located along the Gulf of Thailand and stretches down near the equator, which gives it a tropical feel—continual humidity, the way perpetual summer might feel. You won't see much black or white, but lots of bright colors, fruits and flowers. And the scent of cooking soaks the air: oils and spices. You can smell the flavor as it all cooks. They purchase their food fresh over there, so when they prepare it, you can *smell* the fresh seafood and vegetables. I fell in love with Thai cuisine."

He uttered his words at low volume. Lily noticed he often spoke with her in that manner, as if he had selected his words exclusively for her and wanted to make sure she knew it. Lily felt the heat of Ryder's breath as it settled across her cheek and stimulated the bristles along her neckline.

She moved to a painting of a waterfall that overlooked a calm, narrow river. Tall rock formations surrounded a section of the river and shaded it, while in the background, sunlight seemed to pour forth like a cup of water upon leafy trees. The trees added a slight jungle feel to the scene. In a small boat sat six people, two of whom guided the boat by paddle, weaving their way through the water.

Humor sparked within Ryder's eyes. "Much of this seems uncommon to us. Common versus uncommon works both ways, though. I went to a zoo during my visit. When you go to a zoo here, what kind of animals do you expect to find?"

An obvious question. Lily had visited the St. Louis Zoo on countless occasions, and it had always struck her how the animals represented every corner of the world she could fathom. "Zebras? Monkeys?" she replied. For a moment, her mind wandered to the creatures with the nasty pink butts in the ape house, but she wouldn't admit it to Ryder. Instead, she swallowed her laugh.

"That's what I expected to find, too. I was shocked by some of the animals in the zoo at Thailand: guinea pigs—"

"What!"

"No joke. Along with billy goats, white-tailed deer. Here in America, deer are so common, they get hit by cars. So when I saw them at the zoo, I thought, 'Are you kidding? I see those on the side of the road all the time!' But in Thailand, those animals are unusual. The people are drawn to them. They aren't fascinated by elephants, because some people *own* elephants and walk them down the street to buy groceries. And monkeys—I visited this place where a huge population of them lives in its natural habitat. But deer amaze the people there. Can you imagine? It fascinates me how we human beings can share so much in common, yet our perspectives can be as far apart as the distance between our countries."

The next painting featured a family's house, simple and slim, constructed of natural wood and seated atop a series of stilts grounded in concrete. A wooded stairway led to the home's entrance.

"Did you feel safe there?" Lily asked.

"In the far-northern part of the country, I felt more wary. That region shares its border with Burma, so according to my friend's family, a security issue exists where people sneak across the border into Thailand, commit crimes, then escape back into Burma, never to be seen again. So you'll find a passport checkpoint every half-mile or so if you head up that way. But the farther south you travel, the safer you feel."

"Were they suspicious of an American making a visit?"

"Not at all. They're used to people coming from other countries, though people tend to travel from Australia or Europe. They have a name for Westerners in general: you're a *farang*. But if they find out you're an American, they treat you with utmost respect. Many Thai citizens know America only by what they see in movies. So if you're an American, they look at you like a movie star or someone who can make anything happen in your life. Even though they admire you, many believe improving your lot in life is reserved for Americans but not for them, and as a result, many of them live in poverty.

"The movie-star image is such a stretch, it makes that standard of living appear out of reach when, in truth, upward momentum might be more achievable than they realize. You'll see a dichotomy over there: Parents will point out the wonderful opportunities in America, yet they don't seem to encourage the kids to seek those opportunities at home. It's simultaneous contentment and admiration, each taken to the extreme."

Passion danced along the edge of his voice. After two months of dating him, Lily couldn't get past how down-to-earth he seemed. Honesty and simplicity ebbed from him, which coaxed her into wanting to know him more. And the more acquainted she became with aspects of Ryder's life, the stronger her attraction toward him grew. His words were honey. Swallowing them was delightful.

"Did it make you feel awkward knowing people saw you that way, as someone who has the highest lot in life?" she asked.

Ryder rubbed his chin for a moment. "To tell you the truth, it broke my heart. You look at those precious people with close family relationships, so much potential, and yet many won't allow themselves a chance to improve their lives because of a misinterpretation of what they see. It makes you not want to judge people." He smiled. "They savor life, though. And they love to give nicknames—everyone has one. In fact, it's not unusual to *not* know someone's birth name, especially their last name. Sometimes the nickname carries meaning; on other occasions, the people simply like the sound of it. Oftentimes, siblings in a family will have nicknames that begin with the same letter. In the eyes of the Thai people, a nickname is a gift, something you have the privilege of giving to someone else. And when they give you a nickname, I have to admit, it makes you feel like they've included you, accepted you."

"Does that mean they give you a nickname, too?"

Ryder beamed. "My friend's aunt called me *Law.* So whenever I spent time with my friend's family there, or anytime they introduced me to someone, they called me *Law.*"

"Why did she pick that name for you?"

Ryder blushed. "She considered me handsome, which is what the name means. A handsome young man—or a handsome *farang*," he added with a wink.

Lily studied him from the corner of her eye. She could spend hours in his presence and still desire more. For a moment, their eyes locked and, with one tender motion, Ryder drew her body to his.

CHAPTER 39

WHEN SHE PIVOTED, Lily realized she had overlooked the other half of the room. Breaking contact with Ryder, she sauntered toward an easel, which sat in the glow of a dim overhead light. Upon the easel sat a thin, tan canvas. A fabric drop cloth surrounded the easel and covered much of the room's floor. When she looked to her bare feet, she discovered the drop cloth splotched with paint—and she had stood right on top of several blue drops. Lily jumped back in reflex. *How embarrassing!* She checked the soles of her feet and found them untainted, then squatted to inspect the paint and, to her relief, found it crusty. She followed the splotches and noticed they ended several feet from the edges of the cloth, so the carpet wasn't in danger of damage.

Ryder laughed and padded to her side. "The paint's dry. I splattered it last night as I worked."

Dubious, Lily thought it looked more like the artist had rigged a loaded paint brush to a fan and set the contraption to run at high speed. Upon closer inspection, she discovered the tan canvas was nothing more than a piece of cheap cardboard. In fact, its rough edges indicated Ryder had cut it from a shipping box. The painting looked like a mess. Pale drops of paint had dried in a range of sizes, from small spots to larger clumps the size of a dime. Some drops slid to the bottom of the cardboard surface, leaving behind trails.

"Did you give this painting a title?" she asked.

"Freedom."

As she examined the painting again, Lily clucked her tongue and tried to find and identify a pattern in the work, but wound up clueless.

"No offense," she remarked, "and not to sound ignorant, but it looks like a piece of cardboard with paint splattered on it."

"You deserve more credit for your assessment. You've pretty much sized it up."

"I didn't realize I'd turned into an art scholar," Lily said. Hearing her own voice, she found her sarcasm draped with tender fun.

Ryder's smirk confirmed that Lily's comment hadn't offended him. "When I find myself in a creative block, tossing paint on a canvas helps me channel my emotions," he explained. When Lily shot him another unsure look, he clarified, "It allows me the freedom to create whatever image appears. Every artist has his quirks, I suppose."

Before she could stop herself, laughter burst forth and she covered her mouth to stifle it. "You painted with your fingers? Are you kidding?"

Ryder held out his palms and shot her a grin to match. "Hey, don't knock it unless you've tried it." He padded over to a collection of large, plastic bottles that sat at the far corner of the drop cloth and retrieved a fat squirt bottle. With a few shakes of the blue bottle, he tilted its spout toward Lily's hand. "Go on, try it."

Was he serious? At first, Lily held her palm toward the bottle, then retreated. It struck her as unnatural. She hesitated to touch the paint with her bare skin. Besides, come Monday, she didn't want to arrive at work with blue hands.

But Ryder took her reluctance in stride and appeared to find it humorous. "Don't worry, it's inexpensive tempera paint, the kind you used in elementary school. It washes off of your skin and clothes. Plus, since I don't use it for projects I intend to keep, I dilute the paint even further."

Still hesitant, Lily wondered if this was his idea of a practical joke. After all, Ryder was a quiet guy, and as Lily's dad had always told her, still waters run deep.

Ryder shrugged. "Here, look," he said, and squeezed a royal-blue glob into his left palm. Using the fingers of his other hand, he dipped into the paint and, like a baseball pitcher, sent the drops splattering in front of him.

Lily giggled at the patter of paint on cardboard. Quick and crisp, as if God had set a rain shower in motion and then, two seconds later, changed His mind.

"Come on," Ryder said, a taunt in his voice. "You know you want to."

Yeah, she did.

And she had dressed for the lake, with the assumption she would end up dirty anyway.

She held out her hand and Ryder filled it with the cold, goopy substance, still thick enough not to slip between her fingers. With her eyes shut, she tossed the paint—a wimpy effort for fear of flinging it on his floor—and heard a muffled pitter-patter as most of the paint wound up on the drop cloth. When she opened her eyes, she discovered it hadn't reached the easel.

Ryder had noticed, too. "Oh, come on, Lily! You need to put your heart into it!"

Once again, he flicked paint from his finger tips. His face flushed from the exertion.

If he didn't care, why should she? Lily followed his lead and flung the paint again. Then she flung it a second time...followed by a third, fourth and fifth. Between fits of laughter, she and Ryder bombarded the canvas with an onslaught of blue paint bombs. The tempera's dense scent brought forth memories of Lily's childhood art projects.

To her surprise, she *did* feel free, no longer constrained by façade or ironclad self-consciousness.

Ryder jabbed a playful finger in her direction. "And you thought I was crazy!"

"I stand corrected." She eyed the remaining paint bottles which sat at the edge of the drop cloth. "This masterpiece is too masculine for me, though. It could use a dose of pink."

"No way!" Ryder joked. "I refuse to let you add fluff to my work—"

But Lily had already darted away and filled her hand with another color of paint. When she returned, Ryder grabbed her in jest, which caused her elbows to make contact with the trace of cold paint in his hands. Lily let out a playful gasp. She felt carefree with his arms wrapped around her. As close as his face was to hers, she watched tears of hilarity glaze over his eyes.

"I thought you were all about the freedom thing," she tried to sputter between bursts of laughter, failing to make it all the way through. As Ryder tightened his squeeze on her, his fingers tickled her belly.

Then her belly felt wet.

Ryder must have felt it too, because suddenly, he released her from his grip. His mouth fell agape and he riveted his eyes to her shirt. Lily followed his line of sight to her stomach, where her T-shirt now featured her own handprint in pink.

Ryder tried to repress a snicker. At first, his mouth moved without a sound until he located his voice.

"I'm—hey, I'm sorry," he said, his hands held high in surrender. "I got paint all over your shirt."

"It's an old shirt. Besides, you said it'll wash out."

"I know, but I still feel bad," Ryder said as another chortle escaped from his mouth.

"Accidents happen. Don't worry, I won't hold a grudge," Lily said in a faux trusting manner. Then she clapped her paint-covered hands against his cheeks, smearing in the substance for good measure. "Starting now."

Ryder pursed his lips. "That's it! You're going down, Lily Machara!"

Despite her taking two steps backward as a head start, Ryder managed to grab her in another playful embrace. Lily shrieked with laughter again and turned to face him. Her chin made contact with a handful of tempera from Ryder. Royal blue.

By now, they had speckled the drop cloth with a hearty amount of fresh paint. As Lily tried to wriggle her way out of Ryder's arms, she took another step. By the time her mind registered the slippery spot beneath the sole of her foot, she had already fallen backward and pulled Ryder down with her. He managed to wedge his arm behind her back before she hit the ground, so she landed in his embrace, her head an inch above the floor.

Both Lily and Ryder were smeared with paint. Lily's arms and legs felt smudged and slick, as did his skin against hers. She savored the moment, listened as their breathing patterns returned to normal.

Then her eyes met his. He held her gaze.

For a split second, Lily thought she saw the pupils flutter in Ryder's eyes. Those chocolate-brown eyes. They seemed to beckon her.

Leaning in, Lily closed her eyes and kissed his lower lip.

When she realized she had let down her guard, she felt embarrassed. She wasn't good at the nuances of love. Now she had made herself look ridiculous, kissing him while they were covered in paint. *How romantic, Lily!* As her mind reverted to the Lily in Ryder's artwork, she feared she had burst the image she'd hoped he still found in her.

Lily looked into Ryder's eyes. "I didn't mean—"

But before she could finish, Ryder touched her chin, met her lips with his, then kissed her long and full.

He drew her body closer to his, and Lily's pulse quickened at the sensation of his touch. Her pores prickled along her arms.

She knew her neck and hair were matted with paint, but Lily didn't care.

She was with him.

Staring into Lily's eyes, Ryder ran his fingers through her hair. Their lips met once again. Lily slipped her hands behind his shoulders as he ran his fingers past her waist, cupped her buttocks, and continued his discovery past the bottom edges of her shorts. Her pulse buzzed at the warmth of his palms as they glided along the tender flesh of her thighs. And for the first time, Lily understood how it must feel to step into one of his paintings.

She combed her fingers through his hair to remind herself that this moment was real. And he responded with that tender smile she adored.

Ryder leaned in again, kissed her neck, her earlobe, the cleft behind her ear.

Breathless, she closed her eyes.

"Don't go home," Ryder whispered in her ear.

When she opened her eyes, Ryder's gaze drew her into his world. Lily didn't want to blink. He whispered again.

"After dinner, don't go home. Spend the night with me here."

Lily's heart pounded with such force, she figured he could hear it. She searched his brown eyes for the slightest hint of insincerity but detected none. He brought his hands to her waist and massaged her hips with two strong thumbs.

Without a word, Lily considered his invitation.

He looked so enraptured in the moment. She could tell he wanted this. And Lily yearned for him, too.

She hated herself for fearing his rejection.

His eyes absorbed hers.

And before she could change her mind, Lily answered him with a nod.

CHAPTER 40

"YOU'RE DRIVING YOURSELF crazy," Brooke said at last. "Why don't you sit down?"

No, Lily couldn't bear to do that. Her stomach had become a wadded paper ball. Back and forth, she paced from one end of the living room to the other while Aaron and Brooke watched with amusement from the sofa.

Aaron crossed his arms. "What's the big deal, Lily? It was bound to happen sooner or later."

"This is different," Lily said.

"Oh, horrors, you're right!" Brooke chimed in. "Heaven forbid your *boyfriend* come to town!"

"You don't understand." Lily's cell phone, perched on the coffee table, interrupted them with its bouncy Taylor Swift ringtone. Lily grabbed the phone. Checking the caller ID, she found a number-withheld message on the display. "And these constant phone calls don't make it any easier." She considered ignoring the call but answered with a huff. "Hello?"

"Lily Machara?"

"Yeah. Who is this?"

"Hi Lily. My name is Sandra Bremer, and I'm a reporter with—"

"How did you get my number?"

Either Sandra Bremer didn't hear Lily's question or pretended not to notice it. She continued, "When I heard from a source that you work in marketing, I—"

Marketing?

Lily could recall herself claiming to work in marketing only once: over cappuccinos with Ryder in Cleveland. Had someone overheard them talking in the restaurant?

Lily cut off Sandra Bremer midsentence. "Sorry, but I'm not interested in talking to you." And with the push of a button, she terminated the call. Lily grunted in frustration.

Aaron furled his eyebrows. "What was that all about?"

"Another reporter. They started calling me a couple of weeks ago, a ton of them, from all over the country. A few days after the calls began, I could no longer stand them and put my phone on vibrate. I turned on the sound today in case Ryder calls."

"Why are reporters calling you?"

"They want an interview with the 'Mona Lisa,'" Lily replied, enclosing her honorary title in finger quotes. "It started out exciting, but now it grates on my nerves. Why do they care about me all of a sudden? They didn't give a damn three months ago."

"You weren't dating Ryder Flynn three months ago."

Lily returned the phone to vibrate mode and slipped it into her back pocket.

When Lily began her umpteenth trek across the room, Brooke reached out and grabbed her arm, which brought her to a halt. "Lily, you need to calm down or you'll freak him out." She gave Lily's arm a squeeze. "You love spending time with Ryder! I know it's his first time visiting you in St. Louis, but why are you so stressed about it?"

At last, the energy drained from Lily's body. Her shoulders sagged.

Planting her face in her hands, Lily succumbed to the inevitable.

"I haven't told him I work in the auto shop," she said, peeking through the crevices between her fingers before dropping her hands to her sides in surrender.

Wide-eyed, Brooke and Aaron answered in unison.

"You *what?!*"

"I know, I know! Don't ask me why I do the stupid things I do, because I don't have a clue. I just couldn't bear to tell him."

"Lily, you've dated him for two months! How did you keep him convinced this long? Hasn't the subject come up?"

"We talk about more important things. Life things. And I ask him a lot about his art. He's so passionate about it, he could talk for hours. Anytime he mentions my career, I turn the attention back to his. Besides, I love hearing what he has to say. It inspires me."

"But doesn't he find it strange that you avoid mentioning your job?" Brooke asked.

"I tell him I don't want to talk about it. I open up about everything else, and we dig deep together. He loves being with me and I love being with him. How's that different from you and Jeremy? How much time do you spend talking about work?"

"Well..."

"From what I can tell, it's the last thing he wants to hear about. He wants to be near you. That's all, right? Anyway, your job doesn't define who you are—or it shouldn't, at least. That's what Ryder's paintings are all about when he puts me in them: He sees potential, the person I *could* be."

"Didn't he wonder why you haven't invited him to St. Louis until now?"

"It's been two months, not two years. Sure, he wondered why, but I truly like Osage Beach. We wanted to spend a lot of time on the lake while summer is here."

Aaron scratched his head and grimaced. "Lily, you can't keep this a secret forever. What if you run into someone you know while you're out?"

"Look, he's only here for today. This is a large city. How often do you run into people you know in random places? Besides, we'll be on another side of town."

"I still say you won't be able to keep this up." Aaron shook his head. "The time will come when he'll want to come visit you again. If he's truly interested in you, which appears to be the case, he'll want to know more about you. He'll want to know more about how you spend your time—not because your career defines you, but because it represents a big chunk of your life."

Lily's brain felt ready to steam. They didn't know Ryder the way she did. Why couldn't they give her the benefit of the doubt and let her make her own decisions? She couldn't ask for better friends, but this was *her* life, not theirs.

"Don't you think this rips me up inside?" Lily said at last. "Don't you think I feel guilty? I keep promising myself I'll tell him. I bring myself to try, but then I can't go through with it. And I hate that feeling of weakness."

"But this isn't fair to him, Lily." Aaron put a hand on her arm. "He deserves to know the real you. You're an amazing person. Why won't you let him inside?"

Lily held back a film of tears that tried to gloss over her eyes. She took a slow breath, calmed herself, allowed her nerves to settle. Then she met Aaron eye to eye as a pang drifted to the bottom of her heart.

"Because I'll lose him," she replied.

Aaron and Brooke said nothing in response. Brooke stared at her, while Aaron appeared uncomfortable, inching his big toe back and forth on the carpet.

Lily heard a pleading in her own voice. A quality so unfamiliar to her, it made her uneasy. "When I'm at the auto shop or in my everyday life, there's nothing exciting about me. Most people see me as plain or unattractive, but he sees me differently. He views me as *her,* the girl he paints. That girl is beautiful. She's wanted. That girl is valued, and people don't overlook her. She desires someone, and that someone desires her back."

Tears stung her eyes by now, but she continued to force them into retreat. She'd intended no harm. This wasn't selfishness. It was one little white lie about something inconsequential. It was—oh, she hated to admit it, but Lily suspected it might be insecurity.

Lily sighed. "I know it sounds ridiculous to you, but the woman in Ryder's art—that's the woman I want to be. I've never been that woman before. For years, I've watched others be that person. Do you know how that made me feel?

"No, Ryder doesn't know what I *do* for a living." She put her palm on her chest. Her heart palpitated. "But he knows who I am *in here.* That's what's important. I don't know where it will lead, but I think we have potential together, and I don't want to lose him over some stupid thing like tire rotations."

"Lily…" Brooke began.

"I'll do it," Lily interrupted. "I'll tell him everything. But I'll do it my own way."

"When?"

"I don't know," Lily replied. When that remark earned her expressions of misgiving, she added, "Soon, I promise. But this is my life. So for now, please respect me enough to let me make my own decision, okay?"

Brooke sighed. "Fine, but I think you're making a mistake. If Ryder is the great guy you've made him out to be, wouldn't he want to know the real you?"

"He *does* know the real me—deep down. It's wrapped in better paper, that's all. Which matters more: the birthday gift or the paper it's wrapped in?"

A quick, hollow knock at the door gave Lily a start. She headed for the door. As she unlocked the deadbolt, she shot her friends a stern look and whispered, "Not a word. You promised."

Aaron gave a palms-out gesture of surrender and rolled his eyes at Brooke, who had her hands on her hips. No worries. Lily knew Brooke would return to her bubbly self by the time their visitor walked through the door.

At the sight of Ryder Flynn, the argument melted into the recesses of Lily's memory.

CHAPTER 41

THEIR LIPS MET in a soft, silent kiss that sent a quiver up Lily's arms.

"I missed you," Ryder whispered.

"Missed you too. Come in."

Lily turned to find both Brooke and Aaron wearing shit-eating grins. Lily introduced them to Ryder, whose face lit with recognition at the mention of their names.

Ryder shoved his hands into his pockets and drew his shoulders together. For a guy in the public eye, he appeared timid in this intimate setting. A teenager meeting his date's parents before a high-school homecoming dance. Lily found it adorable.

"Of course. Nice to meet you," Ryder said. "Lily's talked about both of you." He slipped his arm around Lily's waist, and she reciprocated the gesture.

Aaron bit his bottom lip in an obvious struggle to make conversation while trying to avoid what might expose Lily's little white fib. "You do great work, Ryder. We've kept an eye on your paintings ever since we, uh—"

Brooke gave Aaron a patronizing pat on the head. "Aaron here solved the mystery of who was sharing Lily's face with the public. So you can blame him for you and Lily getting together," she said. Sure enough, now that the earlier argument had ceased, Brooke's eyes had resumed their normal sparkle. "And we've heard all about you from Lily. The good things, anyway. You don't have any secrets tucked away in your paint canister, do you, Ryder Flynn?"

Ryder chuckled and gave Lily's waist a squeeze. She felt her cheeks blush. She wasn't used to receiving displays of affection like that, not even in front of her friends. Whatever nervous tension might have resided in Ryder's abdomen when he'd arrived subsided as his muscles rested against her.

"Lily mentioned she and you have been friends since you were kids," Ryder said to Brooke.

"Yeah, we rode the bus together, and the rest is history."

Ryder turned toward Aaron. "And she tells me that she and you work together?"

"Okay..." Aaron replied with a smirk, warming to the challenge.

"In marketing?" Ryder said.

Aaron looked as if Ryder had caught him red-handed, a kid who had sneaked a handful of Oreos and still had a mouthful of evidence. He darted his eyes toward Lily, then returned his attention to Ryder's innocent stare.

Though Lily couldn't look Aaron in the eye, she noticed he had started to run his fingers over his mouth to prevent himself from snickering.

"Same as Lily," Aaron replied. "Whatever she says goes double for me."

Terrific, thought Lily as she sucked air. *He's decided to make a game of this.*

She tapped her foot, a nervous inclination to which she was prone. Upon noticing it, she stiffened her leg and forced her foot to rest.

"Lily didn't mention what *you* do for a living," Ryder said to Brooke.

Brooke, whose two friends had pilfered *her* career, appeared too stunned to improvise. "What do *I* do?" She flung a limp wrist into the air as if an answer might float past. “Oh, I…I’m a…a garbage collector.”

Brooke! Shit.

Aaron covered his face as he shook his head.

Meanwhile, Ryder looked puzzled. “You’re what?”

All Lily could do was fake a laugh, grab Ryder by the shoulder, and nudge him toward the door. “She’s great, isn’t she? Loves to bring people joy with her *jokes* and whatnot.”

Brooke shrugged and wiggled good-bye with her fingers.

Lily followed Ryder outside and, with one final glare at her friends, yanked the door shut.

CHAPTER 42

"I NEVER PICTURED this many cars showing up," Ryder said.

"They always get a nice crowd," Lily replied.

For five years, an annual classic car show had occurred here. Waxed and polished, vehicles from decades past sat at parallel angles on the lawn of an old, brick church. Several vehicles had their hoods open. While some cars were a simple black or white, the majority set the lawn awash with colors of summer and yesteryear. Lily felt like Marty McFly in *Back to the Future.*

Nothing beat the rush she felt when she arrived at these shows. From a distance, vehicles shimmered in the sunlight, swatches of red, turquoise and orange. A rainbow minus the rain shower.

To her credit, prior to Ryder's visit, Lily had decided to take baby steps toward telling Ryder the truth. A car show would set the conversation rolling. It marked progress.

She saw it that way, at least.

She wouldn't have expected Brooke or Aaron to understand anyway. Brooke's personality was a magnetic force field to begin with. Her gorgeous face and figure added to her charm. She never starved for attention from the opposite sex. And Aaron—his circumstances couldn't begin to compare to hers.

The more she pondered her predicament, the more she realized it wasn't Ryder's rejection she feared. Rather, she didn't want *anyone* to cut her heart open again.

Besides, she couldn't imagine returning to a life without Ryder. When he stared into her eyes, she knew she could spend hours soaking in his and never grow weary.

It took less than three minutes for Lily to conclude Ryder knew nothing about automobiles.

But he appeared secure enough to learn from her.

"What kind of car is this?" Ryder asked as he pointed to a yellow beauty.

"A 1969 Corvette." When Ryder reached his hand toward the gleaming, waxed surface, Lily blurted, "You enjoy breathing, don't you?"

"Excuse me?"

"The owner will kill you if you touch his car."

"Oops." He took her remark in good humor as he bent at the waist and studied the black interior through a side window.

"That was also the year they offered a ZL1 model of that car," Lily added, "which was said to be the fastest car available at the time—460 horsepower."

Ryder gave a matter-of-fact nod but said nothing. Lily had hoped to find him enthralled at the sea of history around him. Many guys she knew stopped short of salivating at the dream of owning one of these gems. Yet Ryder struck her as nonchalant. She hoped he found this fun but couldn't gauge him.

By Lily's estimation, hundreds of people had attended today's event. They resembled an uncoordinated army of ants as they ambled from vehicle to vehicle.

Lily and Ryder floated down another row and stopped at a long car, which Brooke would have dubbed a boat. Cherry red, the white-top convertible glistened. Its body sat low to the ground and covered the upper edges of its tires. Lily downplayed her awe as she stared at its headlights, each one a perfect circle, like a pair of full, unlit moons. The front bumper featured a wing at its left and right corners.

Even while stationary, the car's sharp angles and front design lent it an illusion of forward motion.

"This one's a 1956 Caddy." Pointing to the rectangular parking lights near the bottom edge of the front bumper, Lily added, "You can tell it's a '56 model because they embedded the parking lights in the bumper. In the earlier model, its lights were round and located in the grill."

Ryder crossed his arms. That familiar smile enlivened his eyes. "How do you know so much about cars?"

"My dad took me to shows like these when I was a kid." That much was true. So far, so good. "Sometimes you'll catch the owners hanging around their babies, and they'll rattle off the whole history behind the car and tell you all the work they put into restoring it."

"And you absorbed those details over time."

"Right." She shielded her eyes from the afternoon sun so she could concentrate on his eyes, which looked a shade lighter in the sunshine.

Side by side, they moved along. Ryder took her hand in his.

"If you think I sound like I know a lot about it," Lily continued, "you should hear some of these owners talk."

"Fanatics, huh?"

"In a good way. They're walking encyclopedias."

They wandered past a 1933 Roadster, a 1968 Camaro, and a 1955 Bel Air. Finally, Lily had to ask. "You're not much of a car person, are you?"

"I'll admit, you won't find me holed up in a garage, just my car and me." He shrugged. "I guess I've never understood how people can be so fascinated by cars like these people who restore them. I mean, these are fun to see, but I'd bet there are people out there who devote their *lives* to car stuff. They love it that much. Isn't that strange?"

Lily tried to hide the sinking feeling in her stomach. "Maybe they see it as an art form, like your paintings."

Ryder studied the sky as he considered her response. "I suppose. And I'm sure these cars are worth some cash after you've poured money into them." Squinting at the car before him, he rubbed the stubble on his chin. "Then again, if you put a bunch of miles on a car, doesn't it lose value? True art would gain value over time, no matter how many miles it travels around the world."

Oh, no. Had her car-show idea—along with her whole strategy of transitioning their conversation to her career—turned into a blunder? What was she supposed to do now? He had no idea he'd insulted her, and he had misinterpreted her art-form comparison.

Ryder must have sensed he'd said something wrong. He slid his hands into his pockets. "I didn't mean to put any of these people down. But a car will never speak to a person's heart or inspire them in ways that are timeless."

Lily averted her gaze and pretended to study a couple that passed in the distance.

In obvious discomfort, Ryder took Lily's hand again and kneaded her knuckles with his thumb. "Wait, you didn't think I was talking about *you,* did you? Lily, I love that you're interested in these cars," he said. "But you're not like the fanatics out there. You like to look at cars, but you don't devote your *life* to them. It's not like it's your chosen career."

If you only knew.

Lily wanted to groan. She hadn't lost respect for him. Even as an opinionated artist, he had sought to make sure he hadn't wounded her feelings.

He still viewed her as the woman in his paintings—an image she had helped perpetuate.

And even now, she preferred that image. She still enjoyed seeing herself that way.

What was another day or two?

CHAPTER 43

"NOBODY CAN LEAVE St. Louis without visiting Ted Drewes." Lily gestured toward the building's fluorescent lights as they stood waiting for their desserts at one of the restaurant's order windows. "It's a family-owned place and it's been here forever. Best frozen custard you've ever had, I promise."

More than any of the restaurant's qualities, Lily defined it by its rich, full fragrance. She didn't know which ingredient caused the distinctive scent, but it smelled like a mixture of caramel and cream. Traces of the aroma always teased her from a block away and lured her closer. Even tonight, she noticed she had quickened her pace once they turned a corner and headed toward the building.

A seasonal establishment located on Chippewa Street, Ted Drewes looked like a white house with a row of windows that spanned the front of the building. Lily marveled at the fact that with every trip to Ted Drewes, despite an absence of seating for customers, she joined a crowd of at least thirty patrons who waited in line to place their orders.

Yielding to Lily's recommendation, Ryder had ordered a concrete, Ted Drewes's specialty.

"What's the verdict?" Lily asked. "Did I lie to you?"

Ryder closed his eyes as he placed another spoonful of butterscotch custard into his mouth and allowed it to melt on his tongue. "Why did you do this to me!" He gave her elbow a playful jab. "How will I survive knowing this place is three whole hours away?"

Lily grinned. "I came here a lot in high school. My grandpa came here when *he* was a teenager, too. Some things never change."

"Except maybe the employees wore those white paper hats back in his day."

Lily giggled as they ventured away from the yellow neon lighting and along a side street. "Yeah, the olden days. Back then, the waitresses probably wore saddle shoes and had names like Mitzy and Bitzy, right?"

"And don't forget Flo."

Lily slapped her forehead. "That's right! How could I forget? Every place from yesteryear has its Flo! Betcha they keep her on ice in a storage closet."

"And they'll roll out her bones for their hundredth anniversary. Celebration of the century!"

Ryder almost dropped his concrete as he played along. Lily considered his near-mishap endearing. Between that and his lack of interest in cars, it was nice to know the guy had his shortcomings. Why should she settle for perfection, anyway?

They carried their green-and-yellow custard cups a couple of blocks to Francis Park, a city park in the midst of The Hill, a section of town known by locals for its mom-and-pop Italian restaurants. But by Lily's own admission, when she came to The Hill, she craved custard more than lasagna.

They chose a tree and sat beneath it, on the grass, where they could watch passersby in the fading glow of daylight. The sky possessed the appearance of a matte texture, the underside of a lithograph. Even at twilight, the temperature and humidity of the Midwest caused their desserts to melt and drip over the sides of the cups when they tilted them.

"You mentioned your dad introduced you to car shows." Ryder scooted a tad closer to her. "Do you have a close relationship with him?"

Lily inhaled deep. The scent of foliage in the moist July air possessed a soothing quality.

"He passed away a few years ago."

"I'm sorry to hear that."

"It's okay. I've had time to adjust. But yes, we had a great relationship while he was alive. Growing up, I felt closer to him than most of my friends were to their dads," she said. "Without any brothers or sisters, I was Daddy's little girl." Then, as she reflected on what she had said, Lily added, "More like his buddy. I followed him everywhere as a kid, and he started including me in tasks he'd do around the house."

"Like fixing the sink? Making repairs?"

"Car tasks. During spring and summer, we'd wash the car together. Or when he changed the oil, I'd hand him the supplies he needed." Lily took a quick peek from her peripheral vision, hoping he hadn't smirked at her words like the jerks in her past, but Ryder kept a straight face. "We bonded during those times together. I learned a lot from Dad." Lily scooted closer to Ryder, then took another bite of her custard. "Dad and Mom got divorced when I was ten, and I moved in with him."

"You chose to live with your dad?"

Lily nodded. "I loved my mom, but Dad and I were so much closer. Our personalities were more alike. My mom got remarried, and two years later, my stepdad's employer transferred him out of state. From then on, for most of my life, it was Dad and me."

"Did you and your mom get along well?"

"Sure. We didn't have issues between us, but we didn't see each other often after the divorce, due to time and space."

"Did you miss having her around?"

"Some seasons were harder than others. Coming-of-age years are critical, and that's when Mom moved away. I visited her during summer vacation and breaks, but that's different from having a maternal figure around on a daily basis." She glanced at Ryder's inviting eyes and decided to take another step toward trusting him. "By the time I was old enough to drive, I'd gotten used to who I was. And my interests didn't always match up with the other girls in school."

"Like Brooke's?"

"Yeah." Okay, maybe she could ease toward the truth about her job, prepare him bit by bit, day by day. She could make it work.

"When did marketing enter the picture?"

Ugh. She'd sure picked a winning career alibi with that one. As often as he tried to steer their conversations toward it, it must have enthralled him.

"Did you come up with ideas for TV commercials as a kid?" he asked. "Were there early signs that make you look back and say, 'Yeah, I always wanted to handle those products but didn't realize it'?"

Lily stared into the distance and rested her back against the tree trunk.

"I wanted to be my doll when I was a kid." She sniffed at the thought of that comment. Talk about a contrast with reality. Now that she'd admitted it, embarrassment settled in. "Lots of girls do. But when you think about it, it's understandable. A doll has a perfect life, doesn't she? Gorgeous eyes, slim figure, a house on the beach, a job she loves. Always someplace to go, people to clink martinis with. Even her dog has a perfect name like Everett and a collar made of diamonds."

"Only in the movies, huh?"

Lily grinned. "And your paintings."

Ryder leaned forward, took her hand, enveloped it in his.

"That's why I loved spending time with my dad," Lily added. "As a kid, whenever I was around him, I felt like that doll, like nothing could hurt me or tarnish my life." Self-conscious, she covered her eyes for a moment. "Sounds stupid, doesn't it?"

He offered her a single head shake in slow motion. "Nothing's wrong with that. A dream can look foolish to somebody else, but when it's your dream, it forms a piece of who you are."

"It didn't last long anyway," Lily said. "By the time I entered middle school, I knew I'd never be that dream doll, never have her life. I was too different from other girls. Even when I tried to fit in, it was like they could sense a missing quality, a detail that flew under the radar but shouted, 'She's not one of you!' So as time marched on, I withdrew into myself and trusted only a handful of people. My sense of humor took on a sharper edge—Brooke once called it a defense mechanism, but whatever."

Her stomach now felt hollow. She held back the tear that had pooled in her eye. At this point, she had no desire to finish her frozen custard, so she set the remainder on the grass and drew her arms around her knees.

"I guess I never really felt beautiful," she murmured. "That's why I love your paintings. You see something in me that I'd forgotten was there. Or maybe never thought it was there to begin with."

Ryder drew near, wrapped his arm around her shoulder, and she leaned into him. Both Lily and Ryder's fingers were sticky from the custard that had melted, dripped and dried. A cool breeze emerged, which caused Lily's perspiration to evaporate as evening deepened.

"I think you're beautiful," whispered Ryder.

CHAPTER 44

RYDER STUDIED HER for a moment. Then he tilted his head, squinting his eyes as if a revelation had struck him.

"Have you ever been in love?" he asked, his voice low and gentle.

His question caught her off guard. A lump formed in her throat. When had she last spoken about something so intimate or made herself so vulnerable? Years, no doubt, but how many?

"Once," Lily admitted. She focused on silhouettes of individuals who strolled along sidewalks. Judging them too far away to overhear her conversation with Ryder, she tried to relax, but her muscles had tensed in her arms, her legs, her abdomen, and throughout her body. "I was in love once. One guy."

Ryder shifted himself on the grass. "You don't have to tell me if you'd rather not."

"It's okay, I can do this."

She could hear herself swallow. In truth, Lily didn't want to rummage through her past, but she couldn't help herself. She so wanted to confide in the man who sat beside her, who took pleasure in listening, who stared into her eyes as if searching for deeper meaning in every word she spoke.

The way he peered into her eyes, she almost believed she held something worth searching for.

"I was 23 years old, still young enough to maintain a remnant of naiveté. Part of you knows you're an adult, but you're still old enough to maintain an innocent side."

Ryder blinked once, and Lily knew he understood.

"I'd dreamed about falling in love for so long," she continued. "I was never the kind of girl who captured the interest of many guys, but I wanted to be. I'd steal quick glances at guys I thought were cute, imagine the thrill of getting asked out by them or held in their arms or whatnot."

Lily paused. The sky had darkened. Streetlamps dotted the park. The tree under which they sat, so inviting as the sunlight had faded, now loomed overhead and cast an inky shadow over her. To Lily, it felt like a cold, cruel shroud.

"The guy I was in love with? He was handsome. I met him at a Halloween party a friend held in her apartment. I'd dressed up in a simple kitten costume, and he'd dressed as a vampire." She plucked a stiff blade of grass and ran her thumb along its tip. "He had come with a friend of a friend, so at first, nobody knew who he was. We crossed paths while grabbing beers, got to flirting, then dancing, then talking. Hours escaped us, and before we knew it, it was past midnight," she said. "He'd covered his face in white vampire makeup that night, so I didn't realize how handsome he was until we met for lunch the next week. I couldn't help but notice he was interested in me, too. There he was, an older guy at 26, and he found *me* attractive. So needless to say, I entered the situation awestruck, but my fascination faded with time. We grew close. The way he'd speak to me, hold me, desire me…everything was new to me. I'd never felt so beautiful in anyone's eyes."

As Lily spoke, Ryder watched her eyes, followed every flinch she made. She heard him shift his foot against the grass, the kind of movement you make when you're engrossed in the person you're with. In the distance, the park's foot traffic thinned to a handful of silhouettes.

"I invested my whole heart in him," Lily continued, "told him my dreams, confided my insecurities. He worked at a stock-trading company, one of those places with branch offices in strip malls, and had a goal of trading in New York in five years. Real driven, focused on the future. And I found myself thinking about the future along with him. He'd talk about times he'd visited Manhattan, the sights he'd seen. 'When you and I move there, I'll take you to a Broadway show,' he'd say. 'We'll eat at a restaurant near Wall Street, some of the best tenderloin you've ever tasted.' He made me feel like my life would have no limits, like anything was possible, even if it meant riding the coattails of *his* dream." A faint tickle caused one corner of her lips to curl upward as she relived the innocent phase of her past relationship.

"You trusted him," Ryder coaxed.

"Yes, I did. Very much."

When she opened her mouth to speak again, she halted. Her breath felt short. Lily closed her eyes, quivered as she took a breath, then willed herself to continue recounting the memory.

She had decided to trust Ryder. She *wanted* to trust him. Lily picked up a metallic taste on her tongue as its moisture disappeared. "His only downside was a control issue that rose to the surface—not always, but on occasion."

Immediately Ryder furrowed his brow. His eyes narrowed as he leaned forward. "What do you mean by 'control issue?'"

Lily shook her head. "They weren't danger signs. Nothing that would make you worry. He was focused on the future, but he also had a self-centered side to him. And a temper. But he'd try to take his anger out on the punching bag at the gym."

Her heart rate began to accelerate. Not much, but enough for her to detect the change. "That's when I started to notice the anger that simmered beneath the surface of his skin."

CHAPTER 45

"I DIDN'T SEE the signs until months into our relationship," Lily continued, "once we started to spend every free moment together." For a moment, she followed an isolated cloud as the moon painted its edges with cold, bluish light. "Sometimes I think back and wonder if I'd always picked up traces of his rage, but had refused to see them. Not in the one guy who had fallen in love with me—or so I'd hoped. Or believed.

"Eventually, we entered a season laced with conflict. He was under pressure trying to track down opportunities in New York while he worked here. In fact, a potential opportunity arose with a firm up there. They even flew him in for an interview. He was sure he had the job. Then, a few weeks later, it fell through. His dream had burst over his head and drenched him with darkness.

"His eyes turned cold. He withdrew from me. Since the New York deal had fallen through, I assumed he was just depressed, so I stuck with him. I waited for the original version of him to return, the one I'd first gotten to know. The one I had come to love."

A shiver surged through Lily's body, leaving goose bumps in its wake, tiny icicles protruding along her arms.

"One night, we sat in his living room, watching a hockey game on TV. Maybe it was my fault for trying to talk to him during a game, but it hurt to see him so withdrawn. I begged him to open up, to say something. *Anything.* But he barely moved his head, refused to talk about it. So I tried again. If anyone could lead him out of that dark corner in his life, I believed it would be me."

Lily's heart plunged, her stomach soured, as the memories reopened old wounds.

"But in spite of my good intentions, our conversation didn't go the way I'd hoped. His coldness escalated into a snowball on fire. Soon we were on our feet, standing toe to toe. He started to shout and I shouted back. I wasn't angry at him, just desperate. I pleaded with him to open up."

Lily wiped tears as they strayed from her eyes. She tightened her lips in a fruitless attempt to suppress her emotions. "He was steamed at me, Ryder. I could see flashes of resentment in his eyes. I begged him to listen to me, to lean on me, but he refused. 'Stop it!' he shouted. 'You don't know what's going on inside me!'" Before she realized it, Lily drew her hands to her ears as his voice echoed in her mind. "I'd never seen him in such a severe state. I was frightened, so I backed off and apologized, but I don't think he knew how to stop himself."

Her eyes felt hot. Tears pooled along her lower eyelids and trickled down her cheeks as Ryder drew her close. He wrapped her in his arms, and the firmness of his embrace, the warmth of his skin, made her feel secure.

And bold enough to admit the truth.

"That's when it happened," Lily said. "I felt a flash of pain as his hand struck my face."

CHAPTER 46

"YOU DON'T THINK it can happen to you until it does," Lily admitted. "I just stood there. Stunned. My face burned from the sting of his touch as my brain tried to register what had happened. He couldn't look me in the eye. And I didn't want him to."

Ryder leaned his face close to hers, his nose and lips against her cheeks. As Lily heard the steady determination in his breaths, she knew Ryder would have done anything to absorb her pain and erase the memories from her heart.

Lily's voice quivered as she took a breath.

"I ran out the door and never went back. Never answered his phone calls, never talked to him again. A few months later, when my lease ended, I moved to another side of town. It had happened to me once, but I'd never let it happen again. And with that, a piece of my heart hardened. It was tough to let another person inside."

Her tears had began to dry. The onslaught of emotions had exerted pressure on her body and caused a slight headache, but nothing she couldn't ignore.

"The morning after the incident, when I looked in the bathroom mirror, the first thing I saw was a bruise on my cheekbone, below my eye, where he'd hit me. I was shocked."

"Didn't anybody wonder what happened?" Ryder asked. "They must have noticed the bruise on your face."

"People asked, but I told them a friend had run through a stop sign. I said I was in the passenger seat when it happened, that I'd knocked my cheek against the dashboard. If I had told them it happened in my own car, they would've wondered where the damage was. But since I claimed it had happened to someone else's car, no one questioned my explanation. And nobody suspected abuse because they'd never seen any strange black-and-blue marks on me before then."

Downcast, Lily shook her head. To this day, she could envision the plum-colored blemish. For evidence of such a harsh encounter, its edges had looked soft and subdued, like a watercolor.

She parted from Ryder's embrace and looked into his eyes.

"That relationship had started out like a fairy tale come true. For the first time in my life, I had known how it felt to be beautiful. But when I looked at my bruised face, and considered the betrayal and hurt that it represented, I'd never felt more *unbeautiful*—not only on the outside, but on the inside, too. Even after the mark faded, my feelings of insignificance lingered, the belief that I would never matter to anyone."

Highlighted from the glow of a nearby streetlamp, Ryder clenched his jaw. Lily knew that, given the chance, he would have put her ex-boyfriend in a body cast. While relieved she hadn't revealed the guy's name, the notion that Ryder would protect her enhanced Lily's confidence. All these years, she had kept this secret to herself, but with tonight's admission, a cleansing had occurred. Ripples of relief fluttered within her.

"That's why I put on such a tough front when you and I first met," she said. "And who knows? When I smacked you that night a few months ago—maybe it was a defensive thing. Maybe I wanted to keep from getting hurt again."

With tender strokes, Ryder rubbed her arm, the spot where his hand rested.

"Some guys wouldn't treat you that way," he said at last. "I couldn't imagine doing so."

Lily turned to face him. "The truth is, I don't understand all your paintings of me. I don't know how you could see me as beautiful, because I don't even see *myself* that way," she admitted. "But when I look at those paintings and consider myself through your eyes, part of me wants to believe what I see, to believe there's a side to me I haven't considered. I want to be that woman. I want to believe your paintings show me who I truly am."

"It *is* who you truly are." Ryder laid a soft kiss on her cheek. "I recognized you were special the first night I saw you, before you ever saw me."

Cicadas buzzed in the tree branches above them.

In the moonlight, Ryder wrapped his arms tighter around Lily as she allowed herself to drift to sleep in his arms.

CHAPTER 47

JUST HER LUCK.

With all the parking spots occupied within the vicinity of her apartment building, Lily circled around and coasted past them a second time, growing more aggravated as she went. Visitors owned most of these cars, she knew. But normally, this predicament occurred on Sunday afternoons, when people stayed home to watch football games, not on evenings in the middle of the week. The lot should have been less populated tonight.

She ended up parking her car on the far side of the lot. To punctuate her irritation, she checked her watch and confirmed that, sure enough, it took her a full minute to trek to her building.

She heard the slamming of a car door behind her. Its driver must have parked there a while ago and frittered away the minutes in their car before climbing out of it.

Lily's workday had turned sour late that morning. A customer's car had stopped running while en route to her job and had arrived by tow truck. The customer had hoped for a quick fix at a hundred bucks. Unfortunately, when Lily drew up a cost estimate approaching seven hundred dollars, the woman ranted about overpriced car repairs, then all but labeled Lily a bloodsucker who had inflated the cost and so she could pocket the difference. In the end, though, the customer knew she had no choice and agreed to the fix. Lily verified the auto shop's supplier had the part in inventory and could deliver it that afternoon.

Around lunchtime, the supplier, embarrassed, called back to explain a glitch had occurred in the inventory software. He didn't have the part in stock. He could secure the part from a third party, but delivery would take a day or two. Lily dreaded informing the customer but had no choice.

The customer was livid. Lily listened to an onslaught of insults and had to bite her tongue to prevent herself from firing back on all cylinders. By mid-afternoon, with her day ruined, Lily counted the minutes until she could leave the shop and put this rotten workday out of its misery.

Lily's day was about to get worse.

By the time she reached the wooden staircase at her apartment building, she heard the click of heels on concrete behind her. Determined steps, drawing closer.

Her neighbors didn't wear heels. Whoever this person was, she didn't live in Lily's building.

Lily stopped at the foot of the stairs and turned around. A woman in a navy-blue blazer and knee-length skirt approached her. Tall with long, brunette hair, she carried a small notebook.

"Are you Lily Machara?" the woman called out, her pace quickening as if Lily might make an about-face and dart up the stairs.

"Yeah." Lily didn't recognize her. "Do I know you?"

"Rebecca Dodd," the woman replied when she caught up with her. "I'm a reporter from the *New Haven Voice.* Do you have time for a few questions?"

CHAPTER 48

ANOTHER REPORTER? LILY was sick of them. In the last month, countless reporters had called her, and Lily had declined every interview.

This reporter, however, had tracked her down in person. That was a first.

New Haven? She had traveled all the way from Connecticut? In an instant, Lily felt her world shrink to the size of a gumball. Antifreeze traveled up her spine in alarm.

The phone calls were bad enough, but now that a reporter had shown up in her own neighborhood, Lily wondered if she should expect to awaken to the flash of a camera through her bedroom window. Would a reporter climb a ladder to get a photo of the Mona Lisa as she slept?

Lily feared the Mona Lisa obsession had spun out of control. She wondered about her safety, yet she hadn't received threats, nor did she expect to. So what was she supposed to do? Complain to the police because a reporter approached her on a sidewalk? Or because others had dialed her phone number? Each call was a one-time occurrence by that individual. No one had called twice. Nobody had stalked her. As far as she knew, at least.

"How do you know where I live?" Lily knew the ease with which you could track anyone down, but after a day of frustration, she refused to make this easy for Rebecca Dodd, who stared at her with determined, silver-blue eyes.

"I located your address online."

Lily wanted to probe further, to find out how Dodd knew her name and which city's address records to scour, but decided against it. Better not to drill a hole in that dam.

Instead, in a curt tone, she said, "I'm not interested in an interview." With that, she turned and started to climb the stairs. All she wanted was an hour of silence.

But Dodd had different ideas and shadowed her anyway. "When did you first learn of your appearances in Ryder Flynn's art?"

"I don't want to comment."

"Prior to meeting Mr. Flynn, did you consider pursuing legal recourse for use of your likeness without your permission?"

"I said, no comment."

When Lily reached the top of the stairs, she fumbled through her keys. Her hands jittered.

Rebecca Dodd stood twenty inches behind her. Lily could feel the reporter's eyes pinned to her shoulder blades.

"Has Mr. Flynn discussed future compensation for—"

Exhausted, Lily forgot to measure her words. Instead, she went on offense, the mode she adopted during arguments at the shop, when she wanted one of the guys to shut the hell up.

Lily spun around. "Do you have a microphone with you?"

"I have a voice recorder in the car—"

"Good. Go grab it and shove it up your ass."

Great. Lily could picture the headline now:

MONA LISA HAS THE TONGUE OF A SAILOR!

She knew reporters witnessed shocking, even grotesque, things over the courses of their careers. So, as offensive as her comment was, Lily didn't believe it would dumbfound this reporter. She didn't expect Rebecca Dodd's mouth to drop open. And it didn't.

But the reporter's left eye twitched.

At the thought of her rude outburst, a tinge of regret settled into Lily's gut. She wished she could retract her remark and try a different tactic. Then again, this reporter had invaded *her* privacy, not the other way around. Granted, Lily had a salty tongue when she joked around at the shop, but in general, she didn't relish insulting comments. Truth be told, she didn't like herself much when she responded to people that way.

With a sigh, Lily shook her head and poked her key into the lock.

"Sorry," she muttered, then headed inside and shut the door.

CHAPTER 49

"ARE YOU READY yet?" Lily heard Ryder call from down the hall.

"Almost."

In the mirror of his guest bathroom, she scoped herself out and cast a hesitant eye upon an unfamiliar image: Lily in a black dress.

Earlier that week, she had broken down and asked Brooke to help her select the garment. Lily wasn't convinced she could pull off this look, but when she'd tried on the dress at the store, she had noticed a boost in her confidence. From any given angle, tiny sparkles twinkled in the light and made her smile. The dress complemented her bust and posterior, which was a plus. She felt like her alter ego, Ryder's Mona Lisa, the one she'd grown to prefer. And for the first time in longer than she could remember, instead of twisting or tying her hair in some manner, Lily allowed it to rest upon her shoulders. It curled in natural wisps at the end.

Ryder had told her to bring a nice change of clothes for a romantic evening. She had spent the last hour showering and getting ready.

Why had he told her to dress up for tonight?

Lily had no idea what he had planned.

But whatever it was, she looked forward to it.

Upon arriving at his home, garment bag in hand, she had knocked on the door and heard the clink of a cooking utensil against metal. Moments later, a barefoot Ryder, dressed in a printed T-shirt and shorts, had met her in the doorway. As soon as she had walked inside, Lily had picked up the scent of spices cooking, something exotic and invigorating, maybe with an Asian flair.

With a hearty breath and curiosity on the rise, she had turned toward the kitchen, but he had placed his hands on her shoulders and turned her around, a playful glint in his eye.

"No, you don't," he had told her. "This is a surprise. I have some work to do in the kitchen, so why don't you head into the bathroom and do whatever it is you do to get ready?"

"It could take a while," she had said.

"Take your time," he'd replied.

And so she had. She had showered, dressed, applied some basic makeup, and fixed her hair. Then she paused, tilting her nose toward the door.

The aroma of whatever Ryder was cooking had been so prominent when she'd arrived. Now she picked up a trace of it, nothing more. Strange.

Her mind returned to her image in the mirror. If she didn't know any better, she might consider herself attractive.

Her pulse quickened. She inhaled the scent of ginger that lingered in her hair.

He's waiting for you, Lily.

She gave herself a final once-over—a stalling technique, by her own admission. Ryder wouldn't mind if she left her things in the bathroom. She didn't want to walk out wearing a dress like this holding an armload of chaos. Lily prayed Ryder would like what he saw. She'd brought a pair of black flats, but Ryder had insisted she'd enjoy herself more barefoot, which continued to pique her curiosity.

Well, here goes nothing...

One long exhale before she turned off the bathroom light and stepped into the hallway.

Ryder stood six feet away—barefoot, sure enough—dressed in a black sport coat and a tie the color of charcoal. He had groomed his hair with extra care. It appeared to have more body than usual, as though he had combed in a dab of gel, the way she had seen him in a recent photo. A far cry from how he'd looked when she'd arrived earlier.

For a split second, Lily's heart buzzed.

Yet, as handsome as he looked tonight, he couldn't seem to tear his eyes from *her.*

The unconscious way he shook his head, the kind where you try to convince yourself you're not walking through a dream, suggested something about her had enraptured him. As he took in the sight of her, inch by inch, the respectful sweeping of his eyes from her toes to the top of her head, reminded her of how one might behold a diamond cut to perfection.

Ryder groped for words. "You look…stunning."

"Thank you." The hairs along her arm, almost invisible to the naked eye, bristled with exhilaration. Lily couldn't help but emit a slight giggle. "You know, technically, you've already seen me like this."

"I have?"

"You've painted me this way, haven't you?"

Ryder pondered her words for a moment. Then his face grew taut. Resolute.

"No," he replied in an earnest tone. "You look more beautiful than a paintbrush could hope to capture."

That got her. Had any other guy said it to her, she would have dismissed it as a pick-up line. But with Ryder, she knew it was genuine.

Her confidence on a slow rise, Lily laid her hands upon his shoulders and a kiss upon his lower lip.

"You look nice." She brushed a fleck from his shoulder. "I don't think I've ever seen you in a sport coat. Not in person, anyway."

With a wink, he took her hand in his. "I took some liberty and decided we should eat outside. I hope you don't mind."

Lily nodded in approval. Together they made their way down the hall, through his studio and the sliding-glass door, and stepped onto his patio. At eight-thirty in the evening, sunset had begun and the temperature had cooled to a comfortable level. But when Lily saw the patio furniture—and the empty table—she was puzzled.

CHAPTER 50

GLANCING BACK AT Ryder, she could see he'd not only anticipated her confusion, but he delighted in it. He chuckled.

"This way." He nodded toward the lake and, once again, led her by the hand.

He guided her across the grass, which, though soft, poked her ankles as she treaded upon it. At the far edge of the lawn, a patch of large rocks served as a border between the grass and the lake. Lily spotted a pontoon boat, docked beneath canopied shelter, bobbing upon the water. A breeze tickled her neckline and caused the hanging edges of the canopy to flutter.

Ryder climbed into the boat, then helped her aboard. As he pulled her toward him, his grasp felt firm, reminding Lily of the security she felt when he held her in his arms.

She gained her footing, peered over her shoulder, and discovered a card table at the opposite end of the boat. Covered with a white tablecloth and a place setting for two, the table fit perfectly between the boat's booth-style seats. At the center of the table, a pair of candlesticks sat aglow, their flames swaying in a tango.

Ryder had covered their dishes, which sat on opposite sides of the candlesticks. Atop a stool beside the table, a bottle of Riesling chilled in an ice bucket.

Ryder was still in the kitchen when Lily arrived at his house. That meant, in the time it had taken her to get ready, he had finished cooking, showered, changed clothes, and carried dinner outside.

Maybe women *could* spend an eternity preparing for a date.

"I'll let you pretend I've pulled your chair out for you," Ryder said as he gestured toward the booth.

"And they say chivalry is dead," Lily quipped. "Thank you."

The foam seat cushion released a puff of air when she sat. He had offered her the seat with a breathtaking view of the lake, which must have stretched a mile before her. Facing west, she could catch the waning sunlight, a burst of color, the sun too far below the horizon to blind her. The sunset cast a reddish glow upon the water.

Lily spotted rolling hillsides, filled with leafy trees, across the water. Lights from houses speckled the perimeter of the horizon. A pine tree sat a few feet from Ryder's dock.

Lily marveled that such a view resided outside his back door. Although vacationers jammed the lake and roads of Osage Beach, boaters avoided Ryder's cove and gravitated toward the lake's primary vein. Lake of the Ozarks is not a round body of water. On a map, it looks like a jagged river that winds for miles, with legs resembling a centipede's in shape and abundance. As a result, no matter where you stand, you can see the other side.

Lily returned her eyes to the table. "Metal covers for the plates?" she said. "Like room service. You came equipped."

"A friend of mine works at a resort a few miles down the road." Ryder lifted the silver covers to reveal a cup of soup and dinner plate for each of them. Setting the covers aside, he took a seat facing her.

A natural scent, one Lily recalled from her first visit, wafted toward her. She felt her muscles unwind amid the pleasant aroma.

They reached for their napkins at the same time and placed them on their laps. Ryder removed the wine cork with an alto-pitched pop and poured her a glass. "I hope you like white wine. It goes well with the entrée."

No man had ever cooked a romantic dinner for her. Ryder could have served sloppy joes and she would have felt as special as she did tonight. Not only had he ushered her into yet another first experience, his dinner was about to take her on a tour of the Orient. She'd never eaten these items. She didn't even know what they were! But they looked delicious.

"The culinary angle is a nice touch," she said. "Should I be worried you're trying to seduce me, Ryder Flynn? Need I remind you we've already spent the night together?" she said with a smirk.

Ryder laughed. "I prefer to cover my dinner plates *and* my bases. I'm always afraid my luck will run out." Lifting his glass, he said, "To us."

"To us."

With a clink of their glasses to seal the deal, Lily swept her eyes over the spread.

Then it hit her. The paintings of Thailand in Ryder's studio! She couldn't believe it had taken her this long to figure it out.

"Is this Thai food?"

"Indeed."

"And the mysterious link to your past continues."

"Normally, the Thai people put all of the items in the middle of the table so everyone can take what they want, but I wanted this to be more like a date," Ryder said. "I prepared common dishes. Try the soup first," Ryder said. "It's called Tom Yum Goong, a spicy soup with a chicken-stock base. I made it with a dash of coconut milk, but some people prefer not to add that ingredient."

Lily shrugged. "I'll try anything once." Small shrimp floated on top, along with what Ryder called kaffir lime leaves. The soup was a visual delight, bursting with red, green and white. Her first taste brought the hearty flavor of lemongrass, but she also detected a hint of garlic and red chilies. The soup soothed her. "And I'll gladly try this any other time you decide to make it."

Ryder's eyes gleamed at her reaction. "I'll take that as a compliment," he said, then sampled his work himself.

Flattered by Ryder's attempt to make this evening a unique experience for her, she asked, "How did you learn to cook Thai food?"

Ryder closed his eyes as he swallowed, as if his taste buds would carry him overseas. "I craved the cuisine ever since I returned from my visit to Thailand. My friend's mom knew how much I loved it and invited me to their house for dinner a lot, which tied me over for a long time. Then, several years ago, I bought a Thai cookbook and a wok, and practiced until I reached the point where my cooking matched my memories.

"You'd be surprised at the variety of food they cook over there. Every province or town has a specialty for which it's known. Along the shoreline, you'll find a lot of seafood. Fishing boats head out early in the morning. Hours later, they gather at the docks to sell whatever fresh seafood they caught that day: lots of different types of fish, along with crab, squid, stingray—"

"Stingray!"

"I kid you not. Whatever seafood they catch, they keep it in a tub of water and sell it alive, so it's nice and fresh. The scent hangs in the air and sends hunger pangs to your gut. Whatever doesn't sell that day, they'll dry it and sell it that way. They're a practical group of people. Meanwhile, in the northern, landlocked provinces, it's not unusual for them to prepare insects to eat—junebugs, cicadas."

Call her a Westerner, but Lily cringed at the idea. "How do they eat them? Raw?"

Based on the way he chuckled in response, Ryder must have anticipated her reaction. "Deep fried. They taste better than you'd expect."

"You ate them?"

"Of course."

"And you've *kissed* me with those lips?"

With a glance toward her side of the table, he noticed her empty soup bowl. "Try the Pad Thai. It has chicken and shrimp over rice noodles. Another classic dish."

"After the crash course in insect consumption, I'm not sure I want to."

"You're safe with this one. Trust me."

Lily teased him with a wary expression, then picked up her fork. Assuming it was similar to Chinese food, she speared a chunk of chicken breast which, unlike her Chinese take-out, did not have breading on it. With her first bite, the sauce burst with sweet and tangy tones. Ryder had sprinkled ground peanuts on top of the entrée, which she crunched between her teeth. "It's delicious," she said. "The tastes all blend together."

Ryder nodded. "In Thai cooking, you'll find a careful balance between sour, sweet, salty and spicy."

Upon closer examination, Lily noticed green onions and bean sprouts mixed into the dish, too. The long rice noodles were fun to chew. In fact, they had such a delicate texture, Lily realized one noodle still hung from her mouth. "Oops," she muttered, tucking it in with her fork, which sparked a mutual snicker with Ryder.

"The fruit in Thailand has such exotic colors and textures, too." Ryder took a bite of his Pad Thai, followed by a sip of wine.

"Like what?"

"Take bananas. In our grocery stores, you can buy only one kind. But in Thailand, you'll find a range of bananas there, from the size of your finger to much larger than a human hand. The smaller they are, the sweeter they are," he said. "You'll also find durian there. It's the king of fruits."

"And why does it get to be king?" she teased.

"Hey, I don't make the rules," Ryder replied, palms out, the pose of an innocent bystander. "It looks like a yellow football with spikes all over it, but when you cut it open, it has the texture of a banana. It smells so awful, I've heard it's illegal in Singapore. But some people love it."

"Are you trying to ruin my dinner?"

Ryder shrugged. "Whenever I'd visit someone, the first thing they did was sit me down and serve tea and fruit. With so many different fruits over there, I doubt I ate the same one twice. I loved mangosteen, the queen of fruits. It's small with purple, fleshy skin on the outside. But inside, it has puffy, white segments like an orange. It's very sweet."

Once again, Ryder seemed to lose himself as he relived fond memories. Lily enjoyed watching his face fill with exuberance. As he delved into details, she studied the way he pursed his lips and narrowed his eyes, a man on a quest to select his words with precision.

A bean sprout crunched as Lily speared it, along with a shrimp, with her fork. "Of all the places you visited there, do you have a favorite?"

"I'd have so many to choose from. Pattaya is a coastal city a couple of hours south of Bangkok. Although it has some seedy parts with brothels and drugs—New Orleans's Bourbon Street is tame by comparison—Pattaya itself is gorgeous. One side is filled with hotels, malls, restaurants—I liken it to Las Vegas. Some restaurants sit high on a rocky cliff that overlooks the ocean, or you can walk down the stairs and eat on the sand. The other side of Pattaya is separated as a beach area.

"I loved the historical aspect of Si Ayutthaya, which is northeast of Bangkok. It was Thailand's ancient capital and contains a lot of old architecture. In one spot, I saw piles of burnt, blackened brick lying around and wondered why no one had hauled it away. As it turns out, those bricks are the ruins of the king's ancient palace. When the Burmese invaded the city centuries ago, they set fire to the palace—and its bricks are *still there,* after all this time. Can you imagine coming across something that old in North America?" Ryder shook his head in bewilderment. "I even rode an elephant in Si Ayutthaya."

"Weren't you scared you might fall off?"

"I was nervous, to say the least!" He watched his wine for a moment as he swirled it in his glass. "But I'd have to say my favorite spot was Amphawa. It's located near a river." His voice grew softer. "It has a tree I like to call my inspiration tree. Amphawa is known for its fireflies, and they gravitate to one particular tree. So, at night, if you travel down the river in season, you can see this tree from far away. It looks like it's filled with Christmas lights, but even better—the tree glows so bright, it looks like it's on fire."

Lily was lost in Ryder's world. The image struck her as romantic. She leaned forward on her elbows, rested her chin on her clasped hands. From behind the flickering candlelight, Ryder's brown eyes appeared not only brighter, but intense, like windows into his soul.

He focused on the flame before him. Lily could only imagine the memories that must adorn the canvas of an artist's mind, the emotional tones that accompany its colors and strokes. After a brief silence, Ryder peered up, and for a moment, their eyes locked.

"Romance in Thailand carries such innocence," he said. "They mature much slower in their perceptions and behavior. They maintain a level of naiveté well into early adulthood. In fact, it's not unusual to find a 28-year-old woman who has never been kissed, never been touched in a romantic way by a man. The beauty of it all struck me—I mean, it was…*pure.* When a woman marries a man, she *gives* herself to him. Not in a male-domineering way; more like a dedication. He's her one and only. How special is that?" Ryder pondered another moment, then added, "I can't turn back time, but it does make me evaluate everything closer. I look at how I've failed at relationships in the past, how I couldn't quite reach the point where I'd commit my whole heart, and…" His voice trailed off.

Lily paused, then reached out and took his hand in hers. "You've given me a peek at your whole heart," Lily said, "and I haven't found failure in there."

Ryder offered no reply, but his eyes softened, and Lily knew the truth she'd spoken had touched his soul.

CHAPTER 51

THE CORNER OF Ryder's mouth curled upward in a grin.

"So what about you?" he asked. "If you could leave right now, travel anywhere, where would it be?"

Lily sniffed. Ryder had jaunted halfway around the globe. Her dream seemed so small by comparison. Prior to her involvement with Ryder Flynn, Lily had given minimal thought to places beyond North America, vacation or otherwise. His experience stretched farther than that of anyone else she knew. Her acquaintances spoke of heading to Florida for a week or, at best, a Caribbean cruise.

"It's not as exotic as Asia," she replied with a brush of her hand. "You wouldn't be impressed."

"Doesn't matter." Ryder leaned forward with his palm on the table and gazed into her eyes, a man on another quest. "What's your idea of beautiful?"

When he gazed at her that way, she was willing to answer anything he asked. "Jamaica," she said at last. "It sounds clichéd, I know. Everybody wants to go there."

With a shrug, he bit the edge of his lower lip. "I think Jamaica sounds quite nice." His eyes remained fixed upon hers, an invitation for her to tell him more.

"It's not the cliché that interests me, though. I don't pull up my Bob Marley playlist and say, 'Gee, I want to drink a Red Stripe and call people *Mon.*'"

"Then what is it? What draws your soul to Jamaica?"

"The ambience, I suppose. The aura. I want to step into it the way I want to step into one of your paintings." Lily's eyes gleamed as she pictured the warm environment, reggae music soaking the background. She closed her eyes. "Steel drums…clear, Caribbean water…a cool, salty breeze sweeping in from the sea…to walk along the shoreline and feel grains of sand between my toes…"

For all she knew, her description hadn't done the place justice. Nevertheless, when she opened her eyes, Ryder appeared rapt with her words as he concentrated on a focal point ten feet beyond her shoulder. Had he started to bring her description to life on the canvas of his mind?

He joined her on Jamaican sand as he added in a daze, "…the sounds of waves lapping and fizzing on the sand…the scent of love and margaritas drifting through air so moist you can feel it on your forehead…"

With a fingernail she'd painted red the prior night, Lily leaned forward and traced circles on the tablecloth. She scrutinized each circle and felt a bit lightheaded from her third glass of wine. "I've never been to a beach before."

"Never?"

Lost in thought, Lily shook her head. The candles' flames continued to sway. For a while, neither Lily nor Ryder spoke.

When she lifted her head, she found Ryder lost in thought. When he looked into her eyes, he entered them, yet did so in the manner of a gentleman, treading with care by way of soft, confident steps.

The hue of Ryder's irises fluttered from dark to vivid as the firelight flickered.

And as Lily watched them dance, she realized she had fallen in love.

She felt a tug in her belly, a subtle pang.

"Ryder, I—there's more to me that I want you to know."

Ryder took her hand in his. Kissed her finger. "About what?"

She tried to find the words but felt weak. More than anything, she feared losing his love.

"I'm not the woman in the paintings."

"Lily, I know that."

"No, I mean—"

Ryder placed a finger over her lips, then caressed her cheek.

"Lily, I know you. I know everything I need to know." He brushed her upper lip with his fingertip and planted a soft kiss there. "I promise. You don't need to say anything more."

"Okay, but…"

"Do you trust me, Lily?"

She studied his countenance and found such calm. Lily relaxed as reassurance filled her heart. If nothing else, Ryder had seen greater depth in her than she had ever found in herself. Maybe he was right. Maybe that was all he needed. After all, what did she know about love?

"Yes," she replied, "I trust you."

"All I want is to—"

A flash of light exploded. Lily gasped. For a split second, the whole pontoon boat lit up in a bright, bluish white, the color of starlight. But the light hadn't originated in the sky.

It had come from much closer. Too close.

Lily caught movement in her peripheral vision. A silhouette of dark against dark, somewhere in the blackness of Ryder's backyard.

Ryder, too, detected the movement and shot to his feet. He ran across the floor of the pontoon boat, jumped onto land, and darted across his lawn.

CHAPTER 52

FRIGHT RACED UP Lily's spine. She squinted and tried to discern the intruder, who now stood still. Lily tracked Ryder's movements. When he noticed the intruder hadn't tried to escape, Ryder slowed to a brisk walk.

"Hey!" Ryder shouted, his voice forceful and clipped. "You! What the hell do you think you're doing?"

The intruder took a few steps back, into the harsh, eerie glow of the moonlight. Lily recognized a camera that hung from a strap around the man's neck and assumed it had caused the flash. The intruder had already gotten what he wanted. Hands empty, the slim man held them at shoulder height as if in surrender. Lily breathed easier at the sight, now that she knew the man didn't intend to cause Ryder physical harm.

Ryder approached the man, faced him chest to chest. "Did you hear me? What are you doing here?"

"No worries," replied the man, "I'm not looking for trouble."

Step by step, each time Ryder came within an inch of bumping against his chest, the man moved backwards. Considering Ryder's anger, Lily wondered why he hadn't hit the man, then wondered if Ryder, in the wake of his fame, had become suspicious of attempts to bait him into trumped-up charges of assault.

"Who are you? What was the photo for?"

"It's a public lake, man."

"But the lawn isn't. You're standing on private property. Move your ass along before I..."

Knowing Ryder was safe, Lily, although stunned, took inventory of her surroundings on the pontoon boat. Just in case the argument escalated and they needed a makeshift weapon for self-defense.

At first, the force of Ryder's reaction to the intrusion had caught her by surprise. He'd had his picture taken on numerous occasions and had grown accustomed to it. She understood his displeasure at this photographer's gall, but the man's action had ignited in Ryder a rage she had never witnessed. Hadn't he himself admitted he no longer possessed anonymity? It was a consequence of his career, he had explained.

Lily returned her attention to the lawn, where the intruder had turned and begun to walk away as Ryder, arms crossed, stood firm and monitored his departure.

At that point, a revelation hit Lily.

Ryder hadn't gone after the photographer in self-defense.

He had done it for Lily.

He had protected her.

CHAPTER 53

FROM WHERE LILY lay in bed, she could glimpse the full moon, electric chalk glowing on the other side of the window. In the shadows of the bedroom, Ryder's cream-colored sheets appeared midnight blue.

With a quick glance at the clock, Lily discovered it was well past midnight. After dinner, she and Ryder had extinguished the candles and carried their dinnerware to the kitchen sink, where they would rinse them and load them into the dishwasher in the morning.

Words couldn't match the invigoration Lily had felt earlier, as Ryder ran his tongue along her lower lip before they made love, right here, in the cascade of moonlight. She recalled the way they had gasped during their final moments of intimacy. She relived the minutes that followed, the way they had fallen back against the pillows, each fighting to breathe, and the sensation of their perspiration, which had mingled upon her belly, as it cooled beneath the sheet.

That was less than an hour ago.

Lily fanned her face with the edge of the sheet. Although a draft of chilled air blew through the vent overhead, the Midwestern humidity caused her to perspire. She wanted to crawl out from under the sheet, but didn't want to leave Ryder's presence and couldn't get used to the idea of sleeping on top of it unclothed.

She listened to his heavy breathing. The slight, nasal tone revealed he was asleep.

Lily turned toward Ryder and eased closer, careful not to awaken him. He smelled like sandalwood, the aroma of someone who had come indoors after spending a few hours in nature. She stroked his sandy-brown hair with her fingertips.

Yes, she loved him.

After all these years spent wondering whether she would find love, love had found *her* when she hadn't even searched for it.

Now she couldn't imagine life without this man.

Lily had never felt so content.

And on the boat earlier that evening, as she had soaked in his eyes, she could see he loved her, too.

PART THREE

SEEKING LILY

CHAPTER 54

MONA LISA REVEALED!
AMERICA'S MODERN-DAY MUSE—
WHO SHE IS AND THE RELATIONSHIP
THAT BROKE HER HEART

THE HEADLINE CAUGHT Lily's eye a few weeks later, on a Sunday afternoon, as she waited in the supermarket checkout line.

Minutes before, she had mused at how bare her grocery cart looked with nothing more than some fresh asparagus, broccoli and a gallon of fat-free milk. She had expected the express lane to move faster, but the man two positions ahead of her had sneaked in with a cartload of groceries. Before the cashier noticed the shopper's load far exceeded the twenty-item limit posted on the sign above, the shopper had already tossed half of his produce onto the conveyor belt. With a shrug and a mouthed apology to the remaining shoppers, the cashier feigned ignorance and proceeded with the checkout.

Lily, meanwhile, swept her eyes across the other lanes in search of a shorter line but wound up, as she often did in her life, at the pointy end of the stick. And so, while waiting, she filled her idle minutes by scanning the shelf beside her, the one aimed at impulse buyers: Individual packages of bubble gum. Travel-size snack packs. A horoscope digest, which she had never seen anyone purchase but pictured its buyer as a woman who owned 25 cats and recycled her toilet water.

Then Lily turned her attention to the row of tabloid magazines. It took her mere seconds to scan the front-page headlines before she turned away.

Then she froze as one particular headline replayed in her mind.

Lily groaned. Her shoulders limped in defeat as she pivoted on her heel to reread the bold, white headline, its font an inch tall against a black background.

How stupid of her to think the truth wouldn't come out.

In a few days, she had promised—or rather, convinced—herself, she would tell Ryder. *Soon. Next week. When I find the right words.* Lily had lost track of time as a few days turned into a few weeks, and a few weeks became a few months. She had grown so comfortable with him. He had seemed content with how he perceived her. And in the meantime, moment by moment, she had become the woman in his artwork. She had wandered into a fantasy world where dreams weren't supposed to burst.

Ryder had told her he knew everything he needed to know because he knew her deep down. He'd promised. Lily had tried to tell him more, but he didn't seem interested in knowing more.

"Trust me," he had said. So she did.

Unfortunately, Ryder didn't know what he was asking.

Lily had reached a sense of peace with Ryder. Now she wished she *hadn't* honored his request to trust him. How naïve of her! She wished she could change the past.

How would Ryder react to this? Would he understand?

REVEALED!, said the headline.

And when she saw the phrase *MONA LISA,* she wanted to vomit. She snatched it from the rack. Whatever the story was, accurate or not, she knew it couldn't be good. When she reached the cashier, Lily avoided unnecessary eye contact, paid for her items—including the rag mag—and hauled ass out of the store.

Through the automatic doors and into a new, scary world. *Alice in Wonderland,* live on the national stage. This new world contained oversized furniture, oversized everything, and it would become Lily's freaking reality. She wanted to shrink and hide, but unlike Alice, Lily would have no magic liqueur to help her adjust to the size.

For Lily, those minutes in the grocery store slowed to such an extent that, had she attempted to speak, her speech would have come out slurred, the way her dad's 45-rpm records sounded when she used to play them at 33-rpm speed for kicks.

Now she sat in the store's parking lot, safe in the driver's seat of her car. But she couldn't bring herself to start the engine. At this point, refrigerating the milk was the least of her worries. Page by page, Lily raced through the tabloid, on a frantic hunt for the article. As it turned out, the editor had devoted prime real estate to the hit piece—a centerfold spread and then some.

Prominent on the left side, Lily found a repeat of the front-page headline, followed by an enlarged photo of Ryder and Lily sitting together on a bench somewhere during daytime. Without the need for a flash bulb, no wonder neither she nor Ryder had noticed anyone snapping their picture. Though the background was a tad blurry, Lily studied it closer and pegged the location as an outdoor outlet mall on Highway 54, not far from where Ryder lived. The photographer must have stood from afar and zoomed in. Was it the intruder from the night she and Ryder had eaten dinner in the pontoon boat?

There they were, a perfect couple engaged in flirtatious conversation, her fingers interwoven with his as she stared into his face. In the photo, she grinned as he spoke to her, though she couldn't recall their topic of conversation. They had ordered iced tea at a little shop that specialized in chocolate and coffee. At least the photographer hadn't caught them on one of their T-shirt-and-shorts days.

Shell-shocked, Lily stared at herself in print. This time, it wasn't a secondhand rendition. This wasn't a sketch or a painting, but a *photograph*—a genuine invasion of her privacy. And in black and white, as though she and Ryder were Bonnie and Clyde, their images slapped onto a *WANTED* poster as they laid low after a bank heist!

She had to read the article three times before the haze dispersed from her mind.

For tabloid fare, the article proved quite accurate. It began with a paragraph about her childhood as the oddball who didn't fit in, followed by some coverage of her middle school and high school years. Assuming the reporter must have contacted a handful of Lily's old classmates, the fact that none of those classmates had turned around and disclosed it to Lily struck her as odd. Maybe the reporter had paid them to keep quiet. It was a rag mag, after all. Then again, she wasn't a popular girl in school, wasn't into social media, and didn't care to keep in touch with many of her former classmates. They had graduated college years ago, and many had scattered across the United States by now. Even if they had stayed in the metro area, they lived in other areas of town, some a good thirty minutes away from her. Brooke, the social butterfly, kept her relationships within a convenient five-mile radius from wherever she happened to live at the moment and had allowed her older friendships to grow stale.

The reporter kept all her sources anonymous, as if those sources found it acceptable to expose Lily's awkward coming-of-age experiences but didn't want anyone to dig into *their* pasts. With only a few paragraphs devoted to that period of her life, however—and with much of the information deducible through some public record or another—the number of sources struck Lily as limited, as if the reporter wanted to imply extensive research before moving on to juicier details.

Next, the article delved into her parents' divorce, for which, Lily presumed, the reporter had scoured court records. It probed Lily's job as an auto mechanic at a local shop, the name of which the article didn't bother to mention. Lily wondered how the reporter managed to track down her employer. Could they access tax records? Had the reporter paid someone under the table? At this point, Lily had no idea how those sleazeballs conducted business, but she assumed their ethical boundaries were as firm and impenetrable as a wet kitchen sponge.

Dave had mentioned a reporter looking for Lily at the shop a while back. Weirder yet, he hadn't mentioned answering any questions. Or maybe those questions didn't strike him as unusual. Maybe the reporter had known more than he'd thought she did.

Lily continued to reread the article as it retreaded the public's fascination with Lily Machara, the mysterious, modern-day Mona Lisa who had become Ryder Flynn's muse at first sight during a chance encounter at a Cleveland hotel six years ago.

How could this reporter know Ryder had spotted Lily all those years ago?

The article culminated with the romance that had budded between the artist and his muse over the last several months, a romance that had caught fire amid whispers and speculation.

Who is the Mona Lisa? The article had answered that question, and it didn't paint an impressive picture of Lily Machara. It depicted a character as plain as Lily had felt until a few months ago. Talk about a letdown for the tabloid reader.

Enter the last part of the article's headline: *AND THE RELATIONSHIP THAT BROKE HER HEART.*

Indeed, buried within the article, not long before Ryder Flynn entered the picture, the reporter focused two paragraphs on the relationship Lily never talked about.

At first glance, Lily had expected the headline to refer to the cruel boyfriend she had left behind. The one she had described on that summer evening Lily and Ryder had spent eating Ted Drewes in a St. Louis park. Yes, such a revelation would have provided much fodder to salivating tabloid readers—if that was the tantalizing relationship espoused by the headline.

But it wasn't.

And now, even after reading the article for the third time, Lily remained stunned.

The relationship that broke her heart.

Once more, Lily repeated the phrase under her breath. It remained surreal.

But when she realized the true damage this story would inflict—the individual who stood to suffer worse from the revelation than Lily herself—a shock bolted up Lily's spine.

The article hadn't exposed Lily's life to scrutiny, but rather, *his.*

Lily's eyelids fell shut as she sunk back into her seat. Her chest felt tight. She fought to breathe as she realized his life had changed in a moment. It would never return to yesterday's form.

Life's floor had just caved in beneath him.

Lily caught her breath. Her heart wrenched for him.

Aaron.

CHAPTER 55

As her car screeched to a stop at a suburban intersection, another yellow-light opportunity turned to smoke, Lily tried his cell phone number again. As with her last several attempts, it went straight to voice mail.

Damn!

Lily fought nausea as she chewed a fingernail, her free hand gripping the steering wheel in a choke hold. The shop was closed on Sundays, so she knew he wasn't working.

She turned right at the next corner and sped into Aaron's apartment complex, its parking lot packed with vehicles, their owners probably watching football on television.

Jogging to the stairwell, she raced down the steps to his apartment, a basement-level unit with a view of the woods, where Aaron lived alone. How many times had she descended these stairs? Yet she'd never felt as distraught as she did now, after a tabloid had taken a hammer and chisel to Aaron's heart.

She rapped her knuckles upon the door. No answer. Lily pressed her ear against the door's surface, which felt colder than a morgue locker, but she heard nothing. Aaron always kept a radio or television on when he was home, but the fact he had neither answered his phone nor replied to her text message had put her nerves on edge. Her instincts kicked into gear. The silence inside his apartment wasn't the silence of an absent owner. It was the silence of solitude.

The kind of silence that accompanies a hard crash.

She lifted the door knocker to announce her arrival again, louder.

"Aaron?" she called out. "Are you in there? It's Lily. Please open up."

Nothing.

With a sigh, Lily let her hand drop to her hip as she scratched a fingernail against her thumb. She shook her head. Then she heard the clunk of the deadbolt.

Aaron stood before her, emptiness in his eyes. Not that he could look at her. He avoided eye contact.

Lily had no idea when the Mona Lisa issue of the tabloid had hit shelves, but judging from his sullenness, she had no doubt he had read about himself that weekend. Minutes ago, she had felt as stunned as he appeared now. Emotionless. Blindsided. Like Lily, the boundaries of his privacy had evaporated in the time it took a gunshot to crack tranquility.

Aaron opened the door wide enough for Lily to make her way past him. The two friends settled, side by side, on his couch. Lily longed to peer into his eyes, reassure him, but his focus darted from her knees to the floor.

Lily sensed the confusion that roiled within him, his soul awash in hurt, fear and fury.

What could she say to dull the wound she had caused him? How could she justify someone sweeping him into the spotlight? Lily hadn't had the courage to face the spotlight herself—not in light of her true self, anyway.

So she followed suit and stared at Aaron's knees, searched for a way to speak from her heart.

"They didn't find out from me," she said at last. Her voice held a notch above a whisper, but it was all she could muster. She drew near, wrapped her arms around him, and felt Aaron's body grow limp as he rested his face upon her shoulder. His misery weighed upon her, the same pressure she had felt once when she'd gotten stuck beneath a car as a little girl.

Feverish-hot tears from Aaron's eyes seeped into Lily's shirt. His body started to tremble, though she felt his muscles tense to try to suppress it.

Tears rose to Lily's own eyes, but she saw no reason to quench them. Her heart wrenched for him.

They held each other without a word. Lily listened to the tick of a clock as it echoed in the hallway bathroom. Together, she and Aaron remained on the couch as time passed, for how long, Lily lost track and no longer cared. She listened as he sniffled, which she coupled with sniffles of her own.

At last, they parted from each other's arms. Lily kneaded Aaron's forearm with her fingers in an absentminded display of affection.

She gazed into his face and hoped he would meet her eyes with his. Though Lily couldn't take a blowtorch and fuse together the wreckage in Aaron's life, perhaps he could see her sincerity.

"I don't know who they talked to," she said, compassion in her voice. "I never outed you, Aaron. I promise, I never told a soul."

She heard him swallow, the heavy kind that follows weeping.

Aaron sniffed once, wiped his eyes against his sleeve. "I know you didn't."

"Do you know who could have given away your secret?"

The way Aaron shrugged revealed his resignation to what had happened. It spoke of a defeated man who knew it was futile to continue in battle. "I didn't tell many people, but there are a couple of them out there besides you. A friend who lives downtown, a cousin in New Hampshire...people I thought I could trust. Obviously, I was stupid to trust one of them. Whoever wrote the article must have found out you and I were together a while back and dug through my past." He exhaled. "It doesn't matter now, does it?"

"I don't know what to say. I never would have guessed this could happen."

Aaron fingered Lily's palm. "I guess we *both* tried to live a lie, didn't we?" he said, an observation more than a question.

He jerked his head back against the couch cushion and closed his eyes. "How am I gonna go in to work tomorrow and face them?"

Lily didn't have an answer for him.

She reached over, took his hand in hers, and held it firm.

Another tear slid from her eye.

Who else would she end up hurting?

CHAPTER 56

THE NEXT DAY, early in the afternoon, Ryder seethed. He gave Lily's apartment door a firm rap with his knuckle. Brooke, who had wrapped up a client meeting and stopped by the apartment on her way back to the office, answered the door.

"Where's Lily, Brooke?" Ryder demanded.

Before she could hide her reaction, Ryder watched her eyes narrow, the fearful look of someone scurrying to calculate her reply.

"She's not here," Brooke said. "She's at work. She gets home around five-thirty."

"Where does she work?"

Brooke blinked, tugged at her earring. "Lily doesn't always spend the entire day at the office. She might be meeting with a client at—"

Ryder kicked the doorframe in frustration. He couldn't help but speak through clenched teeth. "I know the truth about her job! Just tell me where to find her!"

"It's on Patterson Boulevard," Brooke admitted with a sigh. "The place is called River City Auto, but—"

Ryder dashed toward his car before Brooke had a chance to finish her sentence.

"Ryder, wait!" Brooke shouted. "She didn't mean to hurt you!"

He heard Brooke call out to him but refused to turn around. He couldn't stomach whatever concoction she might try to feed him next.

He'd grown sick of hearing about his own life secondhand.

CHAPTER 57

LILY AND HER coworkers kept the garage doors closed. Although it was only September, a cold front had injected a chill into the autumn air. The first frost of the season had arrived around daybreak.

The last two days had proven rough for Aaron. On Monday morning, he had arrived to a mishmash of raised eyebrows and deflected glances, as though the other guys feared getting caught looking at him. Aaron chose not to force the issue, not that he had the willpower to do so. Instead, he had retreated into his own thoughts and said little, even to Lily.

It's like being high school all over again, Lily thought. *How stupid.*

That morning, after two hours of private chats and audible snickers among coworkers, Dave had finally walked up to Aaron and uttered a snide remark, to which Lily had stepped in with a curt reply involving Dave's nether regions and a high-powered microscope. With that encounter cut short, the overt drama had ended. Now the guys avoided Lily and Aaron altogether, saying no more than necessary to get their jobs done. No great loss, as far as Lily and Aaron were concerned.

So, for the rest of the day, Lily and Aaron had partnered on tasks whenever possible.

They exchanged looks of solidarity as she handed him a drill so he could conduct a tire rotation. Lily suspected their coworkers' discomfort would come to an end eventually. Given the tension that hung like humidity in the garage, though, it might take a few weeks.

Lily noticed commotion in her peripheral vision and glanced at the waiting-room window, where her manager, facing away from her, shifted from one foot to the other. Though she couldn't hear the exchange of words, her manager held up his hands and motioned downward as if to calm a customer whose face Lily couldn't see. All she could catch was the sight of the top of a man's head—until the customer darted around the counter, toward the door that led to the garage.

"Oh, no," Lily muttered at the sight of Ryder Flynn. She had intended to call him but, in the midst of Aaron's dilemma, it had slipped her mind. Then again, good intentions and lack of follow-through had become her modus operandi the last few months, hadn't it?

Aaron followed Lily's gaze to the door, which opened with a thud, its sound muted amid the cacophony of drills and engines. Wide-eyed, Aaron loosened his grip on the drill as his hand fell limp at his side.

The shop manager, red-faced at the sudden exertion of energy, followed Ryder through the door. "Sir, you can't walk in there!"

Lily stood speechless. Holding her hand out toward her manager, she nodded to let him know she would calm the situation. Fuming, her manager hesitated, shot her a look of warning, then shook his head and returned to the waiting room.

The abrupt lack of echoes unnerved her. Dead silence, so rare in this garage, seemed unnatural. Lily didn't need to look around to know every coworker's eyes were pinned to Ryder and her. She could perceive it in her chest. Even Aaron, who tried to feign examination of the drill bit, glanced up with a raised eyebrow that suggested he didn't know whether to intervene or not.

Ryder, too, noticed the activity had ceased around him. He had opened his mouth to utter something, but now he stopped short, glaring at the periphery, catching a glimpse of whoever stood in his vicinity. He must have reconsidered whatever he was about to say. Lily could see he hadn't considered the prospect of an audience.

She also saw hurt and displeasure—or, more accurately, a sense of betrayal—in his countenance.

Lily's heart sank. She heard a high-pitched ring in her ears.

She made her way toward him, took gentle hold of his arm, and tried to lead him toward the garage exit, but he slid his arm from her grasp.

"Can we talk outside, Ryder?" She kept her voice soft, but with the surrounding silence and the acoustics of the garage, her words came through as if she had shouted them. Lily swore a whisper would echo.

Sweeping the array of onlookers with his eyes, Ryder tensed his jaw and nodded. They headed toward a door at the corner of the garage and stepped out into the parking lot. No one except the two of them lingered outside. Lily stared at a pair of muddy tire tracks that had dried on the asphalt the prior day.

Crossing his arms, a confused expression on his face, Ryder shook his head. "How long did you plan to keep up the lie? Didn't you think I would discover the truth?"

How many times had she asked herself those simple questions? Lily regretted never having answered them.

She wanted to search Ryder's eyes for some semblance of forgiveness but couldn't face him, given how ashamed she felt. Instead, she focused on the muddy tire tracks. "You don't know how much I wanted to tell you the truth."

"For some reason, I find that hard to believe."

"I couldn't bring myself to admit it, Ryder."

"So you figured I should find out who you really are on the *public* stage instead? So we could all find out together that you'd lied to me the entire time?"

"Every word I told you was true except the job."

"And everything else that stemmed from it, right? 'The client isn't always right, but sometimes you need to let them think they are.' That was great marketing advice, Lily. I'd say *both* of us bought into your bullshit. Quite a deal, eh?"

Lily tensed but forced herself to maintain her composure. A blast of wind caused her to wish she had grabbed her jacket on the way out the door. The overcast sky looked dreary. If it were December, one would assume snowfall was imminent.

She gave the garage a flippant wave. "This isn't who I am. It's just a job."

"No, it's more than that," Ryder said, his hands slicing the space between them. "I could understand it for the first couple of weeks, when we barely knew each other. But after months together, you still didn't feel like you could be honest with me! You didn't even *care* whether I'd want to hear the truth!"

That wasn't true. Despite Lily's shortcoming, her fury spiked at Ryder's remark and she surrendered her poise. "Hey, I didn't ask for this! You brought this scenario into my life! *You* put me into your paintings without my permission! *You're* the one who gave me this...this...celebrity status or whatever it is!"

Ryder took a step back and rolled his eyes. "I can't believe I'm hearing this! You *laughed* when people recognized you in Hannibal. You got a kick out of it!"

"What else was I supposed to do? I didn't know how to respond!"

"So you're being honest with me *now?*"

"You created the version of me that you wanted to see, and I synced myself with it. I put forth an image, the same way *you* put forth an image!"

"Yeah, but I present an image for the public eye. I didn't put forth an image with *you!*" Ryder stopped shouting, but when Lily offered no response, he shook his head. "You know what? This was a mistake. Coming here was a mistake."

Ryder clicked his keychain remote control. His car lights flashed as its doors unlocked. He stormed toward it.

Puzzled, Lily demanded, "Ryder, where are you going?"

Ryder didn't bother to turn around when he waved her off. He climbed into his car and started the engine.

Perhaps out of instinct, Lily darted to her own car and hurried to start the engine. By the time she backed out of her spot and sped toward Ryder, he had already reached the edge of the parking lot. She caught a glimpse as he turned right. Lily's tires squealed upon the asphalt surface as she pealed out of the parking lot in pursuit.

CHAPTER 58

AS LILY SPED down the suburban street, she couldn't help but notice a businessman in the vehicle ahead of her, who gave his rearview mirror a double-take as she approached his tail and zoomed past him. Her calf muscle grew rigid as she floored the accelerator. Soon she caught sight of Ryder's car, in the far-right lane, as it approached the next intersection.

She could tell he was headed for I-270. That gave her a few suburban streets to catch him.

Maybe Lily should have felt sad at the loss of a romantic prospect, but at the moment, she burned with anger. Aaron's humiliation and the collapse of his world arose in her mind, the pain she had seen in her friend's eyes, and she gripped the steering wheel tighter. Ryder acted as if he were the only one who had gotten hurt in the process—the process *he* had set into motion.

Ryder signaled a right turn. Lily had about two hundred feet to get into his lane.

She swerved in front of the car in the next lane, which instigated a long blow of that driver's horn. Lily kept her eyes trained on Ryder's license plate as she made the right turn and heard her tires squeal in the process. She was now directly behind him on a street filled with vehicles and lined with retail stores. She watched the back of his head as he shook it, which angered her further. He had no intention of finishing their conversation.

One block ahead, the traffic light turned yellow. Ryder wouldn't make it through in time. Lily had an idea.

With a jerk of the wheel, she slid from behind him and veered into the left lane. More horns blared. Lily ignored them. Then she and Ryder met, side by side, at the next red light, where they waited for cars to depart the parking lot of an electronics store. From less than ten feet away, she could see how taut Ryder's jaw line had grown. When Ryder peered through the driver's-side window, she met his stare.

Lily saw knives in his eyes.

Join the club, she thought.

When the light turned green, Ryder took off. Lily remained in pursuit. She forced her foot flat, separated from the floorboard only by the accelerator pedal as she remained even with him. She had a plan.

Back and forth, one glance ahead followed by a glance toward Ryder, Lily inched her car toward the side of his. She didn't want their vehicles to collide.

Fortunately, she knew he didn't, either.

Praying she wouldn't pass a police officer during this temporary bout with insanity, she nudged her car, once again, a few inches closer to Ryder's. He glanced in her direction and took note of her proximity, in a clear struggle to keep his attention on her while maintaining sight of the road ahead.

This time, they were on Lily's turf. She knew the roads better than he did.

An expression took shape on Ryder's face—a fusion of panic and incredulity.

Another nudge to the right. Lily's tires crossed into his lane. Her Subaru swallowed the broken white lane markers, which now disappeared from her side mirror.

Lily navigated this street on a daily basis. She knew how much leeway remained at Ryder's right side. And he didn't have much. His tires were a few inches from the shoulder of the road, which would appear even closer from his perspective. She was sure its solid yellow line had disappeared from Ryder's mirror by now.

One quick prayer that Ryder would remain safe, then Lily sucked air and made a sudden shift to her right. Ryder jolted in panic, slammed on the brakes, veered onto the shoulder of the road, which was wide enough to accommodate a car and a body beside it. He shifted his car into park. Immediately, Lily cut into his lane, then joined him on the shoulder, where she threw her car into reverse. She backed up until her bumper sat inches from Ryder's fender, too close for him to pull forward. The steady flow of traffic continued beside them. Not enough time for Ryder to put his car into reverse and get back into the lane without giving Lily advance notice to follow suit.

She had him trapped.

CHAPTER 59

THEY CUT THEIR engines. Lily emerged first. As she marched toward Ryder's car, he climbed out and slammed the door, his eyes on fire.

Arms open, Ryder stormed toward her.

"What the hell are you doing!" he shouted. "You could've gotten us killed!"

"You came here to talk? Let's talk!"

"I have nothing left to say!"

"Well, I have news for you, Ryder: This isn't all about you, your career, your moral high ground!" she shouted. "You've been as selfish as I have!"

"Oh, now I get it," Ryder snorted. "This fight isn't over until our ordeal becomes *my* fault, is that it?"

"My life got completely upended because of your art! You splashed my face all over the United States and, for all I know, the whole world. I woke up one day and found someone had forced me onto a stage. And I'm not the only one whose life you changed with your…your fascination! Aaron's life will never be the same, except his got screwed up even worse. When you read that article, did you stop to consider what he's going through as a result?"

"I feel horrible about what happened to him! I hate that his life fell into the crosshairs of our circumstances. But the fact is, Lily, if you'd have been honest with me from the beginning, we could have taken steps to protect you!"

"*Protect* me? You mean, protect me from the reality that I'm not the woman you presented to the public? To protect me from their disapproval—or to protect you from embarrassment? So you could whisper it to the press? So they wouldn't shout from the rooftops that your muse is an auto mechanic?"

"You know that's not true!"

"Look, you *chose* to live your life in the public eye, but I didn't, and neither did Aaron—you made that choice for us!" Her hands jittered at her sides, but Lily didn't care. She balled them into fists and continued. "You forced me into your public spectacle. You never asked my permission. You could have kept it hidden in your studio and nothing would have happened between us. You could have had your career, smiled for the cameras, and lived your dream life. *I* could have shown up at work each day and lived my life. I wasn't the happiest person on earth, but at least I wasn't confused about how to live day to day."

A pause emerged in their argument. As the tension between them subsided, both individuals started to calm.

Ryder adopted a tone of concession. "Lily, why didn't you tell me the truth? Did I do something wrong?" Lily recognized the earnestness in his eyes. "Why didn't you believe you could come to me?"

Lily unfurled her fists. Her heart surrendered.

"That would've made a great painting, huh?" she muttered. "A woman in a garage rolling a tire across a concrete floor. Not exactly a turn-on, is it?" A wave of emotional exhaustion rippled through her bones. The struggle weighed on her shoulders, but she determined to press on.

"I was content," she continued, then closed her eyes. "Actually, that's not true. I wasn't content, but I didn't *know* I wasn't. I didn't *know* how unhappy I was with my life until I saw those images of myself everywhere and looked into my own eyes—literally. That's when discontentment settled in, because your paintings inspired me. They made me believe I didn't need to settle for less, that even a girl like me could find someone who loved her as much as she wanted to be loved. The same measure of love she dreamed of giving to someone else.

"When we first met, you were so caught up in the way you envisioned me, I didn't have the heart to disappoint you. But once we got involved, I couldn't bring myself to tell you. I tried, I promise I did, but I couldn't go through with it. This auto mechanic thing—I know it's just a job to you, but to me, it represented the opposite of what I thought had brought me to you. You captured my heart, Ryder. For the first time in my life, I knew how it felt to be cherished by someone, and I was scared to death of losing it. I was frightened because, after a lifetime of waiting, the one person I could love—and who loved me back—was the one person who *didn't* know me. And I couldn't blame you, because not even I wanted to accept the truth: I *liked* the way you saw me. I *liked* being beautiful for a change. For once in my life, I wanted to know what it was like to be *that* woman. As long as I was that woman, I knew I was loved."

Ryder sighed under his breath. His shoulders sagged. "Don't you understand? I didn't care about that side of you. I didn't care how you dressed or where you worked. That image I created of you gave me something to grasp. Something to keep you as a part of my life. It represented the beauty I sensed *inside* you." With a shrug, he added in a dismissive tone, "Not that I know who you are."

"Please don't say that, Ryder. You *do* know me." Lily fought to hold back tears. She couldn't break down now.

"Do I?"

"You know my heart," she replied. "No matter where we went, or what we did, or what we talked about, I gave you my whole heart. I loved you." She paused, searched his eyes. "And I know you loved me too."

Ryder ran a hand through his hair. His eyebrows furrowed. He blew out a heavy breath.

"I wish I'd never done such a stupid thing," Lily continued. "Yes, the image was a concoction. But my heart—that was genuine, Ryder. By the time I knew you loved me back, I wasn't scared of losing a romance. I was scared I'd lose your heart. I was scared you'd doubt mine. But I didn't have the guts to admit it to myself because I detested that fear." Lily wrapped her arms across her chest, almost embraced herself. At the moment, she wished someone would. Her eyes fell to her black, steel-toed shoes. "And I was scared you would think of me the way I think of myself right now."

Ryder winced. Lily could tell he didn't know what to think, not that she could blame him. She had betrayed his trust for months and had managed to buy into the fantasy that if she ignored it long enough, this day of reckoning would never come.

Ryder wiped a tear from the corner of his eye, pressed his lips together. Lily thought she saw him lean toward her ever so slightly, as though he wanted to say something but couldn't find the words. Or didn't trust her enough to express them.

Another chilly gust of wind caused Lily's pores to tingle. Ryder started to shiver and slid his hands into his pockets.

"But where does it stop, Lily? How do I know what I see right now is real? I mean, think about it: Even while we were sleeping together, you knew you were keeping a secret from me. What do you expect me to do? You knew I wasn't interested in a one-night stand. You knew I was looking for deeper commitment. And on those nights, you knew I was making love to a stranger. I had no idea, but *you* knew. And you didn't think I had a right to know because you were scared I'd *abandon* you?"

Ryder kneaded his brow with his thumb and forefinger. "Look, Lily, the trust factor is significant to me. You might be willing to bend and mold yourself, change colors like a chameleon, but I'm not. Not in a relationship. That doesn't represent trust to me. And I'm at a point in my life where I don't want another relationship that's doomed from the beginning."

"So you're looking for perfection?"

"Not perfection."

Part of Lily ached, yet another part felt bitter. She nudged her chin a bit higher.

"You'd prefer to believe the fairy-tale version of love," she said.

"Call it what you want." Ryder pursed his lips. "But I'd say that makes two of us."

At that point, Lily knew she had lost him.

All this time, she'd wanted a man to look beneath the surface and discover who she was on the inside. Yet, when given the opportunity to let someone in, she had caved. Ryder was right: She hadn't withheld her job description. She had withheld her trust.

And now it had cost her everything.

Lily glanced at the passing traffic. How fitting that the breakdown of their relationship had occurred in full public view. After all, hadn't most of their relationship unfolded that way since day one? Or, for that matter, since before they ever met?

For Lily, the next minute dragged along, awkward with the ensuing silence. Whether she was angry at Ryder or herself, she had no idea. She knew she couldn't change his mind here. Yet, the fearful side of her found strength, however little, in having the last word.

She walked over to her car, opened the door, and grabbed a car magazine. Then she ambled back toward Ryder.

"Here." She tossed him the magazine, which he caught in his hands. "Something to remember me by. The *real* me."

Tongue in cheek? Maybe. But it was pure Lily.

With that, she climbed into her car and started the engine.

His face knit with concentration, Ryder examined the glossy magazine cover, which featured a photo of the newest sports car out of Italy. In the bottom-left corner, he found a white rectangle with the familiar address of Lily's apartment printed on it. She was a subscriber.

By the time Lily glanced at her rearview mirror and saw Ryder look up from the magazine, she was already at the next intersection.

CHAPTER 60

ALONE IN HIS studio, Ryder shivered in his University of Missouri sweatshirt. December had arrived, and the stone wall made the room feel colder when winter drew nigh. He didn't have music playing. Today's soundtrack consisted of the hum of a space heater to his left and the patter of bristles as he dabbed at the canvas with a small paintbrush. He had already painted the subjects and now added the finishing touches to the background.

He took a long look at the image and chuckled. This painting would end up on another movie poster, a comedy about two strangers who get stuck together in an elevator at a department store. In the film, the young woman turns out to be a United States Senator's niece who has a fetish for danger. She convinces the protagonist, a man old enough to be her grandfather, to join her on a trip to Vegas, where they outsmart the odds at casino after casino. Their luck attracts unexpected attention from a crime syndicate. And, of course, they fall in love along the way. Blah, blah, blah.

When he'd first heard the film's premise, it had made him grin. He'd taken the job due to the natural response it had elicited. Now, however, the project struck him as flat and clichéd.

In the solitude of his studio, Ryder layered the canvas with more sad, uninspired strokes before he stopped and stared at his creation, a depiction in which the lead actor and actress exchanged looks. The actress, who pursed her lips in an expression somewhere between clever and coy, held playing cards, four aces fanned in her hand. Her other hand rested on her hip, which she angled in the direction of the actor, who grimaced at her like a dimwitted schmuck. He dangled a handgun between his forefinger and thumb, holding it as far away from the actress and himself as possible. He extended his other hand in a gesture that said, *What the hell am I supposed to do with this?* Behind the couple stood a Mafia-looking bouncer, a bulky man with a fat cigar clenched between yellowed teeth.

How ridiculous.

Ryder snorted at this pathetic excuse for art. Then again, he had agreed to an impressive paycheck to capture the humor at play.

He tossed the paintbrush on the desk behind him and laid his palette beside it. He padded into the bathroom to wash his hands, and to the hallway closet to fetch his winter coat. Then back to his studio, where he donned a pair of sneakers he kept beside the patio door. Sliding open the glass door, Ryder crept outside and into his frosty wonderland.

The tang of smoke greeted him. A fire in the fireplace sounded nice tonight.

Zipping his coat, Ryder walked to the edge of the lake. Although cold outside, the temperature lingered around 40 degrees, so nothing was frozen. He listened as the water collided against the shoreline in lazy, eerie laps, their sound a hollow treble. At four-thirty on a winter afternoon, dusk arrived quickly.

A gust of wind, cooled further as it swept over the lake, rushed forth from the west and stung Ryder's chapped cheeks. In the remaining daylight, he peered down at his hands, which, after a few minutes in the cold, had faded to a pallid hue.

Ryder scanned the shoreline, tracing its edge as it bent around his cove and stretched into the distance. Multicolored Christmas lights twinkled from the deck of one home, their glow a welcome contrast to the ashen sky. Half the houses lacked Christmas decorations. Their windows possessed the blackness of vacancy.

Osage Beach had fallen dead with the onset of winter. It happened every year.

For many homeowners in the area, their lake house served as a weekend getaway during warmer months. Ryder had met more local homeowners who lived year-round in St. Louis than he could count. Others owned these homes as an investment and rented them to vacationers. Osage Beach teemed with tourists during the summer. In fact, in recent years, Highway 54 had undergone a major expansion to accommodate the influx of traffic. But once Thanksgiving passed, activity ceased and the streets grew as lifeless as a frozen lawn in January. The nearby outlet mall emptied. By Christmas, the disappearance of humanity was so stark, it brought to mind an image of gradual blood loss that had finally come to an end. On occasion, at this time of year, he actually ran into his neighbors at Panera Bread.

The recurring tranquility was one reason he had purchased a home in the area. Granted, he had also sought inspiration that the surroundings and human activity brought during spring, summer and autumn. But he'd figured the wintertime lull would provide a constructive balance, where fewer distractions would allow him to bury himself in a heavier season of work. He'd expected the stillness to help him focus on his projects.

And it had—until this year.

Until he'd met Lily.

That is, until he'd met her the *second* time.

The real Lily.

CHAPTER 61

FROM HIS PERCH inside a restaurant in Los Angeles, Ryder took in the expansive view of the city below and imagined it after sunset, awash in city lights. A Japanese garden sat one story below. Given the size of the property, Ryder wondered which was more breathtaking: the skyline or the restaurant's property taxes.

The restaurant, Asian-themed with a dash of Hollywood chic, required a reservation, which proved hard to come by unless requested by celebrities or power brokers. Crowded at lunchtime, patrons sat at round tables topped with scarlet tablecloths. The walls were scarlet as well, accented with gold-colored etchings of Japanese calligraphy.

Five years ago, the maitre d' would have turned away Ryder's reservation request. Even today, he had to admit, the reason he received this sought-after table was because word had roared through the grapevine that he and his Mona Lisa had parted ways, making him an even hotter property.

And because he mentioned he would arrive with Kathryn Rae.

Ryder had no clue how phone numbers worked their way from agent to agent, manager to manager, until they made a connection. But in typical form, Kathryn had gotten hold of Ryder's number and invited him to grab lunch. Ryder wondered if the thirty-something actress, an odds-on favorite for an Academy Award nomination in a few weeks, sought to keep gossipers buzzing while Hollywood shut down major production for the holidays.

Her call had come at a perfect time. Christmas was still several days away, so Ryder decided to enjoy a few days of vacation. Why not inject a change of scenery and some Southern California warmth into his life?

From time to time, when Ryder poked his fork into his entree, he thought he caught a glimpse of Kathryn's eyes darting to nearby tables. Ryder still found it silly that anyone would make it a point to be seen with him. Nonetheless, he didn't mind meeting new people, and he made plenty of connections this way.

"I saw your movie last month," he said, "the one everyone's speculating about for the Oscars."

"You did?" Kathryn's blond curls jiggled whenever she shifted in her seat. She leaned forward and studied him through eyes the color of azure. That penetrating stare was her trademark characteristic. "All this award talk has taken me aback."

To Ryder's surprise, pale freckles speckled the actress's cheeks. He'd never noticed them on the screen.

The things makeup could hide.

"You mean you didn't expect it?" he asked. "When you filmed it, didn't you think to yourself, 'Something special is happening here, I can sense it'?"

"To be honest, all I did was put the best of myself into it. I never dreamed critics would consider it a success. Once the speculation started, I had to hear it for a week before I could believe it," she admitted. "I did see something special in the script, though."

"What made it special? The plot?"

She nodded. "The plot, my character, the way the writer crafted the dialogue. All of it swept me into the project." She took a bite of her sushi roll. "Do you react that way when you paint? How do you come up with ideas? When you're not fulfilling a specific request, that is."

Ryder thought for a moment. "Oftentimes, I'll revisit a place in my mind, a place where a piece of my heart lingers."

"Anyplace I'd know?"

With a halfhearted sweep of his fork, he brushed away the explanation and decided to keep his answer vague. "I tend to head overseas in my mind."

"A world traveler, hmm?" Kathryn teased.

Ryder responded with a chuckle. "You could say that. I don't always sell those paintings, though. Many remain in my studio and the other rooms of my house."

With a tilt of her head, Kathryn leaned forward on her forearm, waved her fork in a little spiral, and cast him a let-me-tell-you look. "Well, I hope your mind travels somewhere more exotic than Poland. That's where I'm headed for my next shoot. A period piece," she said, then added, "Warsaw in February. I can only imagine." A roll of her eyes in amusement, then another bite of sushi. "With any luck, if this nomination pans out, I'll jet back to L.A. for the ceremony. Escape the set for a few days."

Ryder found Kathryn delightful and clever. She made him laugh. Kathryn Rae possessed the type of self-assured energy he'd expect to find in a cougar divorcee.

Yet he missed Lily. For a moment, he thought back to Lily's endearing vulnerability. He fought back a smile at the memory of her sense of humor: genuine, yet as unrefined as a slap in the face. The dichotomy had amused him. Back when they were together.

An ache arose in the pit of his belly, the sensation he felt after eating acidic food, yet he welcomed the bittersweet twinge. Ryder regretted the terms by which he and Lily had ended their relationship. Should he call her? No, that wouldn't be good. Three months had passed since they last spoke, and he was certain he had burned that bridge. After all, he had walked out on her. In hindsight, he wondered if he had overreacted.

As if on cue, Kathryn said, "I haven't heard many stories about your Mona Lisa lately. I heard the two of you parted ways."

"Afraid so." He felt awkward talking about his personal life. Then again, Kathryn Rae thrived in the spotlight. She must have considered it a given to have your relationships splashed across websites and television screens. He had read about her love life, including her much-touted breakup with the drummer of a rap-metal band. Ryder added, "We came to a mutual understanding."

Kathryn squinted, once again piercing his eyes with hers. She didn't even blink. "Is it true you met her for the first time at a hotel years ago?"

"Do you believe everything you read?"

"I hope what I read about *that* was true. It's made for film. Are you looking to expand your career?" she asked with a wink. "Your first leading role. You could play yourself."

"More public scrutiny of my personal life? I'm not sure I've handled the existing exposure too well."

"Trust me, we've all been there."

The matter-of-fact tone of her voice hinted at a past wound, but she recovered in seconds. Ryder dug his fork into his Pad Thai—more like Pad Thai with a West Coast influence. He detected a seasoning not normally used in Asian food. Mexican, perhaps, or something you would find in a Southwest bistro. He appreciated the creative ways a chef could unlock variations on traditional dishes, but today, the change made him miss home. When had he last cooked Pad Thai? Was it the night he'd prepared it for Lily?

"I can't fathom the passion that must have driven you," Kathryn said as she tilted her head.

Her remark broke his train of thought. Ryder swallowed a shrimp and a slice of scallion. "The passion?"

"For *her.* Mona Lisa. What's her real name?"

"Lily."

"To have that passion rumbling deep inside you. I mean, I approach my roles with full force. To get where I am today, I refused to take no for an answer. But I can't imagine having that kind of passion for a person you'd never met."

"Lack of passion? In you? I find that hard to believe," Ryder said. "I've read about your relationships. The paparazzi documented the details rather well."

"Sure, I've had relationships. Picture perfect ones, dangerous ones—I've tried them all. Cameras would find us on vacation at a private island in the Caribbean, or follow the rock star and me when I'd join him on his tour bus. To anybody who believes life is perfect, I'm sure they saw matches made in heaven. But it never turned out genuine for me. I've never crossed paths with *the one,* my destiny. But you—" Kathryn pointed at him with her pinky as she took a sip of her sake. "When I looked at paintings of you and that Lily woman, it was like each of you had found your soul mate. Anybody who paid attention could sense electricity between you two."

Ryder laid down his fork. "I've never understood people's fascination with it. Those paintings—the first handful of Lily and me, at least—weren't intended to draw attention from anyone. I tried the two of us in an advertisement and it worked, so I tried it again. But my original reason for painting us was to keep a memory alive, nothing more."

"But that's why people responded to it. They sensed it was real. You weren't a celebrity story that ends with a tabloid divorce where you fight over who gets the Chihuahua. It had simplicity to it, the kind that makes people want whatever you have."

Ryder picked up his fork and poked at the noodles on his plate. "Yeah, well, it did end in a fight. The tabloids weren't around to cover *that.* Their coverage stopped when Lily and I parted ways. I guess they lost interest once they tracked down her identity," he said. "But the passion I felt is a rarity. You're right about that."

"I can understand having that zeal in a general way, though. That drive. That's what kept me hanging on to my career by my fingernails all these years," Kathryn said. "I refused to let them tell me no, even after I hit my thirtieth birthday and my choice of roles began to dry up. You can say no to a lot of things, but you can't say no to your heart. Talk about misery." She stopped short of taking a final bite of her sushi and added, "But in the end, if you hang on to what drives you, sometimes they give you a little golden man on a statue."

Ryder's mind wandered back to July as the sweet tang of his entrée melted in his mouth.

"Yeah," he said, deep in thought. "Maybe so."

CHAPTER 62

MICKEY ROONEY HOLLERED in protest over the loud music.

Six months ago, Lily had expected to kiss Ryder tonight at the stroke of midnight. As it turned out, neither she nor Aaron had found themselves in the mood to go out and celebrate on New Year's Eve. They had holed up in Aaron's apartment instead. Several years ago, when they discovered they shared a penchant for old movies, they invented their own classic-movie marathons on Friday nights when neither had plans. And those marathons were more frequent than Lily or Aaron cared to admit.

"Didn't they lock their windows back then?" Aaron said, waving a forefinger at the television screen as Audrey Hepburn climbed through her apartment window to the fire escape. "I know it was the Sixties, but we're talking New York City."

"Maybe they didn't have a high crime rate where they lived. That rich woman furnished the guy's apartment, right? So maybe it was a nicer part of town. Safer."

They had started the night watching *Dark Victory*. Lily marveled at the mysterious air that engulfed Bette Davis no matter which role she performed. When that film ended, they had popped in *The Philadelphia Story*. The girl who played Katharine Hepburn's tomboyish little sister always struck Lily as someone with whom she would have gotten along well as a child.

Now, in *Breakfast at Tiffany's,* Audrey Hepburn sneaked into George Peppard's apartment to avoid some drunken guy with the voice of a cartoon character. A few minutes later, George awoke Audrey from the bad dream about her brother. When he asked if she was all right, Audrey told George not to snoop in her business. Although Lily could watch this film over and over, she had to admit she found Audrey's reaction humorous.

"She wants him to mind his own business?" Lily remarked. "She just climbed into his apartment and under his sheets!"

"Yeah, really," Aaron snickered, then mimicked, "'Don't worry, Stranger. I'm gonna invade your bed, but don't inquire about my emotional state. Nothing to see here; move along.'"

Talk about a character on a tragic search for her identity, though. Was that how Lily appeared to Ryder?

Lily stuffed a kernel of popcorn into Aaron's mouth. For a dateless New Year's Eve, she and Aaron had kept each other in good humor. She grabbed their champagne glasses from the coffee table and handed Aaron's to him.

"To being grateful this year is finally over with," Lily offered.

"Good riddance to bad endings." And with a clink of their glasses, they sealed their toast.

Aaron eyed her a moment as he sipped his champagne. His curiosity couldn't have been more obvious.

"Have you heard from him since you broke up?" he asked.

"No call. No text message." Lily swallowed. The bubbles teased her throat on their way down. "He was steamed at me. I'm sure he's moved on by now."

"You could try calling him."

"I wouldn't want the national spotlight on me again."

"Too bad. You two made a cute couple."

"*You and I* make a cuter couple anyway. That's why I'd rather spend New Year's Eve with you." Lily sipped her champagne and returned it to the coffee table. This was their third glass, and the alcohol had sent a pleasant wooziness swirling around her brain. "I guess we're what people call 'friends with benefits.'"

Aaron winked at her. "Maybe, but I won't try to get you into bed till we've *both* had too much to drink."

She volleyed his remark with a grin, then recalled what Aaron had endured the last few months.

She took hold of his hand and stared at the intricate lines along his palm. She gazed back into his face. "I'm sorry your secret got let out. It never would have happened if it wasn't for me."

Aaron considered her words, then responded with a shrug that said he had resolved to move forward in life. "It was bound to come up sooner or later. At least the guys at the shop have come around." He offered a devilish smirk. "And understandably so. Look at me. What's not to love, right?"

Lily rubbed her thumb against the heel of his palm. Then she caught his eye and, with all the sincerity she could muster, said, "You're a wonderful guy."

Aaron nodded. Lily caught a slight quiver in Aaron's lower lip before he pressed his lips together.

"Thank you," he said, then admitted, "I needed to hear that tonight."

Lily's warmed within.

Genuine. That was how life was supposed to be. Just like tonight.

"You still miss him, though," Aaron observed.

"Who, Ryder?" Lily said. When Aaron nodded, she replied, "You always see through me."

"You're forgetting I was in his shoes at one point, when you and I were together. I know you better than you know yourself."

"I doubt that." She gave him a playful jab.

Aaron rested his elbow on the back of the sofa, leaned his head against his hand. "Beyond the fantasy, beyond the hurdles, did you see a future with him?"

Lily pondered Aaron's question but knew she didn't need to. "Yes, I did. Through the entire charade, while I'd fooled myself into believing I could become someone else, I loved him." She examined her fingernails, which fallen victim to a manicure when Brooke had dragged her to a salon earlier that week.

"Deep down in my heart," Lily continued, "I believed that, one day, I would come clean with him. It would have been inevitable, but I would've chosen to be honest with him. And I knew he would have accepted me for who I was, but nevertheless, I…held back. Maybe the prospect of being in love seemed too good to be true, too unlikely for me, so I bought into a fantasy where it could exist on *my* terms."

Lily reached for her champagne glass and took another sip. The drink had warmed to room temperature.

"But that doesn't matter anymore, does it?" she conceded. "Ryder's gone."

CHAPTER 63

RYDER HADN'T PAINTED Lily or himself since the day they parted ways.

Ever since their breakup, he had buried himself in a barrage of job requests, from film to sports, from health to live events. He had painted an array of landscapes, products and people, none of which included Ryder Flynn or his famous Mona Lisa.

Now, by mid-January, he found himself deprived of sleep. Ryder didn't know how long he could continue this way, but the torrent of work had lured his thoughts from Lily Machara, and that was what mattered.

His anger toward her had faded. Granted, the hurt and disappointment, the awareness that Lily felt she couldn't trust him, continued to linger. But he determined to smother those feelings. Leave the emotional ash heap behind. Let it scatter in the wind.

Or try to, at least. So far, he'd fallen short.

He couldn't forget her all those years ago.

He couldn't forget her today, either.

Ryder had considered calling her again, but she had made clear she wanted no part of his limelight. Not after she and her friend had gotten hurt. Lily was right; she hadn't sought the public stage. Whatever humiliation she had faced, however, he doubted the media could subject her to it a second time. They had gotten their splashy headlines. They had uncovered her identity. What more damage could they do?

But would Lily believe that?

Perhaps the admission that *he* had caused her humiliation hurt the most.

No, she wouldn't return. Not unless he could win her heart again, on her terms. Ridding himself of the spotlight and rebuilding his career without the free publicity could take years. Would she wait that long for him? Ryder doubted it, so he nixed that option. If Lily would enter his life again, it must happen by her choice, knowing the public might hear about it.

The painting before him depicted a floating market in Thailand. Twenty narrow boats had clustered together. The water appeared greenish-brown in color. In each boat sat its owner, surrounded by piles of vegetables, a wide-brimmed hat on his head to block the hot sun. The food colors added vibrancy to a scene dominated by shades of brown and gray. Some owners had opened umbrellas and propped them up in their boats. Crowds of people sauntered along the dock, interacting with the sea-based proprietors. Ryder could smell the fresh produce.

A busy scene. Yet, to him, a peaceful one.

A tap on glass followed by a sliding of the door. Ryder knew Chase's knock and didn't look up.

"It never got above freezing today," Chase said as he wandered to the canvas and stood behind his friend. Chase cupped his hands, blowing warm breath into them as he studied the painting. "Thailand again?"

"I felt like painting anonymity today. No famous people, no products to promote. Just life."

Chase unzipped his peacoat. "I know you, buddy. You only do Thailand when you want to vacate."

When Ryder responded with a nod of nonchalance, Chase turned his attention to Ryder's desk. From the corner of Ryder's eye, he watched Chase pick up the car magazine Lily had tossed at him the day they had broken up. Ryder forgot he'd left it there. Earlier that day, Ryder had paged through it in an attempt to connect with her in some way, however abstract. He cringed in anticipation of the pointed comment that would follow from his business manager. Chase would know who had given him the magazine since Lily's address appeared at its lower corner.

True to form, Chase waved the magazine at him. "Souvenir?"

"I don't want to talk about it, Chase."

"Come on, man. You've gotta get past Lily," his business partner responded with a sigh. "Things didn't work out. It happens."

Ryder paused and lifted the brush from the canvas, turned toward his friend. "I keep racking my brain, trying to figure out how I could have handled it differently."

Chase placed a hand on each of Ryder's shoulders and looked him in the eye. "Look, man, you didn't do anything wrong. You two come from different worlds, that's all. You're used to the pressure. Obviously, she didn't feel like she could cope with it." He gave Ryder's shoulders a quick jostle, then dropped his hands. "She didn't know what she was getting into. That's what I tried to tell you in the first place."

Ryder mixed a lighter shade of brown on his palette, dabbed his brush in it, and continued working.

Chase paced toward the other side of the studio and fingered the edge of a picture frame. "I had a hunch she wouldn't be able to keep up with your life, and I was right. She retreated into that false persona of hers. I tried to make the relationship work to your advantage, but I didn't know she'd created some *image* for herself. And I certainly didn't know about her friend."

Ryder stopped painting. An army of goose bumps marched up his arms. Hesitant to look at Chase, he kept his eyes glued to one of the boats on the water.

"What do you mean, you tried to make the relationship work to my advantage?"

When Ryder raised his eyes from the canvas, Chase pursed his lips. For a split second, Ryder thought he saw the corner of Chase's mouth twitch. His business partner appeared as stunned by the question as Ryder felt by the remark that had triggered it.

Chase released a heavy sigh that gave Ryder the creeps.

"Okay, here's the deal," Chase replied. "You were already a hot property, but all this Mona Lisa speculation fanned the flame. The public couldn't get enough of it, and it brought you projects right and left. High profile stuff. That kind of publicity is too expensive to buy." Though he looked Ryder in the eye here and there, Ryder sensed that Chase had to muster courage to do so. "All I did was stoke the fire to get more life out of it."

That didn't clarify anything for him. Ryder shook his head, shut his eyes for a moment, and tried to sift through what Chase had told him. He couldn't shake the sense that his friend had tried to dodge the question.

"So what are you saying, Chase?"

Chase shoved his hands in his pockets and sighed. "Look, Ryder, don't be pissed. I mentioned to a reporter that your Mona Lisa lives in St. Louis—"

"You what!"

"Hey, that's all I said! All I did was give her something to nibble on. I didn't tell her anything else. I didn't *know* anything else about her, did I?" Chase's eyes narrowed, the look of someone determined to stand his ground. "And neither did *you*, by the way!"

"You told the reporter where Lily lives?"

"It's public record, no big deal."

Ryder fumed. He felt his blood pressure rise as he glared at Chase. "But you knew that reporter would start to dig once you gave her the tip! You knew they'd delve into Lily's personal life from there!"

"Hey, I was doing you a favor. The public loved you *and* her. Adding fuel kept people talking about you. It kept those top-tier projects coming."

"So what am I supposed to do? *Thank* you? Lily's life got screwed! She never wants to speak to me again. The one good relationship in my life is gone!"

"Get real, Ryder. It wasn't a relationship. It was a mirage!"

Ryder swore his blood simmered. It took all the self-restraint he could muster to avoid lunging at his friend.

Ryder gritted his teeth and forced himself to calm down. Emotional silt settled into his gut. Whether it was due to his friend's betrayal or losing Lily, Ryder didn't know. At the moment, he had to fight just to think straight.

"Get out," Ryder muttered.

"Oh, come on, man."

Ryder threw his paintbrush on the ground. Paint droplets splattered upon the drop cloth that covered the floor. His pulse spiked.

"Get the hell out of my house!"

He shoved Chase. Chase, unprepared for Ryder's physical eruption, stumbled backwards but regained his balance.

"Ryder, you need to gain some perspective—"

Whatever Chase wanted to say, Ryder had no desire to hear it. Over and over, he shoved Chase backward, toward the opposite side of the studio. Chase sputtered, attempted to justify the actions he'd taken, but Ryder grabbed his friend's shirt by one of the buttons and dragged him with fresh force.

When they reached the glass door, Ryder released his grip. The two men glared at each other in silence, daring each other to speak. At last, Ryder reached behind Chase and pulled open the door.

"Just get the hell out," Ryder murmured.

Chase engaged Ryder in one more icy stare.

Didn't Chase understand the damage he'd caused? How could he have the gall to peg Ryder's reaction as ingratitude?

Finally, Chase snorted in disbelief. He thrust his hands into his coat pockets. Without another word, he turned and walked out the door, shaking his head on the way out.

Ryder kept his eyes glued on Chase as the guy walked along the rear of the house and rounded the corner. The final evidence of Chase's presence was a puff of breath which lingered behind, then dissipated in the dark, frigid night.

Ryder slammed the glass door shut and locked it. Still furious, he stormed back to his canvas, grabbed a clean paintbrush, and flung it across the room.

CHAPTER 64

BY EARLY FEBRUARY, Lily had almost convinced herself that she was as content with her daily, mundane routine as she had felt before Ryder Flynn appeared in her life. She seldom wore a dress. The absence of makeup alone had simplified her life.

She punched some data into the computer behind the counter in the auto shop's waiting room, then slid the paperwork and car key into a vinyl project pouch. Lily didn't realize how focused she'd become upon the data until a customer approached the other side of the counter and spoke up.

"So you *are* still alive and well!"

A familiar male voice.

Lily looked up and discovered Evan standing before her, grinning. So absorbed had she become in Ryder once the artist entered her life, she had failed to keep in touch with Evan. She had to admit, however, that despite her nervous reflex at Evan's reappearance, relief coursed through her veins, cool as saline, at his presence. The dose of familiarity was a welcome surprise. She searched for a remark to carry her into what she expected to be an awkward conversation with the man to whom she had once grown attracted. While she wound up speechless, she couldn't help but smile at his comment.

"I know this sounds ridiculous," Evan continued, "but I really did wonder how you've been. I hadn't heard from you for a few months, and—"

"Oh…Evan, I'm sorry I didn't stay in touch."

When he nodded, Lily found that familiar, clever sincerity in his eyes. "I was hoping for a problem with my car so I'd have an excuse to stop by the shop. Unfortunately, you must be great at what you do here, because *that* didn't happen."

Lily giggled. She searched his eyes for reassurance that he didn't hold her lack of communication against her.

Those tender eyes.

"Then I thought about opening the hood and loosening a screw somewhere," Evan added, "enough so I could get here with my car rattling, but not enough to get myself killed along the way."

Lily giggled again.

"You laugh," Evan said, "but I did retrieve the owner's manual to find where they installed the latch to pop the hood." He added with a wink, "It's by the driver's left foot, by the way."

"Thanks, I'm aware of that," she played along. This was Evan, so it was possible he *hadn't* known where the latch was, but she doubted he knew *that* little about his own car. "It's good to see you."

Lily opened her mouth to say something else but couldn't. Maybe her heart hadn't healed from Ryder to the extent she had hoped. But she found such comfort in Evan, her eyes began to gloss over with tears.

If the sight caught Evan by surprise, he gave no indication. He reached out to dry her eyes but must have considered the gesture presumptuous. After reaching halfway, he withdrew his hand, yet Lily found comfort in his intention.

When she said nothing else, concern overtook Evan's face. "Did I say something wrong?"

"No, you're fine. I…I've had some shit going on lately, that's all." Lily pushed her coverall sleeve to her elbow and dabbed her eyes with her clean arm. She noticed Evan's eye landed upon a lone freckle on her arm, one Lily had always found cute, before he returned his gaze to her face. She took a deep breath.

Lily caught sight of a subtle grin as it turned at the corner of his mouth. Evan shot her a knowing gaze.

"You look like you could use a nice dinner," he said.

She chuckled again, more to herself than for his benefit. But once his consideration sunk in, Lily offered him a smile. "Dinner would be nice."

Evan blinked once. And with that single, easygoing gesture, he communicated her value as an individual, an affirmation Lily had desired since her romantic life had collapsed beneath her feet.

CHAPTER 65

THAT EVENING, EVAN took Lily to the same Mediterranean-themed restaurant to which he'd introduced her on their first date. To Lily, that first date seemed like years ago.

She could tell she had grown more confident as a result of her relationship with Ryder, in spite of its heartbreak of an ending. Tonight, unlike her original visit to this swanky restaurant, she felt comfortable. She had gotten used to such places—or envisioning herself in them—while moonlighting as the Mona Lisa.

And Lily's palette expanded in tandem with her confidence. At Evan's urging, she decided to try the roasted lamb. At first, she thought it tasted like burnt hair, but after the first few bites, it grew on her.

"I have to admit," Evan said, "I didn't know which reaction to expect when I showed up at the shop. When I stopped hearing back from you, I figured you might have moved on." Evan winced, a reflex Lily could tell was genuine. "I'm sorry, I hadn't meant to bring that up."

Had he called her? Lily replayed the chain of events from months ago…and realized she had, indeed, forgotten to respond to a couple of his calls. Now she felt horrible as she recalled her misstep. Once she met Ryder, she got so caught up in the momentum of their relationship as it burst into full bloom. Between her job, the frequent phone conversations with Ryder, and the weekend visits, Lily's life had grown so busy that Evan's phone messages fell through the cracks. That was the honest truth, but no matter how she phrased an explanation, it would sound to Evan like an excuse.

"It's my fault," Lily said at last. "I feel awful about not responding. You didn't do anything wrong, I promise. Things got hectic in my life, and I—"

Evan smiled and tapped her finger with his. "No need to explain. What I said slipped out by accident. Besides, I should have tried harder to keep in touch."

Evan took a bite of asparagus and Lily returned to her lamb. When their eyes met again, she discovered Evan taking in her appearance, grinning. He studied her not in a creepy way, but with an air of kindness that touched Lily's heart. He appeared to enjoy the simplicity of her presence.

She couldn't quench her curiosity any longer. "What?"

Evan must have gotten lost in his thoughts before realizing he'd begun to stare. He blushed but maintained his poise. "You look like you're enjoying yourself more tonight than you did the last time we came here."

Lily ran her fork along a slice of lamb. "I've been around the block a few more times since then. Gotten a little more exposure." She took a bite, chewed and swallowed, then added, "And if people look at me like I don't fit in—well, that's minor compared to my recent forays into public opinion."

Evan hesitated for a beat. "Yes, I've read about that." He sipped his wine. "I saw you in a few more advertisements since then, too."

Lily stabbed at a sliced potato but didn't lift it from her plate. Instead, she twirled her fork as she gathered her thoughts, then relented.

This wasn't fair to Evan.

She met his eyes with hers.

"I can't fool you either," she observed.

Evan's inviting gaze returned as realization arose in his countenance. He responded with a smile, the halfhearted kind that accompanies a disappointed soul.

"Lily, you're too honest at heart to fool anyone." Evan peered down at the table as though to gather his thoughts. He fingered a metallic accent along the edge of his plate, then met her eyes again. "You gave me a second shot, though. That's all I could ask for."

Lily swept her eyes over the man who sat across from her. For the first time, despite his attempt to appear self-confident, she sensed she had found a chink in his armor.

Laying down her fork, she leaned forward. Although she was sure it would violate proper table manners, she rested her elbows on the table, interlaced her fingers, and laid her head upon her hands.

She decided to drop her guard and be honest with him. One heart to another. Evan deserved that much.

"I wanted to fall in love with you, Evan. Every part of my logic told me I should. And I could tell how you felt about me..." With that, her voice trailed. She couldn't find words to justify hurting another individual.

"...but your heart couldn't get there," he offered.

Lily paused for a beat. "No, it couldn't," she acknowledged in a soft, sincere tone that took her by surprise.

Evan tried to hide his disappointment, probably for her benefit more than his own. With a nod, he eased back in his chair, and Lily felt more comfortable talking to him now than at any other point in their mutual, albeit brief, history.

"So what's he like?" Evan asked.

"Who, Ryder? The artist?"

"Yeah," Evan replied in a casual, yet earnest, manner. "In all those paintings, it *looks* like he treats you well."

"He's sweet," Lily said, grinning at her lighter memories of Ryder. "It wasn't so much the art or his actions. It was more about the little things, the way he could take something hidden inside me and make it tangible, a nature I didn't know was down there. That's the best way I can describe it. At first glance, before we met each other, he saw something in me that I couldn't even see in myself." Lily's words hung between them in the candlelight. "But that doesn't matter anymore."

She lifted her wine glass for a sip but stopped herself. She laid the glass back on the table.

"Evan, I'm not a liar," she blurted. "I'm really not. But I—well, I managed to lose him. Ryder didn't ask me to be someone I'm not. I *became* someone I'm not." She took that sip of wine. "And now he's gone."

Leaning forward again, Evan shrugged. "Maybe not forever. Who knows? He may come to his senses. And if he does, then follow your heart." He ran his finger across the tip of the candle flame, which crouched beneath his touch. "If things couldn't work out between you and me, I'd want to know you're with somebody who recognizes what a jewel he has."

This time, Lily blushed. "Well, like you said: *if* he comes around. I don't see that happening. He hasn't called in months."

"Maybe not. Then again, I doubt you expected *me* to walk back into your shop. Maybe Ryder will come looking for you again."

"What do you mean?"

"You didn't go searching for love, did you? From what I read, love found *you*. In pictures—like that billboard we saw on our first date." Evan had a glint in his eye. "See, I *knew* you looked familiar."

Lily considered Evan's words. Her life had lurched forward at the speed of a locomotive once she met Ryder Flynn. She never had the chance to stop and ponder how it all came together. She'd taken the situation one step at a time as she responded to his overtures.

"You're right. I wasn't looking," she said. "I never believed love would find me."

"And maybe love will find you again. From what I read, he couldn't forget you. That's what motivated him to put you in his art in the first place."

"That was years ago."

"And he has *more* to lose today. He already lost you once. Do you think his heart will let him lose you *again?*" Evan took a bite of salmon, then chased it with a drink of water. "Look at me: Mr. Sentimental, huh?" he said with a grin.

But Lily was already lost in thought, wondering if what Evan said could be true. Yes, she still loved Ryder. No matter how hard she tried, she couldn't forget him and would never be the same since taking the plunge into love. Lily didn't want to re-enter the spotlight, not after discovering how harsh it could be, but she couldn't ask Ryder to leave it, either. It was an important factor in his career.

She wanted him back, but she couldn't do it on their previous terms. Besides, after her roadside attack the day they ended their relationship, why would he want her back?

When it came to romance, if she never had another date, she would be in no worse shape than before she'd met Ryder. More than that, she had experienced true love with someone who, despite the flaws along the way, managed to discover who she *truly* was inside. Not even she had known that side of her existed.

So where did that leave Lily Machara tonight?

Have faith, Lily, she encouraged herself. *Have a little faith in love.*

And with that, she took another sip of wine.

CHAPTER 66

ON A SATURDAY night in late April, Lily savored the tinge of warmth in the air. She had cracked open the windows not long after reaching Kingdom City, where she had exited the freeway and headed south. The last time she had taken a trip into the unknown was April of last year, the day she had met Ryder in Cleveland.

Talk about a contrast. A degree of familiarity had returned to her life, though it hadn't arrived the way Lily had expected. She'd learned that love was, above all, unpredictable.

And creative.

Now, having reached the end of her trek, she put the car into park, let the engine idle for a minute, and turned off the ignition. Once again, she debated whether this was a good idea. Peering over her shoulder at the house with the stone edifice, butterflies tickled Lily's stomach, much as they had on her first visit here.

To regain her confidence, she picked up the latest copy of her favorite car magazine, the one to which she subscribed, which she had placed on the passenger seat. Though she collected each issue, one copy remained missing from her collection—the one she had thrown at Ryder during their fight, her final act of defiance before she stormed away. Before they parted ways.

Enough daylight remained for her to read in the car. Fanning through the magazine, she landed on page 41, a number she had memorized by now. She knew the page's content by heart, as well, and could re-create it with a pen on a napkin if she needed to. But no matter how often she stared at it, the advertisement continued to fascinate her.

A few weeks ago, Lily and Ryder's alter egos had re-emerged—one more time—in a spot Ryder knew she would see as a subscriber.

But this ad was unique. It didn't advertise anything.

Or didn't *appear* to. Not to the average reader, at least.

Lily had noticed it differed from the previous work in which she and Ryder had appeared. This ad was intended for her eyes alone. Though it appeared before a national audience, only Lily and Ryder could decipher its meaning.

The ad appeared in full color and spanned an entire page. Ryder must have spent a fortune to place it there. In the painting, he and Lily leaned toward each other, their fingers entwined upon a counter at an auto shop. Lily stood behind a cash register. Ryder faced her from the other side.

A small, discreet sign hung behind the counter. One which the average reader would overlook. *Lily herself* had almost overlooked it.

In elegant letters, the sign's message hearkened back to the dinner Ryder had prepared for Lily last summer:

THAI ON THE WATER
3RD SATURDAY IN APRIL, 7:30 P.M.
DRESS CODE: COME AS YOU ARE.

Thai on the water. Lily wondered how many tabloid reporters, if they had even noticed the sign, had trekked halfway across the world to pinpoint a location along the coast of Thailand. She snickered at the thought of the female reporter, the one who had shown up at Lily's apartment, wandering around Asia, trying to get the scoop on a clandestine rendezvous somewhere in the Orient.

Lily returned the magazine to the passenger seat and drew a deep breath. Dressed in a casual top and jeans, she climbed out of the car and made her way toward the house. Upon reaching the front door, she lifted her hand to knock, then repeated the message in the advertisement. *On the water,* it had said.

She would head to the back of the house instead.

Checking her watch, she discovered it was 7:31. Her procrastination in the car had caused her to arrive a minute late. The butterflies continued to brush their wings against her belly. What if she was wrong?

Suddenly, she didn't know what to do with her empty, idle hands. Their dead weight made her feel lopsided, so she crossed her arms over her chest and continued to press forward anyway.

When she rounded the side of the house, Lily froze. She couldn't keep from grinning if she tried.

Ryder stood on the grass in front of the pontoon boat, dressed in a polo-style shirt and khaki pants. His smile, a combination of delight and relief, beckoned her to him. Lily's nervousness wilted. She eased toward him as he extended his hand.

When she met him face to face, Ryder took her hand in his. He caught her eye and held her gaze—a moment frozen in time—before leading her into the boat and to her seat at the table he had arranged for dinner. Wine glasses and porcelain dishes surrounded a pair of lavender-colored candles, all of which fit together to set an intimate tone. Across the water, the sun glowed as it set, painting the horizon a shade of raspberry. The aroma of spring, a fresh scent of renewal, drifted upon a trace of breeze.

As advertised, Lily noticed Ryder had prepared Thai cuisine. Just like last summer.

From the deepest realms of his heart to the deepest realms of hers.

The sound of a popped cork broke the silence. Ryder poured two glasses of champagne.

The couple lifted their glasses.

"To new beginnings," Ryder said.

They clinked glasses and took their first sips.

Brushing a trace of champagne from his lip, Ryder furrowed his brow.

"I don't believe we've met," he said. "My name is Ryder Flynn."

"Pleased to meet you, Ryder. I'm Lily Machara."

She felt more relaxed than she had in a year. Everything had fallen into place. Lily's heart pattered at the thought of a second chance for their relationship. A second chance to be herself.

Honesty felt so good.

Ryder wore a mischievous grin. "I must say, you look familiar. I think I've seen you before—perhaps even *painted* you before."

Okay, she'd play along. "Oh, you're an artist?"

"I dabble in it. What do you do for a living?"

"I'm a car fanatic," Lily replied, "and a part-time muse."

Ryder nodded, as if considering the details the way one might examine the cut of a diamond.

"I think that's beautiful," he responded.

Lily's heart fluttered. She giggled at the remark, then tried the spicy soup.

Ryder leaned forward, and they lost themselves in each other's gaze.

"So tell me, Lily: Do you believe in love at first sight?"

Lily's heart flushed as warm as her now-favorite soup.

"Yes," she replied with a smile, taking in the sight of the man she loved with her whole heart.

"Yes, I think I do."

EPILOGUE

ONE YEAR LATER

WHITE SAND. CLEAR water.

If Lily were to paint the scene today, she would capture those two elements in a heartbeat.

The first time she and Ryder had dined together on his boat, she knew he had invited her into his passion for Thailand, a passion she had associated with him ever since. That evening, Ryder had also asked Lily where she would go if given the opportunity. What was her idea of beautiful?

She had answered Jamaica. Ryder never mentioned it again.

She hadn't expected him to remember it. She hadn't dreamed he would merge her dream location with his imagination from that evening on.

Lily should have known better.

Today, she could see it as she approached.

Another year had passed since Lily and Ryder had reunited. With clear boundaries set for their private life versus their public personas, they had struck a balance.

Though they had set today's plan into motion months ago.

Last night, they had skipped town and caught a red-eye flight to Miami, followed by a connecting flight to Jamaica. Neither had mentioned a word about this day to anyone. And not a reporter could be found for miles. In fact, Ryder hadn't told Lily where they were going until they arrived at the airport and printed their boarding passes. In one hand, Ryder had lugged his suitcase. In his other hand, however, he'd hauled the large, leather portfolio which he used to transport paintings.

He'd refused to tell her which of his works hid inside the portfolio until they reached their destination.

From a hundred feet inland, Lily closed her eyes and listened to ocean waves as they rolled in and fizzled upon the sand. Neither Lily nor Ryder wanted music, steel drums or otherwise. Crashing waves would provide the only soundtrack they needed.

Lily wore a white, unpretentious dress. It was too warm for a veil, not that she was a veil-wearing type of woman anyway. In her hand she held a bouquet of tropical flowers, their hues a vibrant collage of red, peach, yellow, purple and lime.

She made her way toward Ryder, who wore a tropical boutonniere pinned to a white linen shirt, and a pair of khaki pants. His shirt rippled in the Caribbean breeze. Overhead, the sky, clearer than crystal, wrapped its arms around the scene in the purest shade of blue Lily had seen in her lifetime.

Wisps of linen, draped along a white gazebo, waved in the breeze and invited Lily inside. The gazebo sat on a small piece of land that jutted several feet into the ocean. Behind the gazebo sat an endless horizon. Lily walked up two wooden steps and onto a tile-covered floor.

Ryder took her hand in his as they turned to face the minister. Lily and Ryder stood barefoot, their toes coated with a thin layer of sand like a pair of powdered doughnuts.

In their hotel room early this morning—the morning of their wedding day—Ryder had unzipped the leather portfolio he had tugged along. At long last, he had given Lily a glimpse of what he'd placed inside.

Speechless, she had stared at the painting, her eyes brimming with tears.

He had painted it a month after seeing her in her bridesmaid's dress in the Cleveland hotel. All those years ago. Back when all he could do was dream of a woman named Lily and try to bring her to life in his paintings.

But this painting was unique.

Ryder had painted a vision of their future.

He had painted himself in a tuxedo; Lily in a long, flowing gown.

Ryder had painted their wedding day.

And he had vowed to keep it hidden until that day arrived.

Today, it sat before them on an easel behind the minister's shoulder.

Fascinated, Lily took a fresh look at the painting and her eyes moistened once again.

Then she turned to face the man who, mere minutes from now, would be her husband. She gave Ryder's hands an affectionate squeeze as the minister opened the private ceremony by quoting a familiar verse from the Bible.

"Love is patient..."

THANK YOU FOR SPENDING TIME WITH

MONA LISAS AND LITTLE WHITE LIES.

Did you enjoy the book?
Please take a moment to leave a review on Amazon.com!

MORE BOOKS BY JOHN HERRICK

Bestselling Author of *From The Dead* and *8 Reasons Your Life Matters*

JOHN HERRICK

BETWEEN THESE WALLS

A NOVEL

"There is a heart and integrity to Herrick's writing."
– *The Phantom Tollbooth*

BETWEEN THESE WALLS

Hunter is a Christian. Hunter is the man next door. Hunter Carlisle is gay.

At 26 years old, Hunter Carlisle has a successful sales career, a devoted girlfriend, and rock-solid faith. He also guards a secret torment: an attraction to other men. When a career plunge causes muscle tension, Hunter seeks relief through Gabe Hellman, a handsome massage therapist. What begins as friendship takes a sudden turn and forces the two friends to reconsider the boundaries of attraction. Along the road to self-discovery, Hunter's secret is exposed to the community. Now Hunter must face the demons of his past and confront his long-held fears about reputation, sexual identity, and matters of soul. A story of faith, fire and restoration, *Between These Walls* braves the crossroads of love and religion to question who we are and who we will become.

> "Herrick will make waves…with this tale."
>
> — *Publishers Weekly*

> "A compelling read from beginning to end … A sophisticated and deftly crafted novel … Very highly recommended."
>
> — *Midwest Book Review*

> "A story of secrets, self-discovery, and the triumph of the human spirit … A moving story of love's power to cast out fear."
>
> — *Foreword Reviews*

Bestselling Author of *Between These Walls*
and *8 Reasons Your Life Matters*

JOHN HERRICK

FROM THE DEAD

A NOVEL

"Herrick will make waves." — **Publishers Weekly**

FROM THE DEAD

A preacher's son. A father in hiding. A guilty heart filled with secrets.

When Jesse Barlow escaped to Hollywood at age eighteen, he hungered for freedom, fame and fortune. Eleven years later, his track record of failure results in a drug-induced suicide attempt. Revived at death's doorstep, Jesse returns to his Ohio hometown to make amends with his preacher father, a former lover, and Jesse's own secret son. But Jesse's renewed commitment becomes a baptism by fire when his son's advanced illness calls for a sacrifice—one that could cost Jesse the very life he regained. A story of mercy, hope, and second chances, *From The Dead* captures the human spirit with tragedy and joy.

> "Eloquence with an edge. In a single chapter, John Herrick can break your heart, rouse your soul, and hold you in suspense. Be prepared to stay up late."
>
> — Doug Wead, *New York Times* bestselling author and advisor to two presidents

> "A solid debut novel."
>
> — *Akron Beacon Journal*

> "A well written and engaging story. It moves, and moves quickly. … I don't think I've read anything in popular novel form as good as this in describing a journey of faith."
>
> — Faith, Fiction, Friends

"There is a heart and integrity to Herrick's writing."
—The Phantom Tollbooth

The LANDING

A NOVEL

JOHN HERRICK

Bestselling author of *From The Dead*

THE LANDING

The power of a song: It can ignite a heart, heal a soul ... or for Danny Bale, resurrect a destiny.

When songwriter Danny escaped to the Atlantic coast seven years ago, he laid to rest his unrequited affection for childhood friend Meghan Harting. Their communication faded with yesterday and their lives have become deadlocked. Now Danny, haunted by an inner stronghold and determined to win Meghan back, must create a masterpiece and battle for the heart of the only woman who understands his music. As memories resurface, Danny and Meghan embark on parallel journeys of self-discovery—and a collision course to seal their mutual fate. A tale of purpose, hope and redemption, *The Landing* is a "sweet story" *(Publishers Weekly)* that captures the joy and heartache of love.

> "A powerful, absorbing tale, that will touch the heart and the mind as never before. A page turner."
>
> — Doug Wead, *New York Times* bestselling author and advisor to two presidents

> "Exquisite and honest. *The Landing* goes beyond language to pursue that elusive something that, when found, lingers and leaves you changed."
>
> — Phyllis Wallace, Syndicated radio host

8 REASONS

Your Life Matters

JOHN HERRICK

Bestselling Author of *From The Dead*

8 REASONS YOUR LIFE MATTERS

"If I were to disappear, would anybody notice?"

Each of us has asked that question in dark, honest moments.

In his first nonfiction book, *8 Reasons Your Life Matters,* bestselling author John Herrick combines personal struggles with biblical insight. Injecting eight chapters with humor, memoir moments, and a postmodern perspective on life, Herrick shares eight reasons your life matters:

Your Life is More Permanent than Your Struggles
God Sees You Differently than You See Yourself
You Have a Destiny
You are Remembered, not Forgotten
You Were Someone's First Pick
Your Absence Would Leave a Permanent Hole
People Need to See You Overcome
You are Loved and Valued

Eight solid reasons to give life one more chance. Eight reasons your life matters.

HIT

AND

RUN

ANONYMITY WON'T
PROTECT YOU.

JOHN HERRICK

HIT AND RUN

A Short Thriller from John Herrick

Anonymity won't protect you.

On his way home from a much-needed respite in the Colorado Rockies, Gunnar Wakeman loses control of his car and dents a vehicle on the side of the road. When he sees no witnesses—and discovers a dead body inside the abandoned car—Gunnar flees the scene.

But the owner sees the incident. And records his license plate number.

Soon Gunnar finds himself stalked by a John Doe with an insatiable appetite for revenge. Jolted into a realm of paranoia, Gunnar must outmaneuver his enemy and engage in another hit-and-run—where the stakes have escalated and a wrong turn could prove lethal.

Bestselling Author of *Between These Walls, 8 Reasons Your Life Matters* **and** *From the Dead*

JOHN HERRICK

BEAUTIFUL MESS

A NOVEL

"A creative and fresh romp through one of pop culture's most notorious tales. John Herrick's characters become your best friends. His world is keen, compelling and excessively alive."
— **Jeffrey James Keyes**, *New York Times* bestselling author

BONUS EXCERPT
BEAUTIFUL MESS

A fallen star. Four Los Angeles misfits. And the Marilyn Monroe you only thought you knew.

Del Corwyn is an aging relic. An actor who advanced from errand boy to Academy Award nominee, Del kept company with the elite of Hollywood's golden era and shared a close friendship with Marilyn Monroe. Today, however, he faces bankruptcy.

Humiliated, Del is forced to downgrade his lifestyle, sell the home he's long cherished, and fade into a history of forgotten legends—unless he can revive his career. All he needs is one last chance. While searching through memorabilia from his beloved past, Del rediscovers a mysterious envelope, dated 1962, containing an original screenplay by Marilyn Monroe—and proof that she named him its legal guardian.

Del surges to the top of Hollywood's A-list overnight. But the opportunity to reclaim his fame and fortune brings a choice: Is Del willing to sacrifice newfound love, self-respect and his most cherished friendship to achieve his greatest dream?

A story of warmth, humor and honesty, *Beautiful Mess* follows one man's journey toward love and relevance where he least expects it—and proves coming-of-age isn't just for the young.

"A creative and fresh romp through one of pop culture's most notorious tales. John Herrick's characters become your best friends. His world is keen, compelling and excessively alive."

— Jeffrey James Keyes, *New York Times* bestselling author

"THIS IS URGENT, you said?"

Arnie Clemmons, Del's agent, shut the door and settled into his leather chair, which had cracked along the seams. The window blinds were open and exposed a view of the parking lot from the office's second-story roost.

Arnie had managed to salvage his hair along the bottom half of his head, but his bald dome looked waxy as sunlight glinted upon it. A man in his late fifties, Arnie's roster featured a variety of former A-list talent that had fallen from their perches but whose reputations remained respectable around town.

"I have an intriguing prospect for a new film," Del replied as he took a seat. He tapped the manila envelope tucked under his arm, which contained Marilyn's script.

He could've sworn he caught Arnie in the onset of an eye roll brought to a sudden halt.

"What kind of project?"

"A pop-culture type of thing. You could say it has a retro feel to it."

Arnie sighed. "Del, I realize you like to relive the past—"

"This is a winner, Arnie. I guarantee it."

"And what does this winning project involve?"

"Marilyn Monroe. It's a screenplay."

"With all due respect, isn't that a bit clichéd? This would need to be an angle no one else has covered. Many people have done films about Marilyn Monroe, not to mention books and memorabilia and everything else under the sun."

"You don't understand. This isn't *about* Marilyn Monroe." Del felt a surge of adrenaline and couldn't contain himself. He leaned forward and, with great pomp, planted the thick package on Arnie's desk. It landed with a thump. "It's *by* Marilyn Monroe."

Arnie sat open-mouthed as he tried to follow along. His eyes widened in perplexity. *"By* Marilyn Monroe," he repeated.

"That's right."

"Del, what the hell are you talking about?"

With a lighthearted laugh, Del eased back into the chair. "Last night, I rummaged through some boxes I'd stored away long ago. Hadn't looked through them in years. Relics from my heyday. Things I'd forgotten I'd saved. And at the bottom of one of those boxes, I found this."

He patted the envelope, which crinkled at his touch.

"It's a script, given to me in 1962." Del caught Arnie's eye to make sure the man paid full attention. "Written by Marilyn Monroe."

Arnie shot him a skeptical glare, then leaned back in his leather chair. The chair squeaked under his medium-size ass. "And somehow, you have possession of it? Something she wrote?"

"We were close friends."

"I've never heard a word about her writing a screenplay. Not even a rumor."

"She kept it a secret, but she considered herself a true artist. She was shrewd, and had growing ambitions. Remember her film contract, the one that included a provision for films to be produced under her own company, Marilyn Monroe Productions?"

"Marilyn wasn't a writer."

"But she was married to one. Arthur Miller, remember? He influenced her."

Del handed the envelope to Arnie, who grimaced as he took it in hand.

Arnie waved the package with an attitude of indifference. Skepticism continued to fill his glare. "And this is the script?"

"Yes."

"Marilyn's script?"

"Yes, Arnie."

With a sigh, Arnie stared at the envelope, then unsealed it, removed the brass-fastened screenplay, and stared at it as if it were a bowl of cauliflower.

Arnie read the title aloud. *"Beautiful Mess."*

Del watched his every move as he scanned the document's title page and flipped through the first few pages.

"This is a photocopy."

"I put the original in a safe-deposit box. I made one photocopy for you, one for me."

"Unfortunately, we can't prove this isn't a hoax, can we? You *say* it came from her, but how could we prove it? That's the first question anyone would ask." Arnie furrowed his brow and held the script closer. "And what are these little boxes in the corners? The ones with smudges in them?"

"Those are the proof it's a Marilyn Monroe original: her thumbprints."

"The quality doesn't look too good."

"It's just a photocopy. They're crisp on the original. Ink from a stamp pad."

"And these thumbprints are here for what reason?"

"She wrote me this letter in 1962." Del pulled a photocopy of Marilyn's letter from the breast pocket of his blazer, unfolded it, and slid it across the desk. "It explains how the thumbprints prove the original came from her."

Arnie scanned the letter, then examined the script closer. He raised an eyebrow.

"And her thumbprint is the only fingerprint that exists inside these boxes?"

"I assume so. I was careful not to touch them. And according to Marilyn, she was afraid to show the document to anyone else. That would prevent any other prints from interfering with hers."

Arnie rapped his knuckle upon the desk and shot Del a tentative gaze. Del watched the man's skepticism subside as he reread the letter's body.

"Smart move on her part," he said. "She certainly covered her bases."

Del nodded. "She wasn't the dumb blond that she played on the silver screen. Consider how well she constructed her public persona. The woman knew how to strategize and think ahead."

Del caught the first hint of a grin at the corner of Arnie's mouth and knew his agent was on board.

"My only question," Del said, "is how we could verify her fingerprints."

"That shouldn't be a problem," Arnie shrugged. "I'm sure they have her prints on file from the autopsy. Given the circumstances surrounding her death and who she was, they would have wanted official confirmation of her identity to eliminate the possibility of foul play. For the record, if nothing else. And her death predated all that HIPAA crap, so the prints are probably floating all over God's green earth. We'd just need to hire someone credible who can verify that it's an authentic match. At that point, we hold all the bargaining chips when it comes to making a deal."

Arnie's cheeks turned rosy as he grinned at Del. A wide, toothy grin. The discoloration of enamel betrayed a long-entrenched penchant for red wine. He rolled the script and slapped it against his palm.

"Do you realize how many people would dry-hump a flagpole to get their hands on this?" exclaimed the agent. "We're talking history here! Hollywood's best-kept secret!"

Del felt a bittersweet quiver in his gut but suppressed it. His life was about to become interesting again.

Arnie paged through the screenplay further, scanning the dialogue. Several minutes ticked past. Del savored the silence which, in this case, was the sound of power.

"Have you read this, Del?"

"I have."

"Pretty deep shit in here. *Dark* shit, the kind that scares the hell out of you." Arnie skipped to the screenplay's midpoint and read some more. "And talk about explicit. The profanity, the sexual content, everything."

"She made herself vulnerable, no doubt."

"Damn, Del. This woman must've been more fucked up than we thought."

Del winced. "Arnie, cut it out."

"Sorry, I forgot you two were pals." The agent shook his head in an absentminded manner, his mouth hanging open as he read further. "No wonder she didn't show this to anybody else. Can you imagine how people would have reacted to this in 1962? The film would've been X-rated—if ratings had existed back then—and gotten banned from theaters. People would've protested outside. This script would've ruined Marilyn Monroe's career."

"But today—"

"—it'll *resurrect* it."

The men stared at each other for a moment, sizing each other up.

"But why you?" Arnie asked at last. "You said you two were buddies, but she knew tons of people. For all intent and purposes, she bequeathed it to you without realizing it. One of her final acts before she died. Why did she put this into *your* hands?"

Del shrugged. "I never betrayed her."

He made his way toward a mini-fridge Arnie kept behind a bureau door and helped himself to a bottled water. He took a swig and began to pace the room, piecing the puzzle together with each stride.

"Many people aren't aware of this," Del said, "but her emotional state took such a dive, she was forced into a mental institution against her will for a brief period. That event left a permanent scar. Toward the end of her life, she didn't trust many people, especially since people she trusted betrayed her and sent her to that place. Once she escaped, she feared the day would come when they'd lock her up again.

"This script exposed some of the inner workings and torments of her mind. What if authorities used it as evidence of a dangerous mental condition and sent her back to the one place she feared most? It was Joe DiMaggio, another ex-husband, who worked to get her out of there—and she barely made it out. If they had recommitted her, she would have lost her freedom forever."

"But something must have prompted her to give this script to you, Del. If she was so paranoid, why did she risk giving the script to anyone? Why didn't she keep it to herself?"

"She mentioned possible trouble ahead but didn't go into detail."

"You're telling me Marilyn Monroe was a psychic?"

"Of course not. More like intuition. A sense that something was about to happen." Del returned to his seat and crossed one leg over the other. He interlinked his fingers across his knee. "And she was right. A few months later, she died from a barbiturate overdose. Some speculated it was accidental, but the amount of drugs in her system were so high, it was hard to believe it was anything but suicide."

Arnie tapped a pen against a legal pad. Del's heart stirred. The memory of her death threatened to bring tears to the resilient man's eyes.

Del leaned forward and locked eyes with his agent.

"For Marilyn, this script wasn't about business. It wasn't about fame." Solemn, Del added, "This script is my chance to bring Marilyn Monroe back to life, one more time—on her own terms. To position her as a serious artist, the way she craved people to view her."

"Your sentiment is honorable. That said, this revelation will set in motion a feeding frenzy." Arnie paused, and Del caught a glint in his eye. "And I know you, Del. You like the cameras, the adoring fans. You want a career comeback—and this is the best ticket you'll ever get."

"Arnie—"

"All I'm saying is this: I don't doubt your motive to honor Marilyn Monroe's memory, but once we set this in motion, you'll get caught up in the whirlwind. I'm warning you now because I don't want to have to dig you out of a guilt complex later."

"I'll be fine, Arnie. Trust me."

His agent regarded him for a moment, then nodded in resignation. "In that case, we need to set a plan in motion. How do we release the news of this discovery? How do we consider contenders? Where do we set the minimum bar for a deal? We get to call the shots here. They'll need to play by our rules, and this script needs to be on strict lockdown."

"Agreed."

"In that case, the first thing we need to do is establish its authenticity. I'll get the proof lined up and we'll keep it in our back pockets. Next, we'll hold a press conference to announce the existence of the screenplay—but let the press *speculate* about whether it's authentic. We'll hem and haw for a while, tease them a bit, make them think they have us cornered."

Del didn't want to look like a fool in public, regardless of how temporary or intentional, but he was willing to hear the rest of the idea. He stroked his chin and clasped his hands upon his chest. "And what happens next?"

"Then, when attention is at its peak, we release the evidence. It'll be good for another round of marketing. So instead of releasing the evidence at the first news conference, we'll get twice the bang for our buck."

"Makes sense to me." Del felt much more at ease. He exhaled and took a swig of water. The bottle's thin plastic crackled in his grip.

"We'll need some time to strategize this while the thumbprints are verified. I know a guy who can get it done under the radar. Meanwhile—and I'm sure you know this, but I'll stress it anyway—don't breathe a word of this until the day of our big announcement. Not to the media, the studio people, producers—not even to the chef at your sushi restaurant. The element of surprise will strengthen our bargaining position. Agreed?"

"Agreed."

Arnie exhaled, as though in relief, and scratched his bald head. His fingers left behind red streaks. "This is big, Del."

Del's pulse increased with anticipation, yet he maintained his composure. He finished his water and crumpled the bottle.

'Big' didn't do it justice.

This wasn't just Marilyn's final chance.

It was Del Corwyn's, too.

Did you enjoy *Mona Lisas and Little White Lies?*

LET THE AUTHOR KNOW!

Visit John Herrick online
to message him or discover his other books.

johnherrick.net

facebook.com/johnherrickbooks

@johnherrick

goodreads.com/johnherrick

youtube.com/c/johnherrick

amazon.com/author/johnherrick